THE BENEVENT
TREASURE

Titles by Patricia Wentworth

THE BENEVENT TREASURE

PATRICIA WENTWORTH

PERENNIAL LIBRARY

HARPER & ROW, PUBLISHERS, New York
Grand Rapids, Philadelphia, St. Louis, San Francisco
London, Singapore, Sydney, Tokyo, Toronto

This book was originally published in hardcover in 1953 by J. B. Lippincott Company.

First PERENNIAL LIBRARY edition published 1990.

ISBN 0-06-081225-7

90 91 92 93 94 WB/OPM 10 9 8 7 6 5 4 3 2 1

"The fault is yours if fault there be,
The thanks are yours if thanks are owed,
Who led me firmly by the hand
Along this gay, adventurous road."

PROLOGUE

The ledge was about six inches wide. Candida stood on it with her toes stubbed against the rock. Her left hand was clenched on a small projecting knob about level with the top of her head. With the other she was feeling carefully and methodically for something which she could catch hold of on her right. There didn't seem to be anything, but she went on feeling. In the end she had to come back to the shallow crack which she had discarded. It would only take the tips of her fingers. By itself it really wasn't any good, but it did just give the least little help to the hand that was clutching the knob. She stood there and wondered what she was going to do next.

There wasn't very much that she could do. In fact, to be quite frank and plain with herself, there wasn't anything at all. She had got as far as she could. She couldn't possibly get any farther. If she looked up, she could see the ledge which she had been hoping to reach. That is to say, she could see the jutting rock which was the under part of the ledge, and it was like a great stone buttress thrusting out from the cliff and thrusting her away. There were no conceivable means by which she could get past that overhang— not unless she were a fly and could crawl upside down. She didn't let herself look at the beach, because of course that was the stupidest thing you could do. But whether she looked or not, she knew very well what she would see—sharp black rocks, and the tide coming racing in. If it had been deep sea that you could jump off into, she would have let herself go and have tried for a better place to climb, but you would want to know that there was a great deal of water over those rocks before you would take a chance with them. Better think about something else. Quickly.

It was a funny thing about that ledge. Seen from below, it didn't look as if it would be all that difficult to reach. The overhang didn't show like this. She had been quite pleased and confident about reaching it—right up to the very last moment when there was no more foothold or fingerhold and the thing stuck over her head like the underside of a doorstep.

Well, she couldn't go on, and it wasn't any use going back. She wasn't quite sure how far she had climbed—twenty feet—thirty—forty . . . But all the way up from the rocks and the sea there wasn't anything that would be better than this, and it was always harder to climb down.

If you can't go on and you can't go back, there is only one thing you can do, and that is stay where you are. The thing that whispers in your mind and always has something horrid to say said softly, "And how long can you do that?" Candida had been brought up to have a short way with the whispering thing. She spoke back to it with spirit.

"As long as I choose!"

The thing refused to be snubbed.

"It will be dark in less than an hour. You can't stand here all night."

Candida said, "I can stand here as long as I've got to." She clenched her fingers on the rocky knob and called, "Cooee! Cooee!"

Things can't talk to you when you are calling with

all your might, but the sound went out of her against the cliff wall and flattened there. Anyone would have to have very sharp ears if they were to hear it against the noise of the tide coming in.

Stephen Eversley had very sharp ears. He was some way out, because even if you knew the coast as well as he did, you didn't take a boat in past the Black Sisters if you could help it. He was making for the narrow bay which the smugglers used to use. A trap if you didn't know your way, safe enough if you did. Sound carries over water, and the way the cliff curved favoured Candida's cry. He heard it and looking shoreward he saw her dark against the rock in her schoolgirl serge. It was not yet dusk but the air had begun to thicken.

He rowed in as far as he dared. He mustn't make it too far, but he had to get within hailing distance, and he thought he could do that. Without word from her, there was no deciding what to do next. If she had a reasonable foot and hand hold, he could land in the cove, fetch help, and get at her from the top of the cliff. But if she couldn't be sure of holding on, he would have to work along the rock face to the ledge just over her head and get her up on to that. The rope he had in the boat would be long enough. It would mean staying there all night, because by the time they were through it would be too dark to get back along the cliff. It was going to be a tricky business anyhow.

As soon as he got near enough he called out to her.

"Hi! You there on the cliff! What sort of hold have you got?"

The answer came back faintly and in one word.

"Fair!"

"Can—you—hold—on—for—say—forty—minutes?"

Even as he said it, he knew she couldn't.

He got back two words.

"I'll—try."

It wasn't good enough. He would have to make it singlehanded. He called again.

"I'll—get—to—you—before—that! About—a—quarter—of—an—hour! I'll—be—seeing—you! Hold—on!"

It was much easier to hold on now that she knew help was coming. The nasty whispering voice went away and she began to make pictures in her mind. Not the horrid sort which showed you all the things you were shutting your eyes against—a dead drop down to the beach and wet black rocks with points as sharp as needles. Not that kind at all, but the romantic sort out of the old long-ago tales—Andromeda chained to a cliff in Greece with the monster coming in out of a blue sea, and Perseus flashing down with wings on his feet to turn the looming horror into stone.

The time went by.

It was only when she heard Stephen on the cliff that she was afraid again. The sound came from away to the left, and all at once she began to wonder how he was going to reach her, and whether she could go on holding on. Her feet were stiff and numb with all her weight thrown forward. She couldn't really feel her fingers any more. Suppose they just slid away from the stone and she tilted over—outwards—and back—and down. But when he spoke from the ledge over her head and said, "Are you all right?" she heard herself say, "Yes."

A rope came dangling down. It had a noose at the

end of it. What she had to do was to get it under her armpit. She would have to let go of the crack on her right and work the rope along until it was over her head and supporting the shoulder. Stephen lay on the ledge and looked over it and told her what to do. All the things were impossible, but he had the sort of voice that made you feel you could do impossible things, and somehow they got done.

When the rope was round her body, she had to edge to the left along the crack until there wasn't really any foothold at all. She couldn't have done it without the rope. It brought her just far enough out from under the overhang for him to be able to drag her up on to the ledge.

She lay on the rough stone and there was no more strength in her. She felt like a doll with the sawdust all run out—horrid limp arms and legs and a wobbling head. And then a hand on her shoulder, and a voice which said,

"You're all right now. Be careful how you move—the ledge isn't very wide."

Oddly enough, that made her feel worse than anything else. There were pins and needles in her hands and feet, and something that went round and round in her head. Before she knew what she was doing she was feeling for his hand and clutching it as if she would never let it go. That was one of the things she was ashamed about afterwards. As soon as she could get hold of her voice she said, "How much room is there?" and he laughed.

"Oh, I won't let you fall! Just come this way a little and you can sit up with the cliff at your back. We're perfectly safe, but I'm afraid we'll have to stay here until it's light. It's too dark to get back the way I came. I didn't like to leave you long enough to go and fetch help—you were in a pretty bad position. And we'll be all right here until the morning. Perhaps we had better exchange names. I'm Stephen Eversley, and I'm down here on a holiday. I was out watching birds and taking photographs, which is why I had a rope in the boat. I couldn't have got you up without it. I suppose you are on holiday too. I'm on my own, and no one will bother about me, but your people will get the wind up, so we may have a search party along almost any time."

It was nice to feel the cliff at her back. The ledge was three or four feet wide and it ran along quite a way, getting narrower until it disappeared. There was room to stretch out her feet. She looked out over the darkening sea and said,

"Oh, I don't know. They weren't getting down till pretty late."

"Who weren't?"

"The people I was going to stay with, Monica Carson and her mother. We're at school together, and Mrs. Carson asked me for part of the holidays. My train got in at four, and theirs wasn't until six, so I was to go to the place where they had booked our rooms—it's a private hotel called Sea View—and have tea and get unpacked. But when I got there, Mrs. Carson had telephoned to say they were doing some shopping in London and they wouldn't be down until eight o'clock, so I went for a walk."

He gave a half laugh.

"And nobody had ever told you about the tide coming in! You let yourself get caught between the points, and then tried to climb up the cliff. How old are you?"

"I'm fifteen and a half. And of course I know about tides! I asked—I asked most particularly."

"Who did you ask?"

"It was someone in the hotel. There were two old ladies, and they said it wouldn't be high tide until about eleven, so of course I thought it would be perfectly safe to walk along the beach."

"That depends upon how much beach there is. And the tide is high at a quarter to nine!"

She turned and stared at him. Just a shape in the dusk—a shape and a voice. But she wasn't thinking about that—it was what he had just said about the tide. If it was high at a quarter to nine. . . . She cut in, quick and breathless,

"Then why did she say it wasn't high until eleven?"

His shoulder jerked.

"How do I know?"

"She did say high tide at eleven."

"I suppose the simple answer is that she didn't know any more than you did."

"Then why did she say she did?"

He shrugged again.

"People are like that. If you ask them the way, they will practically never say they don't know. They just waffle on, misdirecting you. I thought you said there were two of them. Why do you say 'she'?"

"Well, really only one of them spoke. The other mostly stood there and nodded. I'd been writing my name in the book. There's a little window between the office and the hall, and they came up on either side and looked over my shoulder. One of them said, 'Is your name Candida Sayle?' and I said yes, it was. I thought it was rude of them to look over my shoulder, and I didn't want to go on talking, so I began to walk away. But they followed me, and the one who had spoken said, 'That is a very unusual name.'

7

They were quite old, but they were dressed exactly alike. Honestly, they were odd! I wanted to get away from them, so I said I was going for a walk. And that was when she said it would be nice along the beach and the tide wasn't high until eleven."

"It sounds as if they were barmy."

"It does rather."

He was thinking that strangers ought to know better than to mix and meddle with the tides. They must have been strangers, because anyone who lived here would know that this was a dangerous strip of coast.

If it had been later in the year, Candida would hardly have got very far on her walk without somebody warning her, but on a chilly April evening it wasn't likely that there would be anyone down on the beaches after tea. Candida's old ladies were definitely a menace. He said so.

"And I hope your friend will put it across them for misleading you. It might have been serious."

"Do you suppose they'll say anything? I don't."

"They'll be bound to. Mrs.—what's her name—Carson will be arriving. If you signed your name, she'll know you got to the hotel, and she'll be wondering where you are. She'll be in a state, and your old ladies will be bound to say they spoke to you. Somebody probably saw them doing it. And if they say you were going for a walk along the beach, there's bound to be a search-party out looking for you before long. Quite a bright thought. We're all right here, but it will be cold before morning."

There was no search-party, because Mrs. Carson, having started the day at 6 A.M. and crowded it with a great deal of fatiguing and mostly unnecessary exertion, was overtaken by a rather alarming fainting fit at the moment when she ought to have been catching her train to Eastcliff. She was carried into the Station Hotel and a doctor sent for. Monica, a good deal frightened, rang up Sea View to say that her mother was ill, and that she would ring up again in the morning. The line was not at all clear. Candida's name reached her vaguely. She said, "Oh, I hope we'll get down in the morning, but if we can't, she will just have to go home." After which she rang off.

Stephen and Candida knew nothing of all this. They sat on the ledge and talked. She told him that she lived with an aunt who had brought her up.

"Her name is Sayle too—Barbara Sayle. She is my father's sister. She gardens all the time. My father and mother were torpedoed in the war. Aunt Barbara is a pet."

Stephen was perfectly right about the cold. He made her sit close up to him and put his arm round her. Sometimes they dozed, and sometimes they talked. He was going to be an architect. He hoped to pass his final exam in the summer, after which there was a place for him in an uncle's firm. It wouldn't be a bad job as jobs went, only working for relations wasn't always the best thing for you. Everyone thought you were being let down easy, but sometimes it didn't work out that way at all.

"Richard is all right of course. As a matter of fact he's a very fine chap, but he's going to expect me to be about twice as good as there's any hope of my being—just because I'm his nephew. Of course it's a tremendous chance."

A drowsy voice said against his shoulder, "I don't see why—you shouldn't be—quite as good—as he is——"

He found himself talking about the houses Richard Eversley had built and the houses he hoped to build

9

himself. Her head was warm against his shoulder. It was like talking to himself. Sometimes he knew that she was asleep. Sometimes quite suddenly she spoke. Once she said, "You can do anything—if you try." And when he came back with, "That's nonsense," she went off into a murmur of words which sounded like, "If you—really—want to——"

The night went by.

They woke in the dawn, cold and stiff. Each saw the other clearly for the first time. Candida rubbed her eyes and stretched. The sea was the colour of the pewter plates on Aunt Barbara's dresser. It was very calm and still. The sky was an even grey, with a yellow streak low down in the east where it touched the water. There was no breeze. Everything smelled very cold, and fresh, and clean. There was a salty taste on her lips. She looked at Stephen and saw him stretching too—a tall, loose-limbed young man of two or three and twenty with a lot of sun-burned hair. He wore an open-necked shirt under an old tweed jacket, and he was tanned to almost the same colour. His grey eyes were light against the brown of his skin. They looked back at her. What he saw was a girl with dark blue eyes and chestnut hair in a plait. The hair was all ruffled up where it had rubbed against his shoulder. The eyes were good, the features emerging from a soft roundness, the mouth wide and full, and the teeth very white. They looked at one another and laughed.

CHAPTER 1

More than five years later Candida was reading a letter. It was ten days since Barbara Sayle's funeral, and there had been a great many letters to read and to answer. Everyone had been very kind. She had written the same things over and over again until they almost wrote themselves. What it all added up to was that Barbara was gone. She had been ill for three years, and Candida had nursed her. Now that it was all over, there was practically no money, and she would have to look for a job. The bother was that she wasn't trained. She had left school and come home to look after Barbara.

And now Barbara was gone.

All the letters which she had been answering had been concerned with this one thing, but the letter which she had just opened was different. It wasn't about Barbara at all, it was about herself. She sat by the window reading it, with the wintry light slanting in across the expensive paper and the old-fashioned pointed writing. There was an embossed address in the top right-hand corner:

Underhill,
Retley.

The letter began, "My dear Candida," and it was signed, "Olivia Benevent." She read:

11

"My dear Candida,

"I am writing to condole with you on your recent bereavement. The unhappy quarrel consequent on your grandmother's marriage having interrupted normal intercourse between her and the rest of the family, my sister Cara and I were never afforded an opportunity of making the acquaintance of our nephew Richard and his wife, or of our niece Barbara. Now that they are dead, there would not seem to be any reason why this regrettable quarrel should be carried on into a third generation. As the daughter of our nephew Richard you are our only surviving relative. Your grandmother, Candida Benevent, was our sister. Her marriage to John Sayle removed her from the family circle. We invite you to return to it. My sister Cara and I will be glad if you will pay us a visit. The Benevents come of an old and noble family, and we feel that their last descendant should know something of its history and traditions.

Hoping that you will see your way to accepting an invitation which, I can assure you, is very cordially extended, I sign myself for the first but, I hope, not for the last time,

Your great-aunt,
Olivia Benevent."

Candida looked at the letter with some rather mixed feelings. She knew that her grandmother's name had been Candida Benevent, and she knew that there had been a family quarrel, but that was about as far as it went. What the quarrel was about, why it had never been made up, and whether there were any Benevent relations, she really had had no idea. Perhaps Barbara didn't know either. Perhaps she knew and didn't bother her head about it. She was the sort of person who mightn't. An old quarrel might just not have seemed worth bothering about. And Candida Benevent had died when her children were quite young—there had been no living link with the family she had left behind her.

When she showed the letter to Everard Mortimer, who was Barbara Sayle's solicitor, she discovered that he knew no more about the quarrel than she did herself, but he strongly advised her to accept Miss Benevent's invitation. He was a pleasant young man in his early thirties with a modern attitude towards the family quarrels of two generations ago.

"Cutting people out of wills and washing your hands of them was rather in the Victorian tradition. People are a bit more tolerant nowadays. I think you certainly ought to accept the olive branch and go and stay with the old ladies. You seem to be their only relation, and that might be important. Your aunt's annuity stopped when she died. She had the cottage on a lease, and by the time everything is cleared up you won't have more than about twenty-five pounds a year."

A bright carnation colour came up under Candida's fair skin. It made her eyes look very dark and very blue, and her lashes very black. Everard Mortimer found himself noticing the contrast with her chestnut hair. He found it pleasing. It occurred to him that if she were really going to be something of an heiress— and that was what Miss Olivia Benevent's letter sounded like—she would not lack for suitors. Even with no more than twenty-five pounds a year there might be quite a queue. He had a fleeting glimpse of himself at the head of it. He allowed his manner to become a little warmer.

Barbara Sayle had never spoken of her mother's family. The old great-aunts might have nothing to leave. On the other hand they might have quite a lot. All over the place there were old ladies with property to leave and no very clear idea of how they were going to leave it. He could think of half a dozen amongst his own clients. The making and unmaking of wills was a recreation to them. It gave them a sense of importance, a sense of power. They liked to feel that they would have a hand in the affairs of the younger generations. There was old Miss Crabtree. Her niece didn't dare to get married and leave her for fear of being cut out of her will, and if she would have been willing to risk it, her fiancé wouldn't. There was Mrs. Barker, whose elderly daughter had never been allowed to have either a job or a penny of her own—had to go to her mother for bus fares and didn't know how to write a cheque. And there was Miss Robinson, who made a new will regularly every three months, and put in first one and then another of a large circle of relatives as principal legatee. It was like a game of musical chairs. One day the tune would stop and someone would scoop the lot. Well, the Miss Benevents must be pretty old. It wouldn't do Candida Sayle any harm to make up the family quarrel and pay them a little attention. With that new warmth in voice and manner, he advised her to do so.

CHAPTER 2

Candida arrived at Retley on a February afternoon. She hadn't expected anyone to meet her, and no one did. She found a taxi, tipped the porter who carried her suit-cases, and was rattled away over the stones of the station approach. There was a yellow gloom and a drizzle of rain. The lamps were not yet lighted, and she could not feel that she was seeing Retley at its best.

They passed through a street with some good shops, and a number of narrow ones with tall old houses. After that, the usual jumble of bungalows and council houses, until quite suddenly there were open fields and hedges on either side. They passed an inn with a swinging sign, and a little farther on a petrol station, and then just fields and hedges, hedges and fields. She had begun to wonder how much farther it was going to be, when they turned sharply to the left and the ground began to rise.

Presently she made out a wall with iron gates that stood open. The drive was like a dark tunnel, and when they emerged it was not into the light but into a deep and gloomy dusk. The house stood up before them like a black cliff, and the hill stood up behind the house. She stepped back across the gravel sweep and stared at it. There it was—and that was why the house was called Underhill. The hillside must have been cut away to get a level site on which to build, and the house looked as if it was jammed right up

15

against it. What an extraordinary idea, and how dreadfully dark all the back rooms must be.

She returned, skirting the taxi, to the worn stone steps which went up under the shadow of a porch. For the first time it occurred to her that the house must be very old. These steps had been hollowed out by the passing feet of many generations. It seemed odd to find that there was an electric bell.

The taxi driver said, "I've rung, miss," and as he spoke the door swung in. An elderly woman in a black dress stood there. There was a light in the hall behind her—a dark place fitfully illumined. The woman had white hair. It stood out against the glow like a nimbus. She said in a deep voice and with a foreign accent,

"You will come in. He will carry the cases. I have a half-crown for him. The ladies, they wait you in the drawing-room. I will show you. There—across the hall—the first door. Go in. I see to everything."

Candida crossed the hall. It was hung with tapestry which gave out a mouldy smell. For the most part the subject was lost in gloom and grime, but from a rather horrid glimpse of a sword and a severed head she conjectured that this was perhaps just as well. She came to the door to which she had been directed and opened it.

There was a black lacquer screen, and beyond it a blaze of light. She came round the screen into the room. There were three crystal chandeliers. The candles for which they were made had been replaced by electricity, and the effect was brilliant beyond belief. The sheen dazzled upon the white and gold panelled walls and was reflected back from a ceiling powdered with golden stars. There was a white carpet, white velvet curtains fringed with gold, and chair and sofa

16

covers of thickly ribbed ivory corduroy. The rest of the furniture consisted of gilded cabinets and marble tables with carved and gilded legs placed in stiff symmetry along the walls.

As Candida stood blinking on the threshold, the Miss Benevents rose from two small golden chairs placed on either side of the hearth.

Against all that white and gold they looked very small and black—two little dark women in black taffeta dresses with spreading skirts and tightly fitting bodices. The dresses were exactly alike, and so were the collars of old lace, each fastened by a diamond star. Candida saw the dresses first, but they were not the only things which were alike. There was the strongest possible resemblance of figure, face, and feature. Both were little and thin, both had small features, neatly arched eyebrows, and black eyes, and, most remarkably, neither of them appeared to have a grey hair. They were her grandmother's sisters but the small erectly carried heads were covered with shining black hair quite elaborately dressed. Grey would have been kinder to the little pinched faces and the sallow skins.

They did not move to meet her, but stood there against the background of a portentous marble mantelpiece. Walking up to them was rather like being presented at Court. She had to repress the feeling that a curtsey would be appropriate. Her hand was briefly taken, her cheek was briefly touched. Twice. Each Miss Benevent said, "How do you do?" and the ceremony was over.

There was a little silence whilst they looked at her. From over the mantelpiece a mirror in a gilt frame reflected the scene—Candida in her grey coat, her bright hair showing under a matching beret, and a flush on her cheek because the room was hot and strange and she changed colour easily, and the little black ladies looking at her like a pair of puppets waiting to be jerked into life by an unseen string. They stared at her, and the string jerked. The one on her right said,

"I am Olivia Benevent. This is my sister Cara. You are Candida Sayle. You do not resemble the Benevents at all. It is a pity."

The voice was clear, formal, and precise. There was nothing to soften the words. Miss Cara echoed them on a note of regret.

"It is a great pity."

Seen close at hand the likeness to her sister was that of a copy which has been too often repeated and is blurred at the edges.

Candida wanted to say "Why?" but she thought she had better not. She was unable to feel sorry that she was not thin and black and dry, but she had been nicely brought up. She smiled and said,

"Barbara said I was like my father."

The Miss Benevents shook their heads regretfully. They spoke in unison.

"He must have taken after the Sayles. A very great pity."

Miss Olivia stepped back and pressed a bell.

"You will like to go to your room. Anna will take you up. Tea will be served as soon as you are ready."

Anna was the woman who had admitted her. She appeared now at the door, talking and laughing.

"He is an impudent one, that driver. Do you know what he said to me? 'Foreign, aren't you?'—just like that. Impudence! 'British subject,' I said to him. 'And nothing for you to look saucy about either. I've lived longer in England than you, my young man, and

18

that I will tell anyone! Fifty years I have lived here, and that is a great deal more than you have done!' And he whistled and said, 'Strike me pink!' "

Miss Olivia tapped with her foot on the white hearth-rug.

"That is enough, Anna. Take Miss Candida to her room. You talk too much."

Anna shrugged her shoulders.

"If one does not talk one might as well be dumb."

"And we will have tea immediately. Joseph can bring it."

Candida followed Anna into the hall. The stair went up on the left-hand side to a landing from which a passage ran off on either side. They took the one on the left, Anna talking all the time.

"Of all houses this is the most inconvenient. All the time you must look where you are going. See, here there are three steps up, and presently there will be two steps down again. They must have wanted to break someone's neck when they built like this. Now we go round the corner and up four more steps. Here on the right is a bathroom. This is your room opposite." She threw open a door and switched on the light.

The room which sprang into view was oddly shaped. It ran away into an alcove on one side of the hearth, and the whole of the recess was lined with books. Perhaps it was this which made the place seem dark, or perhaps it would have been dark anyhow with its low ceiling crossed by a beam, curtains and bedspread of a deep shade of maroon, and a carpet whose pattern had become indistinguishable. The walls were covered with what she afterwards found was a Morris paper. At first sight it merely presented an appearance of general gloom, but by the light of day and a more particular inspection it disclosed a pattern of spring flowers massed against a background of olive green. She was glad to see that a small electric fire had been imposed on the narrow Victorian grate. Anna showed her the switch.

"You will turn it on when you want. Thank God, we have a good supply. For ten years I lived with paraffin lamps. Now, no thank you—I have better things to do with my time! You will turn on the fire, and so you will not find it cold. It was put in specially for you. Three years since anyone slept here, but with this good little fire you will not be cold."

Candida looked past the fire at the alcove.

"What a lot of books! Whose room used it to be?"

There was the sort of silence which you can't help noticing. Something made Candida ask her question again.

"You said it hadn't been used for three years. Whose room was it before that?"

Anna stood looking at her with her hair very white above the olive skin and dark eyes. She made an effort, looked away, and said,

"It was Mr. Alan Thompson's room. He has been gone three years."

"Who was he?"

"He was the ladies' secretary. They were very fond of him. He was ungrateful—he disappointed them very much. It will be better you do not speak of him—it is better no one speaks."

But Candida went on speaking. She didn't know why. It just seemed as if she had to.

"What did he do?"

"He ran away. He took things—jewels—money. He took them, and he ran away. Their hearts were

20

broken. They were ill. They went away and they travelled. The house was shut up. They do not speak of him ever—we should not have spoken of him. But you are of the family—perhaps it is better you should know. And they are happy again now. Mr. Derek makes them happy—he is young, he is gay. They do not think about that Alan any more. He is gone, and for us too. I speak too much—they have always said so. See, here is the bell. If you want anything, you ring it and Nella will come. She is my great-niece, just as you are to Miss Olivia and Miss Cara. But she has been born in England—she does not even speak Italian any more. She speaks like a London girl, and sometimes she is saucy. She is one of the new-fashioned ones—service is not good enough for her. She only comes because I say so, and because I have money saved and she does not wish me to leave it to my brother's grand-daughter in Italy. Also the wages are very good. There is a young man whom she wishes to marry, and he encourages her to come. 'Think what everything costs,' he says, 'and think how you can save—good money coming in every week and not a penny going out! We will buy the suite for the lounge.' And Nella, she tosses the head and she says if the money is hers, it will be for her to say what way it is spent. But she comes. It is true that she grumbles every day, but she will stay till she has saved the money for the suite, and perhaps a little longer because of my brother's grand-daughter in Italy." She broke off laughing. "It is true what Miss Olivia says, I talk too much. If you want anything, you ring for Nella, and if she does not do everything you say, you speak to me and I scold her. Now I go and tell Joseph to bring the tea."

CHAPTER 3

Joseph had started life as Giuseppe in a newly arrived Italian family some fifty years before. He had now been Joseph for most of that time, and he spoke with much less accent than Anna. They had married as a matter of convenience. He was dark and of medium height, with the manner of a superior upper servant. When he had set down the tea-tray and gone out of the room, the Miss Benevents told Candida all about him and Anna, speaking in alternate sentences.

"He served in the first world war and was wounded."

"He was lame for quite a long time."

"He has been with us ever since he recovered."

"He was, fortunately, too old to be called up in the last war."

"He is not at all suited to being a soldier."

"He and Anna got married instead. It is more convenient that way."

"It is much more convenient."

They did not give Candida time to say anything. She sat on a small gilt chair and balanced a fragile cup upon a slippery saucer. The china was very good and very thin. The saucer was the kind that has no hollow to keep the cup in its place.

Miss Olivia continued the discourse.

"We are very fortunately situated as regards our staff. Anna's niece Nella looks after the bedrooms, and a woman comes out from Retley on a bicycle."

"Or in the bus if the weather is bad," said Miss Cara.

"It is all very convenient. Let me cut you some of this cake."

"Anna makes very good cakes," said Miss Cara.

As they sat one on either side of her, Candida was obliged to keep on turning her head. It seemed rude not to look at the aunt who was speaking, but she had no sooner turned towards one than the other took up the tale. They were really very much alike, but she thought that she would know them apart. Miss Olivia had a more decided voice and manner than Miss Cara, and she definitely took the lead where Cara merely echoed and agreed. Olivia had a small brown mole high up on her right cheek like a patch. Candida wondered if they were twins. And she wondered just how long she was going to be able to bear this visit.

Miss Olivia poured a second cup of tea from an ornate and capacious pot.

"This tea-service came into the family in 1845 when Gerald Benevent married Augusta Cloudsley. Her mother was the Honourable Fanny Lentine, a daughter of Lord Ledborough, but her father was a wealthy City merchant. The tea-service is handsome and valuable, but we have always regarded the marriage as something of a mésalliance."

"It is the only time that we have ever been connected with trade," said Miss Cara.

The room was very warm and the lights very dazzling. Candida began to have that slightly floating feeling which comes with the onset of sleep. She had had many wakeful nights in the last days of Barbara's life, and since her death she had been working very hard, cleaning, clearing, sorting, and packing up.

Last night she had been too tired to sleep at all. The lights shimmered overhead and the voices of the little black ladies came and went.

She must have slipped from waking into sleeping, because just for a moment the white drawing-room was gone, and the glittering chandeliers. Instead there was a narrow dark hall with a little window through into a room next door. She had been signing her name in a book which lay on a ledge in front of the window. The ink in the pen which she had laid down was still wet. The name was black on the page of the open book—Candida Sayle. She turned away from it, and there were two little black ladies looking over her shoulders, one on either side, in the dark hall. She couldn't see them well because the hall was so dark. One of them said,

"Candida Sayle—a very unusual name," and the other one nodded.

She woke up with a jerk. Her cup was sliding in the smooth flat saucer. The dream could really only have lasted for a moment, because the cup would have started to slide at once, and it hadn't had time to fall. How awful if it had fallen on to the carpet! She could almost see the puddle of tea and broken bits. The shock of it woke her right up. She put down the cup and saucer on the tray, and heard Miss Olivia say,

"The china is French. It belonged to my grandmother. Not one piece has ever been broken."

A sense of the narrowness of her escape quite swamped the memory of the dream. After a few more particulars about the tea-set and its original owner, who must have been her own great-great-grandmother, the conversation drifted to other objects in the room. The mirror over the mantelpiece had been brought from Holland by Edward Benevent in 1830. The mantelpiece itself had been imported from Italy by his father.

"He did not, of course, go there himself," said Miss Olivia. "No Benevent has ever set foot in that country since our ancestor left it in the seventeenth century. While their rights were not admitted and the relationship ignored it would have been beneath their dignity to do so. However strongly the ancestral tie is felt, however strongly the family tradition is observed, we could never consent to visit Italy except on the clear understanding that we are true and legitimate descendants of the ducal house of Benevento."

Miss Cara shook her head.

"We could never consent."

Since Candida had not the slightest idea what they were talking about, she thought she had better not say anything at all. There was, apparently, no need for her to do so. Stiffly upright behind the heavily embossed tray, the teapot, the water jug, the enormous sugar-basin of Augusta Cloudsley's tea equipage, Miss Olivia continued to talk. She may or may not have noticed a slight vagueness in Candida's expression, but she stopped suddenly in the midst of some observations on the value of family traditions and the necessity of maintaining them, to say in a sharpened voice,

"You are, of course, acquainted with our family history."

Candida's colour rose.

"Well—I'm afraid——"

"Incredible! I could not have believed it! Your grandmother was, after all, our sister. I believe that she did not die until her children were nine and ten years of age—quite old enough to have been grounded in the historic facts. But of course her marriage—my father would neither acknowledge nor condone it—she may have found the subject too painful."

Miss Cara raised a lace-edged handkerchief to the tip of her nose and sniffed.

"Oh, *yes*."

Miss Olivia threw her a reproving glance.

"It will be for us to supply the deficiency——" she began, when the door opened and a young man came into the room. He was of medium height with brown eyes, very dark hair, and a most charming smile. He was, in fact, an extraordinarily handsome and vital creature. The Miss Benevents' faces lighted up at the sight of him, their small pinched features relaxed, and the air of solemnity was gone. Speaking both together, they said,

"Derek!" Miss Cara adding, "My dear boy!"

He came up to the table and bent to kiss them both. Miss Olivia introduced him.

"This is our secretary and adopted nephew, Derek Burdon. He is compiling a history of the family. He has recently been in Italy and has returned with some very valuable additional material. He has not been able to sort and arrange it yet—these things take time. We thought perhaps it might interest you to help him in his labours."

Candida thought, "Well, it will be something to do." She met a sparkling glance of the brown eyes, and the prospect brightened a little. He looked as if the family history would not bulk so largely as to preclude the possibility of a few lighter moments. In fact he was young, and he looked as if he might be fun. She was to learn that he was adept at getting his own way with the old ladies and at putting off until at least the day after to-morrow whatever he did not incline towards doing to-day. To the suggestion that he and Candida might get to work on some of the Italian material in the morning he came back with,

"But if you want her to have driving lessons she really ought to start at once. I thought if we went into Retley after breakfast she could begin right away. There's no time like the present. I spoke to Fox about it this morning."

Candida had a bewildered feeling. She looked at Miss Olivia, and received a slight wintry smile.

"I suppose that you do not drive."

"No, but——"

She would have liked to say, "How on earth do you know?" but she restrained herself. Only if Candida Benevent and her descendants had been so completely dismissed from the family consciousness, how on earth did her sisters know whether Candida's grand-daughter could drive or not?

Miss Olivia answered the unspoken question.

"John Sayle was not a man of any means. His son and daughter were brought up in a very moderate manner. Barbara would certainly not have been in a position to own a car."

Miss Cara said, "Oh, dear no," and Miss Olivia resumed,

"My father would not allow of any communication, but he took steps to inform himself of such events as births and deaths. When he passed away we continued on the same lines. We have thus always been aware of our niece Barbara's circumstances and whereabouts. Since your parents died young and were in no position to provide for you, your education must have been quite a strain upon her resources. There would have been no money left over for such things as a car."

"Oh, none at all," said Miss Cara.

Her sister went on as if she had not spoken.

"But we feel that being able to drive may now be considered a most useful accomplishment. We thought that you would perhaps like to have lessons and qualify for a driving-licence during your visit. We had intended to lead up to the subject, but Derek has forestalled us."

He laughed ruefully.

"I've put my foot in it again!"

Both ladies beamed at him.

"You are sometimes too impetuous, dear boy."

There was a point in Miss Olivia's speech when there had been a pricking of angry tears behind Candida's eyes. Never for a single moment had Barbara allowed her to feel herself a burden. They had been happy together—they had been happy. She clenched her hands until the nails ran into the palms.

Miss Olivia went on talking for long enough to let that pricking anger subside. She had always wanted to learn to drive, and the lessons would probably save her life. They would mean going into Retley and getting away from Underhill for at the very least an hour at a time, and with any luck a good bit more than that. If she and Derek were to go off on their own, she thought there might be ways and means of spinning out the time—letters for the post, errands to the shops, morning coffee. She met Derek's eye and found it sparkling with mischief. Her spirits began to rise. She listened intelligently whilst Miss Olivia told her how Ugo di Benevento fled from Italy in the middle of the seventeenth century, taking with him what had come afterwards to be known as the Benevent Treasure.

"He had got into some trouble of a political nature—it was so very easy in those days—and the family cast him off in what we have always considered to be an extremely cowardly manner. It may perhaps account for the misfortunes which fell upon them afterwards. As you will no doubt remember, Napoleon in 1806 bestowed what had been the ancient Duchy upon the upstart Talleyrand, with the title of Prince of Benevento. At the fall of Napoleon the province became once more a part of the Papal territories until 1860, when it was united to the kingdom of Italy. Our ancestor was well received over here. He married an heiress of the name of Anne Coghill and built this house. There have been alterations and additions of course. This room was, for instance, extended and greatly improved during the eighteenth century. In the generations since Ugo there have been many advantageous marriages. The Italian ending to the name was dropped, and Benevents have married into some of the noblest families in England. My father's indignation at Candida's mésalliance arose from this fact. John Sayle's father was, I believe, a mere yeoman farmer. That his son took orders can hardly be said to excuse her."

Candida resigned herself. The great-aunts existed in the past—useless to try and disinter them. She really felt a good deal prouder of the yeoman farmer than of Ugo who had run away with the family jewels and married an heiress, but it was no use saying so.

Miss Olivia continued to rehearse the births, marriages, and deaths of the Benevents, with Miss Cara nodding assent and occasionally putting in a word or two. It all felt very stiff and unreal, but in a sort of a way it was interesting, like those stiff medieval pictures which it was so hard to relate to the living, breathing human beings who had sat for them. They had had real joys and sorrows, and hopes and fears. They had lost people whom they loved. They had lost their hearts, their heads, their lives. They had fought and conquered, or fought and been defeated. There was a kind of fascination about making them come alive and be real again. Her mood changed insensibly. After all, these were her people too—she ought to know something about them. Her eyes brightened and her colour rose.

Derek Burdon watched her with genuine admiration. She might have been a pale, flabby girl with dead-fish eyes, or one of those skinny little things with bones instead of curves. Whatever she had been, he would have had to follow her round and amuse her. As it was, his luck was in.

The discourse on the Benevent family went on and on.

CHAPTER 4

Candida went up to bed that night with the feeling that it wasn't going to be so bad. The evening meal had been formally served by Joseph in a cavernous dining-room from whose gloomy walls dark family portraits frowned upon the scene. But the meal itself was beautifully cooked—a soup, a fish soufflé, a sweet. And then the white drawing-room again.

It appeared that Derek had a pleasant voice and a

light touch upon the piano, a lordly grand in a cream enamelled case. Candida found herself diverted to that end of the room, asked if she knew this or that, persuaded to join her own voice in a light duet. The Miss Benevents beamed approval and the evening passed very pleasantly.

When she got up to her room there was a girl there putting a hot water-bottle in the bed, rather pretty with a dark lively look. Candida had a friendly smile.

"Oh, thank you. Are you Nella?"

There was a slight toss of the head.

"Well, that's just Auntie—her fancy Italian way of saying Nellie." The accent and the laugh were authentic cockney. "It riles me a bit, but what's the use?"

"Your name is really Nellie?"

"That's right. My old Gran that I don't remember, she came over with Auntie about the year one, and she married an Irishman, and my Mum who was their daughter, she married a Scotchman called Brown, and they lived in Bermondsey, so how much of the Italiano have I got? Proper Londoner, that's what I am—born there and brought up there and don't want to be anything different! It's no good saying that sort of thing to Auntie—she don't understand. Only how she can go on year in, year out in a nasty dark country hole like this"—she gave an expressive shrug—"well, it passes me!"

Candida laughed.

"You don't like the country?"

"Like it!" The London voice was shrill. "It gives me the pip! And I wouldn't be here, only Auntie made such a point of it, and the doctor at the eye hospital he said if I didn't knock off a bit and rest my eyes I'd be sorry I hadn't done what he said. I'm

31

an embroideress—but the work's too fine, I'll have to find something else. As a matter of fact I'm getting married, so when Auntie made a point of it and the money was good, I thought, oh, well, I can stick it out if I've got to—for a bit anyway. Is there anything else I can do, Miss Sayle?"

"Oh, no. I'm going to love the hot water-bottle."

The girl flashed her a smile as she went out. Candida had a feeling that it wouldn't be very long before she heard all about the boy friend and the lovely suite. The bed was comfortable and the hot water-bottle was really hot. But before she had time to luxuriate in these thoughts they were blotted out by the rising tides of sleep. She went down under dreamless waters and lost herself.

A long time afterwards, when the turn of the night was past and a thin white mist lay ankle-deep on the low-lying fields beyond the garden, the tides began to go down again. They thinned away and left her in the place where dreams can come and go. She was asleep, but she was not unconscious any more. The dreams came and went. In the first one she had gone back nearly six years. A knob of rock cut into the palm of her left hand. With the nails of her right hand she dug into a shallow crack and clung there. Her feet tiptoed on a narrow ledge. At any moment she was going to fall to the bare black rocks below. The dream was not a new one. During the years it had come and gone again—when she was tired— when she was troubled—when something reminded her. But it had come less and less. In her last year at school it had not come at all. Then, with Barbara's illness, it had started again. Sometimes it ended with the fall, sometimes it changed in a flash and she would be up on the ledge above, with Stephen saying, "You're all right now." When she fell, she always woke before she got as far as the rocks. Tonight she did not fall, nor did she reach the ledge. She heard Stephen calling from the sea, and she turned her head. She couldn't have done it really—not without losing her hold, but in the dream it was all quite easy. She looked round and saw him coming to her across black water with wings on his feet, like Perseus in the story of Andromeda. She saw the wings quite plainly—they were bright and fluttering. He had light wind-swept hair, and he had on old grey flannel slacks and an open-necked shirt and a tweed jacket. And then all of a sudden he was gone, and so was the sea and the cliff. There was a wall with a window in it, and an open book on the windowsill. She had just written her name in the book, Candida Sayle, and someone said, "That is a very unusual name." There were two old ladies standing one on either side of her and looking at the book. One of them said, "It's a very nice walk along the beach," and the other one nodded. One of them said, "It is not high tide until eleven." And she woke up.

The room was dark. She had pulled back the curtains, and she could just see the shape of the window. She sat up straight in bed with her heart beating fast. Her hands pressed down on the mattress on either side of her. There was a trickle of sweat in the hollow of her back, a cold running drop. Her heart beat because she was afraid, and she was afraid because in the moment of waking she remembered three things and they all rushed together. There was the dream from which she had just waked up. There was the dream which had come and gone in the moment when sleep had reached out and touched her under the lights in the white and gold drawing-room. And there was the thing that wasn't a dream—the thing that had happened more than five years ago, when two old ladies had stood in the hall at Sea View and told her what a nice walk there was along the beach, and one of them had said, "It won't be high tide until eleven."

These three things rushed together in her mind and became one thing. It wasn't a dream any longer, it was fact. It was the Miss Benevents who had looked over her shoulder and read her name in the hotel register. It was her great-aunt Olivia who had told her about the beach and the tide, and it was her great-aunt Cara who had nodded assent.

Sitting up in bed in the dark room, she said, "Nonsense!" There was a shaded light beside the bed. She switched it on. She had her mother's watch, and it lay on the table under the lamp. The time was half-past five, the sort of time you did have thoughts like that. She left the light on and lay down shivering, with the clothes snuggled up about her neck. She began to get warmer at once. The bed was soft and the light friendly. The dreams receded. The two old ladies at Sea View were just any old ladies who had muddled up the times of the tides. The hall had been dark—she hadn't really seen them at all clearly. And she hadn't ever seen them again, because when she and Stephen had got off the cliff and back to Sea View there was no more than time for her to snatch some breakfast and catch a train home. Monica had telephoned to say her mother was really ill and would have to go into a nursing home. She herself would stay with an aunt in London. She was dreadfully sorry. Mummy would send a cheque for the bill, and there was nothing for it but for Candida to go home. So Candida went. And she didn't see the old ladies again. And she didn't see Stephen Eversley.

She lay in the shaded light of the lamp and thought about all these things. It was quite easy to see how she had got the old ladies mixed up with the great-aunts. Two old ladies in black in the hall at Sea View—two old ladies in black in the white drawing-room at Underhill. One taking the lead and the other following. Wasn't that the sort of thing that would be bound to happen when sisters lived together all their lives? The idea that the old ladies at Sea View had been her Benevent great-aunts was just one of the fantastic things that happen in a dream, like Stephen in grey flannel slacks with wings on his feet. She slid into sleep again, and only woke when Nellie came in with the early morning tea.

CHAPTER 5

They breakfasted in the dining-room. Candida wouldn't have believed it possible, but it was even gloomier by daylight. The Miss Benevents appeared to take a certain pride in the fact.

"It is one of the original rooms, and as you see, it looks out towards the hill." Miss Olivia might have been introducing a View.

It would have been difficult to avoid seeing the hill, since there was no more than twenty feet between it and the two narrow windows. The intervening space was paved in stone. It formed a small square court-yard with figures in each corner and a rather larger one in the middle. The one in the middle represented a naked lady brooding over an urn. All the figures, as well as the paving-stones, had acquired a film of damp green slime.

"This is the oldest part of the house," said Miss Olivia, pouring out coffee. "Several of the other rooms have been added to, but this is just as it was built. Perhaps you will help yourself to milk and sugar. We have been employing a young architect to advise us about the preservation of all this part of the house. We have been a good deal disturbed by the appearance of one or two cracks."

"Very alarming," said Miss Cara.

Miss Olivia went on as if she had not spoken.

"We fear that they must be attributed to the bombs which fell in the neighbourhood from time to time during the war."

"These things do not always show themselves at once."

"So we thought it wise to have expert advice. Mr. Eversley is very well known in the neighbourhood."

"Lord Retborough employs him at the Castle."

"We had hoped for his advice, and he came for a preliminary survey, but the actual work will be supervised by his nephew, who, he assures us, is fully competent."

"Mr. Stephen Eversley," said Miss Cara.

Candida heard herself saying, " I think I met him once when I was at school." She had no idea why she should have put it like that. The words said themselves, and it did not occur to her that they might be misleading, until she found Miss Olivia enquiring whether the head mistress had been satisfied with his work. She did her best to clear the matter up.

"Oh, I didn't mean that he came down to the school. I just met him once in the holidays."

Miss Olivia looked at her rather coldly.

"He probably will not remember you."

It was at this point that Candida should have narrated her adventure on the cliff, and she simply couldn't do it. Last night's dream got up and wouldn't let her. The Miss Benevents looked at her, and she said nothing at all. She just couldn't think of anything to say.

And then the door opened and Derek came in, wreathed in morning smiles.

"I'm late again! I don't suppose it's any good my saying I'm sorry." He kissed Miss Olivia. "I make good resolutions every night and break them every morning." He kissed Miss Cara. "You shouldn't have such comfortable beds—I just can't wake up."

As a topic Stephen Eversley was superseded.

They got off to Retley by ten o'clock, with Derek at the wheel of a good-looking Humber.

"Pre-war, but she hasn't done a big mileage and she has always been very carefully looked after. This is her original paint, but she's just had an overhaul and she goes like a bird. You know, I could have taught you just as well as Fox, but the old dears wouldn't hear of your practising on her. They let me drive because if they didn't the car would never go out. And they think you should have lessons from a qualified instructor, so if you don't mind, I'll just hand you over to Fox and be off on my own. I should get the jitters if I had to sit behind and watch you doing all the things you're bound to do to begin with. People who give driving lessons must have nerves of iron. Mine aren't, and I should only make you nervous. You don't mind, do you?"

Candida said, "Why should I?" She thought there was a discrepancy between his professed willingness to teach her himself and this advertisement of a lack of nerve. She thought that he had other fish to fry, and that it was none of her business. It did not surprise her when he suggested that it might not be necessary to obtrude the fact that he had not superintended the lesson.

"You'll do a lot better if you haven't got my eyes boring into the back of your neck. But they wouldn't understand about that, so if you don't mind——"

Candida met a laughing glance and found herself laughing too. There was that sense of escape, of having secrets from the elders, which is not always left behind with childhood. If she couldn't help wondering what he was going to do with himself, she asked no questions.

"Look here, I'll meet you at the Primrose Café, just opposite the garage. Half-past eleven, and whoever gets there first can order coffee for two."

Mr. Fox was a red-headed young man with a lot of cheerful self-confidence. He informed Derek that he could do very well without a passenger in the back seat—chipping in as likely as not and making the learner nervous.

"And now, Miss Sayle, if you'll just pay close attention, we'll start with the dashboard."

Candida was interested and quick. She got all the gadgets sorted out in a remarkably short time, after which he made her move over and took the wheel until they were out of Retley on an empty road with wide grass verges.

She hadn't known that it would be so thrilling to feel the wheel under her hands. Power and speed—everything running smoothly—control—it was like having a new sense. It was like having wings. She turned with sparkling eyes, her lips parted to say so, and only Mr. Fox's large freckled hand on the wheel kept the car on the road. He said in a tone of reproof,

"Now don't you go looking round! You keep your eye on the road!"

The lesson went very well. They were out for an hour, and she passed six cars, two lorries, and the Ledbury bus. Mr. Fox dismissed her with words of approbation, and she went across to the Primrose Café feeling a good deal pleased with herself.

The café was twentieth-century Olde Englishe with beams that only just cleared your head and bottle-glass in the windows. This made the interior so dark that it was more than easy to fall down the two steps which separated the front of the premises from the back. Candida, having had a narrow escape, stood still and looked about her to see if there were any more traps. There were a lot of little tables with tops made of yellow tiles, thus saving table-cloths. There was pale yellow china, and a waitress in yellow linen with a mob cap. The place was very nearly empty, but sitting alone at a table in the far corner was a tall man. He had on a tweed jacket, and she couldn't see his face because he was bending forward over the table and writing in a notebook. All she could see was the top of his head, and because she had dreamed about Stephen Eversley last night and had heard him talked about this morning he reminded her of Stephen. Just the thick light hair, and perhaps the tweed coat. Her eyes were getting accustomed to the bottle-glass dusk. The jacket was brown, and the hair was the colour of sun-dried hay, or it would be if you allowed for the greenish tinge in the light.

She walked slowly towards the table next to the one at which he sat, and just as she came level with him he looked up, and it was Stephen. She thought that it was odd he should be so exactly like the dream. He was, and it puzzled her, because after all they were more than five years older. She stared right into his eyes and said, "Stephen!" in a sort of jerky whisper, and he stared back and said, "What on earth are you doing here?" He was looking up, and she was looking down. Her knees wobbled and she sat down on the nearest chair. She hadn't thought that he would recognise her—she hadn't really had time to think at all. Five years was five years, and she was only fifteen when he was Perseus to her Andromeda. She found enough breath to say,

"But you don't know who I am." And he laughed and said in an everyday careless sort of voice, "But of course I do! You're Candida—Candida Sayle."

She had a warm, bewildered feeling. It was nice to be recognised, but how did he do it? She was glad of the chair, and she was glad to reach out and hold on to the table. When five years have been suddenly telescoped, it makes you feel giddy.

Stephen said, "You look as if you had seen a ghost."

She shook her head.

"Oh, no—not me. I knew you were somewhere about. Did you know that I was? Because if you didn't——"

"I didn't."

"Then I can't see how you recognised me."

He laughed.

"But you haven't changed a bit. No plait, but otherwise just about the same. What are you doing here?"

The giddy feeling was passing off. There are people whom you have to get to know again every time you meet them, and there are people with whom time doesn't make any difference—if you didn't see them for twenty years you could begin again just where you left off, in the middle of a sentence if necessary.

Candida began to have this feeling about Stephen. They had only met once, and that was nearly six years ago, but they didn't feel like strangers. They weren't doing any of the things that belonged to having met only once before.

It didn't occur to them to shake hands or say, "How do you do?" She just sat and looked at him with the blue of her eyes dark and troubled, and he looked back and smiled.

"Well?"

"I'm staying here with some great-aunts. They asked me on a visit. Barbara is dead."

He said, "I'm sorry."

The way he said it was nice—as if he really meant it—as if he was really sorry that she had lost Barbara and was all alone. It took away some of the aloneness. She said,

"You did go into your uncle's office? You told me you were going to."

"Yes—that's why I'm here. I'm doing a job on an old house that got shaken up by the bombing in the war. It belongs to two Miss Benevents."

Candida said, "Yes."

"Why—do you know them?"

"I'm staying with them."

"They're not your aunts?"

"My great-aunts. My grandmother was their sister. Her name was Candida Benevent, and their father cut her off and cast her out because she married my grandfather who was the son of a yeoman farmer— 'although he had taken orders.'" She spoke in a quot-

41

ing voice, and he laughed.

"You mean he was a parson?"

She nodded mournfully.

"But it didn't make up for his being a farmer's son."

"Is that what the old ladies say?"

He remembered liking the way she smiled. Her lip curled up a little more on one side than on the other, and there was just a glimpse of those very white teeth. She said,

"Oh, yes. So there wasn't any communication, but he took means to inform himself when anyone was born or died. And the aunts went on doing it, so they knew when my grandmother died, and my father and mother, and Barbara. And when there was only me, they asked me to come and stay, and I did."

Stephen was frowning.

"I was at Underhill two days ago. How long have you been there?"

"I came yesterday."

"And how long are you going to stay?"

"I don't know—it was a bit vague. They're giving me driving lessons. It's very kind of them."

He said abruptly, "Who is teaching you? Not Derek Burdon?"

"No, it's Mr. Fox from the garage over the way. He's very good."

"Like it?"

Her smile flashed out.

"Oh, yes!"

It was at this moment that Derek made his belated appearance. He said he had had a puncture, hoped she had not been waiting long, and, rather as an afterthought, became aware of Stephen Eversley.

"Oh, hullo! Do you know each other?"

Stephen said, "Oh, yes," and Candida put in, "Of course we do. I said so at breakfast."

"You said you'd seen him once at school."

"Not at school. I said I was still at school when I met him. I was fifteen and a half."

Derek laughed.

"And now we've got that settled, what will you have—tea or coffee? I'll go and have a wash while they're bringing it. I got filthy changing a wheel."

When he had gone, Stephen said,

"Did he drive you in?"

"Yes."

"But he didn't go out with you and Fox?"

"No."

"Why?"

She laughed.

"He said it would make me nervous. But I think——"

"Well?"

"I don't think I'll say it."

"You mean you don't get on?"

"Oh, no, we get on very well."

"Then what?"

"Oh, just that I think he likes to get off on his own, and he's quite good at doing it."

Stephen said, "Oh, well——" And then, "What does he actually do?"

"Family history, I think. We are supposed to be going to work on it together."

The quick frown came again.

"How long did you say you were going to stay?"

"I didn't say. I don't know."

"How do you mean you don't know?"

"Well, I shall have to get a job. The bother is I'm not trained for anything."

43

He said abruptly, "No money?"

"Not very much."

He looked as if he was going to speak, but checked himself.

Derek appeared in the offing.

Stephen said quickly, "Lunch with me to-morrow."

"I don't know—"

He said with energy, "You mean you've got to ask leave?"

"Well, yes—in a way."

"Then begin the way you're going to go on. If you start by knuckling down you won't be able to call your soul your own—nobody who works for them can. Lunch to-morrow—twelve-thirty here. The food isn't at all bad. Make your driving lesson a bit later, so that it fits in."

The last words were spoken as Derek came up. He caught them, because when Candida hesitated he laughed and said,

"Why not if you want to? We can fix it up with Fox all right. Join us and have some coffee, won't you, Eversley?"

But Stephen got up.

"No thanks—I was just putting in time—I've got an appointment. Twelve-thirty to-morrow, Candida."

She watched him go. His head just cleared the central beam. Derek had stooped though he had a few inches to spare. Stephen's careless stride took him under it without any regard. Derek said, "That's a near shave," and dropped into a chair as the waitress came in with the coffee.

It was when they were driving home that he asked,

"He wants you to lunch with him to-morrow?"

"Yes."

"Well, I don't know that I'd mention it at Under-hill."

She turned in surprise.

"But I must."

She got a charming smile and a shake of the head.

"Much better not. They won't like it. Architects don't cut any ice socially."

"What nonsense!"

He shrugged.

"Victorian outlook—influence of poor papa—it's never worn off. And what's the use of upsetting them? I told Fox you'd be out for your lesson at a quarter past eleven, and all we need say is that we're lunching in town. They'll be quite pleased about that."

Candida had a feeling of distaste.

"No, I couldn't do that."

He laughed.

"Just as you like! But you know one can't really carry on according to Papa, and what the eye doesn't see the heart doesn't grieve over."

Her colour rose. She shook her head vehemently.

"I'm not going to tell lies about anything at all! Why shouldn't I have lunch with Stephen?"

He shrugged again.

"Oh, have it your own way. But don't blame me if there's a blight."

She wondered what his own plans would be, and she thought he was running a risk. If the Miss Bene-vents were to find out—— The thought broke off. They wouldn't like to feel that he had kept them in the dark. It looked as if there might be a girl whom they wouldn't approve of. His affair, but he needn't feel that he was going to drag her into it.

She went into the house as he was putting the car

away, and found Miss Olivia at her writing-table in a dark little den lined with bookshelves. As she opened the door she heard Miss Cara say in a plaintive voice, "She is really quite pretty, and there is no reason why he shouldn't take to her. It would be much better that way."

Whatever Miss Olivia's reply would have been, it was arrested by Candida's entrance. Instead, she enquired about the driving lesson, and was pleased to hear that it had gone well.

It was Miss Cara, in a chair by the window with a newspaper in her lap, who appeared to be embarrassed. She produced an embroidered handkerchief, rubbed her nose with it, and sniffed. Candida had not allowed herself time to wonder about what she had overheard. She went directly from the driving lesson to the programme for the next day.

"It was lovely. I enjoyed every minute of it. It is so kind of you. And bye the bye, I ran into Stephen Eversley. He asked me to lunch with him to-morrow. I hope you won't mind."

There was the sort of silence which means that you have put your foot in it. Miss Cara sniffed and chafed her nose. Miss Olivia laid down her pen. When the pause had had time to sink in she said in a restrained manner,

"It is not exactly a question of minding."

"Oh——"

"You are naturally inexperienced. It is, of course, hardly to be expected that you should be otherwise, but Mr. Eversley should have known better than to presume on his professional position."

Candida's colour rose brightly.

"Aunt Olivia——"

Miss Olivia's manner became very grand indeed.

"We will say no more about it. The mistake was an excusable one on your part. We have his telephone number. You can ring him up and say that we have made other arrangements for you."

Candida had the feeling that life at Underhill would be impossible if she did not stand up to Miss Olivia. She said,

"No—I don't think I could do that."

There was another pause. The handkerchief was crushed in Miss Cara's hand. But after a moment Miss Olivia gave a small wintry smile and said,

"Well, since the engagement was made, you must please yourself."

CHAPTER 6

The Retley train jogged on without any uncomfortable effect of hurry. Miss Silver, in a corner seat with her back to the engine, was really finding it very restful. Third-class carriages were sometimes badly crowded, but her only companion was a quite elderly gentleman who was immersed in a book. Even if she had been nervous, his aspect would have been reassuring, to say nothing of the fact that it was a corridor train. She felt able to relax and watch the soothing if rather monotonous country-side go sliding by in a procession of fields and hedgerows, country paths and lanes, a farmstead here and a cluster of cottages there, with an occasional pond or stream to brighten it.

After about half an hour she opened a capacious

knitting-bag which lay on the seat beside her and took out four steel needles from which depended about six inches of grey stocking. Her niece Ethel Burkett's three boys, now all of school age, were continual in their requirements, and Ethel had never yet been obliged to buy them a single pair of stockings or of socks. Removing her gloves, she settled herself and began to knit easily and rapidly, her hands held low in the continental fashion.

On the opposite seat Mr. Puncheon was observing her over the top of his book. He had been doing this for some time, but he hoped that she had not noticed it. It would be really dreadful if she were to imagine that he had any intention of annoying her. It was perhaps foolish of him to have followed her into this carriage, but when he had recognised her at the terminus it really did seem as if it was an Opportunity. He had followed her, and he had said to himself that if nobody else got into the compartment he would take it as a Sign. But now that they were alone together a natural diffidence caused him to hesitate. If she were to consider that he was taking a liberty— a lady travelling alone——

He looked at her over the top of his book, and was reminded of a great-aunt of his own now many years deceased. She would, of course, have been a great deal older than Miss Silver if she were still alive, but he was very strongly reminded. There was the black felt hat trimmed with loops of purple ribbon, and there was the small bunch of purple flowers of some species not easily identified. Mr. Puncheon was an enthusiastic gardener, and even in the preoccupation of his mind he refused to accept them as violets. He could dimly remember Aunt Lizzie with a similar bunch upon her bonnet. The hat ought not to have reminded him of the bonnet, but it did. Then there was the black cloth coat, the kind of garment which looks as if it had never been new, and as if it would never wear out. And the tippet of yellowish fur grown pale with age. He could not remember that Aunt Lizzie had had a tippet, but all the same he was very strongly reminded.

The precious moments were slipping away. The Opportunity was escaping him. He looked out of the window and sought for a Sign. If there was a haystack before he could count up to sixty, he would speak. There was no house. If there was a black and white cow? There were three black and white cows in a field. He turned his head with a jerk and said,

"I beg your pardon, madam——"

Miss Silver gazed at him in a mildly enquiring manner.

Mr. Puncheon, having taken the plunge, struck out for the shore.

"If you will forgive me for addressing you. You will not know me, but I recognised you immediately."

Miss Silver continued to knit and to maintain the enquiring gaze.

"Yes?"

"You are Miss Maud Silver, are you not? I used to see you when you were staying with Mrs. Voycey at Melling at the time of the Melling murder. I had a bookshop in Lenton, and you were pointed out to me. It was said that it was due to you that the matter was cleared up. My name is Puncheon—Theodore Puncheon."

Miss Silver observed him. He was of medium size and he stooped a little. He had thick grey hair, and he wore old fashioned pince-nez with steel rims. Behind them were a pair of good brown eyes with an anxious expression. She said,

"Yes, Mr. Puncheon?"

He took off the glasses and rubbed them with a silk handkerchief.

"If you will excuse me for addressing you—when I saw you like that on the platform and you got into the Retley train, it did seem like an Opportunity. So I got into the same compartment, and when no one else got in—I hope you will not think me superstitious, but I felt that it must be *meant*."

Miss Silver's slight cough was of the kind intended to recall a speaker to the point.

"In what way, Mr. Puncheon?"

He laid down his book upon the seat.

"Well, you see, I have a Problem, and speaking as a professional man myself, and without wishing in any way to intrude, I did understand that you were consulted professionally in the affair of the Melling Murder—you will correct me if I am wrong."

"No, Mr. Puncheon, you are not wrong."

There was a discernible sigh of relief.

"Then will you kindly allow me to consult you professionally?"

Miss Silver pulled on the ball of wool concealed in her knitting-bag.

"I am going down to Retley to stay with a connection. She is not very robust, and she has a good deal of family business on her hands. I do not know to what extent my time may be taken up."

Mr. Puncheon adjusted his glasses, and left them crooked.

"I feel that it would be of great help to me if you would allow me to talk to you about my Problem. I do not know if there are any steps that could be taken, but I feel that it is laid upon me to find out if there is anything that can be done. So the Opportunity having occurred——" He paused and looked at her in a hopeful manner.

Miss Silver's needles clicked.

"Perhaps if you would tell me what your problem is——"

Mr. Puncheon allowed himself to relax. He leaned forward, his stoop a little more pronounced.

"I told you that I had a bookshop in Lenton, but I have lately moved to Retley. My wife died about a year ago—she had been a sad invalid—and at about the same time my sister was left a widow. Her husband had a bookshop in Retley, and she suggested that I should sell my business and join her. As she said, why should we both be lonely when we might be together?"

"A very sensible remark."

"My sister is a very sensible woman. To cut a long story short, I did sell my business and I joined her. She is a very good cook, and we could be very comfortable together were it not for the Problem. You see, my late wife had a son."

"You mean that he was your step-son?"

"Exactly—her son by her previous marriage with a Mr. Thompson, a solicitor's clerk."

"And this son is the problem?"

Mr. Puncheon sighed.

"You might put it that way. His father died, and his mother spoiled him. She had a soft heart, and he was a very good-looking boy. At the time of her marriage to me he was fifteen and it was too late to control him. He was a bright boy at school, and as he grew older he proved very attractive to young women. I don't blame him entirely, because they ran after him, but it ended in a scandal and he left Lenton. He was about two-and-twenty at the time. He didn't write, and my wife took it very much to heart. And then, after some months, we had news of him. He had got a job as a secretary to two old ladies near Retley. It was through my sister that we heard about it. These Miss Benevents came into the shop with him, and she said they were in a fair way to spoiling him as much as his mother did. It was Alan this and Alan that, until she said it would have done her good to box his ears. Mind you, he hadn't seen her since he was a child, and he didn't connect her with us, or they wouldn't have got him into the shop. But she knew him all right. We had sent her snapshots from time to time—to say nothing of the way they were calling him by his name. It was, 'Alan dear!' and 'Dearest boy!' and, 'Mr. Thompson would like to see what you've got in reprints of so-and-so's novels!' My sister said she didn't know how she bore it, but she thought it best not to say anything. Well, his mother wrote off at once, and Alan wrote back as cool as you please. He had found himself a good job and he was in a fair way to doing very well for himself, and he didn't want his relations coming round and interfering. The old ladies had high ideas, and it wouldn't do him any good to have it known that he was connected with trade."

Miss Silver used her strongest expression of disapproval. She said,

"Dear me!"

"Well," said Mr. Puncheon, "I don't mind saying that I was angry, and my poor wife took a turn for the worse. Then about six months later my sister wrote and said it was the talk of the town that Alan had helped himself to things that didn't belong to him and run off, and not a word as to where he had gone. I went down to Retley, and I went to see the Miss Benevents. They've got an old house called Underhill about three miles out. Yes, they said, Alan had run off. He had taken money and a diamond brooch. They had trusted him as if he were one of the family, and he had deceived them. They wouldn't prosecute him, because they were too upset. They were going off abroad to try and get over it, and they hoped never to see or hear of him again. Well, I felt rather the same way myself. I went home and told my wife, and I think it killed her—not just at once, you know, but that's what it amounted to."

Miss Silver looked at him kindly.

"It is a very sad story, Mr. Puncheon, but not I fear an uncommon one. The loving mother who spoils her child is preparing an unhappy future for both of them."

Mr. Puncheon said, "Yes." And then, "But that is not all. If it had been, there would be no Problem to trouble you with. It has arisen quite lately, since I have come to Retley."

"Something has happened?"

Mr. Puncheon adjusted his glasses.

"I suppose you might put it that way. My sister is a good Chapel member. A little while ago it came to her knowledge that a Mrs. Harbord who attends the same Chapel was lying ill and in a bad way and asking to see her. So Ellen went. There was a daughter-in-law looking after her, and what you would call sufficient care, but the woman had something on her mind. When she was alone with my sister she began to cry and to say that she had got it on her conscience to have let a young man's character be taken away. Ellen said what did she mean, and she said wasn't it true that she was in a way connected with Alan Thompson? Ellen wasn't best pleased, and she said, 'My brother was married to his mother, if that is what you call being connected.' Then Mrs. Harbord said was it true that I was coming to live with her and taking over the business, and she began to cry and said she didn't know he had relations in Retley. Ellen has a quick tongue, and I suppose she came out with something about not having any reason to be proud of the connection, and Mrs. Harbord catches her by the wrist and says, 'You think he stole those things and ran away, but he didn't!'"

"How did Mrs. Harbord come to know anything about it?" said Miss Silver.

Mr. Puncheon gazed at her mildly.

"Didn't I tell you that? Of course I should have done. How very stupid of me. You see, Mrs. Harbord obliged the Miss Benevents—went up every day on her bicycle and did housework and cleaning for them until she got ill—so of course she knew Alan quite well. And when she said about his stealing and running away I'm afraid my sister took her up pretty sharply, and then she couldn't get any more out of her. Mrs. Harbord just lay there and cried and said he never did it. And the daughter-in-law came in and said she couldn't have her upset, and would Ellen please go, and she went. Well, she didn't tell me about it until getting on for a month ago, and I don't seem to get it off my mind. Ellen says it means no more than that he'd made the same kind of fool of Mrs. Harbord as he had of his mother and of any other woman that was fool enough to let him, and it was no good my thinking she was one of them, because she wasn't. I told you she had a sharp tongue."

Miss Silver said quietly,

"In what way was it on your mind, Mr. Puncheon?"

"In the way of thinking that we may have done Alan an injustice—taking what those old ladies said without any question. Afraid—that's what we were, and we swallowed it all down and sheered off in case of anything worse coming to light. And that isn't justice—now is it? A man may be a thief and he may be a liar, but it ought to be proved against him before you believe it and go cutting him off. Well, we didn't ask to have it proved to us—we believed it right away. Even his mother believed it, and it killed her. Perhaps if I had gone into it more, she wouldn't have believed it and she wouldn't have died. And it began to come to me that I ought to try and do something to make amends. If Alan didn't steal and run away, it wasn't right for people to go on thinking that he did. I began to feel I'd got a duty to get back his good name for him. You see, he was all the world to his mother, and even if she wouldn't know about it I came to feel that it was something I could do for her." Mr. Puncheon let his glasses fall and looked at Miss Silver with sad, defenceless eyes. "You see," he said, "I was very fond of my wife."

Miss Silver returned the look with kindness.

"When did all this happen, Mr. Puncheon?"

He seemed a little surprised, as if it was incredible that there should be anyone who did not know what had made so a great a difference to himself.

"Do you mean about Alan? It was three years ago in February."

"And when did Mrs. Harbord speak to your sister?"

He put on his glasses again.

"It would have been about three months ago, because it was before I took over the business, and I made the move to Retley over the Christmas holidays, so it would have been sometime late in December."

"And after your sister had told you what Mrs. Harbord had to say, did you try to see her?"

"Oh, yes, I did, but the daughter-in-law wouldn't let me in. She said my sister had made quite enough of an upset without having any more of the family coming around. So what could I do?"

"Then you do not really know whether Mrs. Harbord had any grounds for what she said?"

He shook his head.

"Only what I have told you. Ellen said she just kept saying over and over that he never went away from Underhill."

Miss Silver stopped knitting for a moment.

"You did not tell me that."

"Oh, didn't I? That is what she kept on saying."

"Mr. Puncheon, if that was true, have you thought what it would mean?"

He looked startled.

"How could it be true? Why should the Miss Benevents say he was not there if he was?"

She said gravely,

"I think Mrs. Harbord ought to be asked to answer that question."

CHAPTER 7

Candida's second lesson went extremely well. Stephen, waiting in the Primrose Café, saw her come in with a glowing colour and starry eyes. She made a brightness in the shaded place. He had a rush of feeling which surprised him. It was as if a light had sprung up to meet her, and when she came to him and they looked at each other the brightness was round them both. He said, "Did you have any difficulty in getting away?" and she said, "Nothing to speak of," and then they both laughed.

When they were seated he went on, with the remains of the laugh in his voice.

"Your aunts are a bit formidable, you know—at least Miss Olivia is. I had an idea they wouldn't think much of my asking you out to lunch."

Candida's already bright colour rose. She said,

"Oh, well—" And then, as much to change the subject as anything, "Stephen, such a funny thing— do you know, Aunt Olivia isn't the elder. Anyone would think so, wouldn't they?"

"You don't mean to say it's Miss Cara!"

She nodded.

"Yes, I do. And I'll tell you how I found out. Derek and I were turning over a lot of old music yesterday evening. It was in the drawer of the music-stand— old songs, you know. And right in the middle of them there was a photograph of three little girls in white party frocks and their hair tied back with bows.

57

I could see that two of them were the great-aunts—because of the dark hair and the dark eyes, and their features haven't changed a lot. And I guessed that the third one must be my grandmother Candida, so of course I was very much interested, and I turned the photograph over to see if there was anything written on the back."

"And there was?"

She nodded.

"Their names and their ages behind each of them. And this is how they went. Caroline aged seven and a half—Candida aged six—Olivia aged five. So you see, Olivia is the youngest. You'd never think it, would you?"

"No, you wouldn't. I expect she got spoilt, and it made her bossy."

"I don't think anything *makes* you bossy—you just are. And there's only two and a half years between the three of them. By the time they were grown up that would hardly make any difference at all, and now when they are old you can wash it right out."

They went on talking about a lot of different things. Stephen's work—

"Nothing very exciting to be done, with all these restrictions on materials. It's not very inspiring to be having to think how you can get five pounds off the cost, or where you can cut out half a dozen bricks or a foot or two of timber. And when you look at some of these old houses and see how lavish they were, it fairly makes your mouth water. Underhill is an interesting bit of patchwork. Those back rooms have practically never been touched. Actually, it is time they were. I've got a horrid suspicion there's some dry rot knocking about, to say nothing of death-watch beetle in some of those old beams. By the way, they are very cagey about the cellars. Miss Olivia didn't consider it would be necessary for me to inspect them, and when I said I couldn't report on the foundations unless I did, she went all *grande dame* and nearly froze me to death. I stuck to it, and she took me down herself, attended by Joseph with a candelabrum. No electric light, though why they didn't have it put in down there whilst they were about it I don't know, and I had a feeling that I had better not ask. Anyhow, all I got was a cursory glance by candle-light and the conviction that I'd only been allowed to see what Miss Olivia chose. Do you suppose there's a secret passage, and that they are afraid of my stumbling on the Benevent Treasure?"

Candida looked up with a startled widening of her dark blue eyes.

"The Benevent Treasure?"

"Haven't you heard about it? Everyone in Retley has. There was an ancestor who ran away from Italy with the family plate and jewels in the seventeenth century. He or his son built the house, and the Treasure is supposed to be hidden in it somewhere. My informant is an old cousin of mine who lives here—the sort of old pet who knows all the stories about everyone in the county and has them patched together and embroidered on to a quite incredible extent. There isn't a dull moment, but you can't bring yourself to believe that any of it is really true. Which is just as well, because most of the stories are pretty scandalous. Amazing, isn't it, how old ladies who have never done anything wrong in their lives can believe and repeat the most awful things about their neighbours."

"Does your cousin know the great-aunts?"

"She knows everyone. Her father was a Canon at

the Cathedral, and his father was a Bishop. It's a sort of aristocracy of the Church, and the Miss Benevents condescended to a visiting acquaintance. My cousin's name is Louisa Arnold. At the moment she is entertaining a female sleuth who is a relation on the other side of the family. I am bidden to sup with them tonight. I met her in the street, and she asked me at point-blank range. Bye the bye, she wants to know whether the Miss Benevents have ever had any news of Alan Thompson. He was their secretary before Derek took it on."

Candida said, "Oh!" And then, "Yes, I know! He ran away with some money and a diamond brooch, and nobody is supposed to mention him."

"But they mentioned him to you?"

"No, it was Anna. She let it out, and then she said I mustn't ever speak about it, because they had been dreadfully upset."

"Well, Louisa wanted to know if they'd had any news of him, because her sleuth, whose name is Maud Silver, had met an old boy in the train who said he was Alan Thompson's step-father and he was a good deal worried about him." He broke off to laugh. "It sounds a bit like 'The stick began to beat the dog, the dog began to bite the pig, the little pig jumped over the stile, and so the old woman got home that night,' doesn't it?"

Candida laughed too.

"Can you say it all through? I used to be able to."

"I don't know—that bit just came into my head. It works up to a butcher killing an ox and water quenching fire, as far as I remember. Anyhow, to get back to Alan Thompson's step-father, there's a good deal of hush-hush about it all, but he wants to know whether anyone has ever heard anything since what may be called the official disappearance."

"I shouldn't think so from what Anna said."

"Well, if you get an opportunity you might ask her. It must be tolerably unpleasant to have a relation disappear into the blue with a suspicion of theft tacked on to him."

Stephen duly supped with Louisa Arnold, and was introduced to "My cousin, Miss Maud Silver." It turned out to be a very distant connection indeed, and he had to listen while Miss Arnold traced it out through her mother's step-brother's marriage to a Miss Emily Silver who was first cousin once removed to Miss Maud Silver's father. As all this information was embellished and diversified by a considerable fund of anecdotage, it took the most of the way through supper. There was an alarming story of the ghost seen by an uncle of the step-brother in question, an apparition so horrifying that he was never able to describe it, and its exact nature had therefore to be left to the imagination of the family. There was the romantic story of the step-sister who met and married a shy and tongue-tied young man and discovered on her return from the honeymoon that he was the heir to a baronetcy and a fortune. There were other beguiling tales.

Miss Silver, contenting herself with an occasional sensible remark, enjoyed the excellent food provided by Louisa Arnold's cook, an old retainer inherited from the Canon, well up in years but still able to invest the post-war ration with the glamour of the now almost mythical years before the war.

It was not until after supper, when they had moved to a drawing-room cluttered with furniture and gazed upon by generations of family portraits, that Stephen found himself invited to a place on the sofa beside

Miss Silver. She was wearing the dark blue crêpe-de-chine bought at the insistence of her niece Ethel during a visit to Cliffton-on-Sea. The price had shocked her, but, as Ethel had insisted, both the material and the cut were of a very superior nature, and she had never found herself able to regret the purchase. She had filled in the "V" at the neck with a net front and wore to fasten it a brooch in fine mosaic which depicted an oriental building against a background of bright sky-blue. A work-bag lay between them, and she was engaged with four steel needles and a boy's grey woollen stocking. It did not appear to be necessary for her to watch her work, for when Stephen addressed her she looked at him in a very direct manner. They were for the moment alone, Miss Arnold having disclaimed all offers of assistance and retired to make the coffee.

Stephen said, "I hear that you are anxious for news of Alan Thompson, but I am afraid that I have none to give you."

Miss Silver gave the slight cough which indicated that she had a correction to make.

"It is his step-father who is anxious for news of him. He thought it possible that the Miss Benevents might have heard something."

"If they have they don't speak of it."

Miss Silver pulled on a ball of grey wool.

"There was a song which was very old-fashioned even when I was a girl. It began:

" 'Oh, no, we never mention her,
    Her name is never heard.
    Our lips are now forbid to speak
    That once familiar word.'

"It would seem to describe the situation?"

He nodded.

"I have been lunching to-day with a niece who is staying with them, and she says he really isn't supposed to be mentioned. The old maid told her he had run off with money and a diamond brooch, and she mustn't speak of him because the Miss Benevents had been so dreadfully upset about it."

Miss Silver was silent for a moment, after which she asked no more questions about Alan Thompson, but to his subsequent surprise he somehow found himself talking to her about Candida. He did not realise the fact that he had arrived at the point where it was not only extremely easy to talk about her, but quite difficult to avoid doing so. To this frame of mind there was added an as yet undefined uneasiness on her account. The Miss Benevents depressed him, Underhill depressed him. To think of Candida in association with them produced a feeling of repulsion. Old thoughts, old images rose from the deep places of his mind. They did not quite break surface, but they were there—something about children of light and hidden works of darkness—all very vague, coming up out of the depths and going down into them again.

Miss Silver said, "You do not really like her being there, do you?" and he had no more than time to say, "No, I don't!" when the door opened and Louisa Arnold came in, pushing an elegant tea-wagon. Stephen sprang up. Louisa was voluble on the subject of how long the kettle had taken to boil, and it was only afterwards that it occurred to him that Miss Silver had taken a great deal for granted. She had, for instance, assumed that he had not only a special but a proprietary interest in Candida, and his reply

63

had admitted as much. The odd thing about it was that not only did he not resent this admission, but that it should give him a feeling of exhilaration. All the time Louisa Arnold was explaining that the coffee service was Georgian and quite valuable, and that the cups had belonged to the Canon's mother, this feeling persisted.

"She was a Miss Thwaites and she came from Yorkshire. That is her portrait over the bookcase. Those tinted drawings were all the fashion in the 1830s and '40s—just a little colour in the lips and eyes, and some dark shading in the hair. Ladies used a stuff called bandoline to get that very smooth effect. You see it in the very early portraits of Queen Victoria. My grandmother had naturally curly hair, but her daughter, my Aunt Eleanor, never discovered it until her mother was over eighty. She had kept it banded down all her life, and do you know, it still curled! My aunt persuaded her to let her fluff it up, and I can remember her with lovely silver waves under a lace scarf."

It was some time before Stephen could stem the tide, but they reached the Miss Benevents in the end. Once there, she was profusely reminiscent.

"Oh, yes, we used to play together as children. They were brought up in rather a peculiar way, you know. Their mother had one of those long illnesses, and their father was rather a frightening person—so different from my own dear father, who was the soul of kindness. Olivia always had the upper hand of poor Cara, even though she was nearly three years younger. Candida used to stick up for her, but it wasn't much good, you know. When anyone has such a yielding disposition you can't really do much for them, can you? Candida was the middle one. She wasn't much like the other two—taller, and not so dark. I liked her much the best of the three. But she ran away with a curate who came to do temporary duty at Stockton, which is just on the other side of the hill. Papa's friend, Mr. Hobbisham, was the Vicar, and he was dreadfully upset about it. Now what was the young man's name—would it have been Snail?"

Stephen laughed.

"I expect it was Sayle!"

His Cousin Louisa beamed upon him. She had pretty white hair, surprisingly blue eyes, and a pink and white complexion.

"Yes—so it was! How clever of you, my dear boy! Candida met him at a concert which was got up by the Dean's sister in connection with a Chinese mission. He had a very nice tenor voice, and she was playing all the accompaniments. Candida, I mean of course, not Miss Wrench, who was a woman I never did care about and a terrible thorn in Papa's side, because nobody could possibly help seeing that she was doing her best to marry him, and she was such a determined person that there was always a chance she might succeed, poor darling—and I'm sure it would have killed him. Now let me see—where was I?" The blue eyes gazed at him trustfully.

"Candida Sayle." It gave him pleasure to say the name.

"Oh yes—of course! She married Mr. Sayle, and Mr. Benevent quite cut her off. I know Papa considered it very harsh of him, because Candida was of age, and there was nothing against Mr. Sayle's character. He even had a little money of his own—not very much, but enough to help them along until he got a living. I believe he had the promise of one when they were married. But Mr. Benevent wouldn't allow Candida's name to be mentioned, and I didn't see so much of the other two after that, because she was always the one whom I liked the best. And if it is her grand-daughter who is staying at Underhill I should very much like to see her."

Stephen felt tolerably certain that he had not mentioned Candida whilst Louisa Arnold was in the room. He said, "Oh, yes," and waited for more. It was forthcoming.

"Now who was it was telling me? Someone at the Ladies' Guild—not Miss Smithers or Mrs. Brand—I think it must have been Miss Delaney, because it is connected in my mind with a knitting-pattern for a cardigan, and it was Miss Delaney who gave me that. She said the quarrel must be made up, and about time too, because the girl was staying at Underhill and she had her grandmother's name. Now of course she would be able to tell us what Maud is anxious to find out on behalf of Mr. Puncheon, whether anything has been heard about Alan Thompson. Living in the house, she would know whether they speak of him at all."

"I gather they don't."

Louisa Arnold opened her blue eyes very wide indeed.

"How very extraordinary! But Olivia had a most determined nature. He must have offended them very much, for they really were quite foolishly devoted to him. In fact people did say—well, I hardly like to repeat it, Papa was so very strict about gossip and there is always a good deal in a cathedral town— but they did say that no one would be surprised if Cara were foolish enough to marry him."

Miss Silver said, "Dear me!"

Louisa Arnold nodded.

"There was quite a lot of talk—I heard it myself. Of course there was the difference in age, but you do hear of such things, do you not? There was the Baroness Burdett-Coutts—I remember Papa telling us how displeased Queen Victoria was. And to come down to quite a different walk of life, old Mrs. Crosby who had the sweet shop in Falcon Street was married again within the year to quite a young man who came round as a traveller. They ran the business together and made a very paying thing of it. People said it wouldn't come to any good, but they seemed to get on quite well. But Olivia would never have let Cara do anything so foolish. And now of course there is this other young man, Derek Burdon, but I believe he calls them Aunt, which is a great deal more suitable. Only of course it wouldn't be easy for them to provide for him unless they can do it out of their savings, because if anything happened to Cara, this grand-daughter of Candida's would come in for everything."

Miss Silver stopped knitting for a moment. Her hands rested on the four steel needles and the half-finished stocking.

Stephen said sharply,

"Not Miss Olivia?"

Miss Arnold shook her head.

"Oh, no, I believe not. It has always been a sore point. Everything was quite strictly tied up by their grandfather. I remember Papa saying that it was all very well for Mr. Benevent to talk of cutting Candida off, but nothing he could do would prevent her or her children inheriting if Cara died without marrying and having children. So he said the quarrel was not only unchristian but foolish."

Miss Silver said quietly,

"It is not an easy position for Miss Olivia."

"Oh, well, it is quite all right for her as long as things go on as they are. Underhill and most of the money may belong to Cara, but it is Olivia who manages everything. I don't suppose poor Cara would have the least idea about what to do. As a matter of fact, I happen to know that Olivia makes out all the cheques and Cara just signs them."

Miss Silver gave the slight cough with which it was her custom to indicate disapproval.

"Not at all a satisfactory practice, Louisa."

"Oh, no. Papa did not approve of it at all. He always said Olivia had too much influence. And now, you know, they do say that she has got this young Candida Sayle here to try and marry her to Derek Burdon. You see, it would provide for him if anything happened to Cara, and Olivia would naturally expect to go on having a say in everything."

Stephen said in a voice of cold fury,

"What a perfectly monstrous idea!"

Miss Louisa looked surprised.

"Oh, I don't know, my dear. He is a very good-looking young man, and not as spoiled as Alan Thompson. They might take a fancy to each other. But of course it might not turn out at all as Olivia hoped. There was that rich Mr. Simpson at Ledford—he made over his house and nearly all his money to his son in order to escape the death duties. He was quite old and beginning to be infirm, and he made sure they would look after him, but almost at once the daughter-in-law began to treat him as if he didn't matter. She was very gay and smart, and she filled the house with a very fast set. Papa said it was a most shocking case, and just like King Lear! But it all goes to show that you can't tell what young people will do, so it might not turn out at all as Olivia had planned."

It was at this moment by the light of a blinding flash of anger that Stephen became aware he was in love with Candida Sayle.

CHAPTER 8

It was next day that Miss Silver met Mr. Puncheon in the street. He was hurrying along and had already passed her in a short-sighted manner, when he seemed suddenly to recollect himself and turned back.

"Miss Silver—I really beg your pardon! I have been wanting to see you—I was immersed in my thoughts. Indeed I was hoping very much to see you. I suppose you could not spare a little time? My shop is just there. I had only stepped out to post a letter—the answer to an enquiry about a somewhat rare book."

Miss Silver's errand not being of a pressing nature, and her own thoughts having been to some extent occupied with Mr. Puncheon's Problem and some kindred subjects, she acquiesced in her most gracious manner and found herself presently entering a shop with a gabled front and every appearance of having been there for some hundreds of years. Inside it was dark and crowded with books from the uneven floor to the low black beams overhead. Mr. Puncheon took her through to still gloomier depths at the back, where he opened a door and disclosed quite a tidy office with a modern writing-table and some comfortable nineteenth-century chairs. After allowing her to precede him he paused on the threshold to address an elderly woman in black.

"I shall be a little time, Ellen. Do not disturb me unless it is really important." After which he came in and shut the door.

A gas fire burned on the hearth. Miss Silver having seated herself, he took the opposite chair, made a small vexed sound, and remarked that he had left the fire on again.

"And of course it is no economy if you do that. But having been always used to a coal fire, I find that I go out and leave it, and of course that annoys my sister."

Miss Silver smiled.

"It is not so easy to form new habits. I find the fire very pleasant. Was there something you wished to ask me, Mr. Puncheon?"

He took off his glasses and looked at her in a defenceless manner.

"Oh yes. I want to ask you whether you would advise and help me professionally. What you said in the train—I haven't been able to get it out of my head."

"And what was it that I said, Mr. Puncheon?"

"It was in reply to something that I said myself. We were talking about Mrs. Harbord who had worked for the Miss Benevents. I said she had told my sister that my step-son Alan never went away from Underhill. It was a strange thing to say, wasn't it?"

"Very strange."

"She kept on saying so. Ellen thought it was all nonsense. Why should the Miss Benevents say he had gone away if he hadn't? That's what Ellen said. But when I said it to you, Miss Silver, you said—well, you said that you thought Mrs. Harbord ought to be asked to answer that question."

Miss Silver looked at him and said gravely and clearly,

"Yes, I remember. I still think so, Mr. Puncheon."

He was rubbing his glasses with a large white handkerchief. The initial embroidered across the corner did not look like professional work. It went through Miss Silver's mind to wonder whether it had been the work of his dead wife. He said,

"Yes—yes—that was what I was coming to. You said that she ought to be asked. And I think so too, but I really can't bring myself to do it. The daughter-in-law was really very disagreeable—one of those boisterous women. My wife—my late wife I should say—was an extremely gentle person. I really do not feel at all able to cope. And I thought if you would perhaps accept the commission—on a professional footing——" He did not seem able to get any farther than that.

Miss Silver looked at him seriously.

"You wish me to interview Mrs. Harbord?"

The word obviously startled him.

"Well, I thought—perhaps—you would see her. And if you did not mind, I think it would be better not to say anything to my sister about it. You see, she took such a very decided line, and strife in the house is not what I've been accustomed to."

A few preliminary enquiries informed Miss Silver that Mrs. Harbord, though no longer confined to her bed, was still in a very weak and melancholy way, and that the widowed daughter-in-law whose children were of school age went out to work by the day.

Miss Arnold, it appeared, knew all about her.

"Oh, yes, she goes to the Deanery. Mrs. Mayhew says she is an absolute treasure. Of course she is Chapel. How shocked dear Papa would have been at the idea of employing a dissenter, but people can't pick and choose as they used to, and she is a marvellous worker—never stops for a moment and gets through about twice as much as anyone they have ever had. Mrs. Mayhew says she is more than worth the extra sixpence an hour she asks."

With this and other helpful information at her disposal, Miss Silver considered that an early hour in the afternoon would be the most suitable time for a call.

The appearance of the small house in Pegler's Row certainly bore out the character ascribed to the younger Mrs. Harbord. The front door step was whitened, the four windows, two up and two down, looked as if they had just been cleaned, and spotless curtains screened the rooms behind them from the public eye. The small brass door-knocker shone. Miss Silver used it. After an interval she heard a slow, dragging step in the passage behind the door. It opened a very little way and a tall, stooping woman came into view—at first no more of her than a poking head and a hand, but after a moment the whole bent figure in a decent black dress with a grey shawl caught about the shoulders. At the sight of Miss Silver she stepped back and said in a hollow voice,

"If it's for my daughter-in-law, she won't be in till five."

Miss Silver smiled pleasantly.

"Oh, no, Mrs. Harbord, my visit is to yourself. But you should not be standing at the door. May I come in?"

The days are long when you are alone during most of the dragging hours. Mrs. Harbord no longer felt well enough to engage in the active household tasks with which she had been used to fill her days. By the time she had dressed herself and made shift to do her room she felt fit for nothing but to drop into a chair and mind the kitchen fire. On a good day she would get the children's dinner, but mostly Florrie would leave everything ready, so that she only had to have it hot by the time they came home. She had never been a reader, and there were a great many hours in the day. Miss Silver would be someone from the Chapel—she had heard that the minister had an aunt coming to stay—or perhaps someone from the Ladies' Guild. Anyhow she would be someone to talk to.

"If you wouldn't mind coming into the kitchen," she said. "It's warm in there. We've a nice front room, but the fire isn't lit."

A poor thing she might be, but she had yet to be ashamed of taking anyone into her kitchen. All nicely tidied up it was, and the children back at school. She had her chair by the fire and a footstool in front of it, and a second chair that could be pulled up for the visitor. She was glad to get back into the warm, and that was a fact. It was cold in the passage, and she felt the cold these days.

Miss Silver looked at her in a sympathetic manner and said,

"I am afraid you are not very strong, Mrs. Harbord. You must not let me tire you. My name is Silver— Miss Maud Silver. I thought perhaps we might talk for a little. It must be lonely for you here with your daughter-in-law out all day and the children at school."

Mrs. Harbord said,

"Yes, it's lonely. Only I don't know that I could do with the children all the time—two of them, and twins. And I don't know which of them makes the most noise, the boy or the girl. Just turned eight they are—and lively—you wouldn't believe it."

Miss Silver smiled in a friendly manner.

"It sounds as if they were very strong and healthy."

A gleam of pride appeared on Mrs. Harbord's face.

"Oh, they're healthy," she said. "They take after their mother. Now my poor son, he was always ailing from a baby. Died when the twins were three months old, and what we'd have done I *don't* know, only I had my health, and Florrie went out to work. My old mother was alive then, and she'd mind the babies. I didn't think I'd come to being the one to sit at home and be a burden. The doctor, he says there's no reason why I can't get well, but I don't, and that's a fact."

"I am sure you did not think your mother a burden when she was looking after the babies and making it possible for you and your daughter-in-law to work."

Mrs. Harbord shook her head. Her mother had been a very decided old lady. She would have made short work of anyone who set up to consider her a burden. Even Florrie had been under her thumb.

"She was able for more than what I am," she said.

Before she knew quite how it came about she found herself telling Miss Silver all about her mother. There were incidents which she had not recalled for years. Miss Silver displayed great skill in steering her past deathbeds and family illnesses to such cheerful occasions as weddings, christenings, and outings. Mrs.

Wild had appeared at the twins' christening in a bonnet with two black ostrich feathers which nobody knew she possessed.

"Down in the bottom of her box she'd got them, and a wonder the moths hadn't been at them. 'Why mother,' I said, 'wherever did you get those feathers?' And it seems my Uncle Jim brought them from South Africa when he came home after the Boer war. And just to think she'd never had them out all those years! Not when poor Father died, nor my husband, nor poor Ernie. And she tosses her head and says feathers is for joyful occasions, not for funerals, and she's going to wear them for the twins, poor little fatherless things, and may be they'll bring them a bit of good luck." She broke off to give a heavy sigh and say, "Oh, well, I had my health then. I could bicycle out the three miles and do a day's work and not so much as feel tired at the end of it."

Miss Silver said in a sympathetic voice,

" You used to work at Underhill, did you not, with the Miss Benevents?"

Mrs. Harbord's flow of reminiscence was arrested. She looked sideways and said,

"I'm sure I never mentioned it."

"There was no reason why you should not do so."

"I left on account of my health." Mrs. Harbord's voice shook. "And I was never one to talk."

Miss Silver looked at her.

"What would there be to talk about?"

Mrs. Harbord's hand went up to her lips and stayed there. Her eyes shifted. She said,

"I don't know, I'm sure." And then quite suddenly words came pouring out. "I don't know anything—why should I? I just went there for the cleaning—there wasn't anything for me to talk about."

It was no use, she couldn't go on looking away. She had to turn her eyes back again to meet Miss Silver's. She did so, and found them very clear and kind.

"Pray do not distress yourself, Mrs. Harbord. But when you have something on your mind, I think you know that you cannot get rid of it by pretending it is not there. I think that you have something on your mind. I think it has been there for a long time, and that it is frightening you and preventing you from getting well. You began to tell Mrs. Kean about it, did you not, but you did not go on."

Mrs. Harbord still had that shaking hand pressed against her lips. It came down now and went out groping to the arm of the chair. She said in a startled voice,

"Ellen Kean—did she send you? I thought——"

"No, she did not send me. You asked her to come and see you because you were very ill and you had something on your mind, but when she came you did not tell her very much."

Mrs. Harbord said in a choked voice,

"She came in—and she sat there—and she didn't believe a word I said. She come like it was her Christian duty to come, and because I sent for her. She'd gone up in the world, and I'd gone down, but we went to school together. There isn't much I don't know about Ellen Kean, and her duty is what she'd always do. But when it comes to bowels and mercies, Ellen hasn't got them, and that's a fact. Sat there and looked at me as cold as ice and told me I was talking nonsense. So I don't have any more to say."

"That was when you had told her that the stories about Alan Thompson were not true?"

Mrs. Harbord's voice sharpened.

76

"I don't say there wasn't plenty that might have been true. Favour is deceitful, and beauty is vain, and the way the young women ran after him was enough to turn anyone's head. And not only the young ones neither, but I'm not talking about that. Only what I had on my mind and what I told Ellen Kean was gospel truth, and she hadn't any cause to disbelieve me. You said you didn't come from her?"

Miss Silver made a slight negative movement of the head. Her voice, her look, her manner were having a tranquilizing effect. Mrs. Harbord's breathing was more normal and she no longer clutched the arm of her chair. The time had come for a more open approach. She said,

"I am not acquainted with Mrs. Kean. It is Mr. Puncheon who had asked me to come and see you. He is very much troubled at the stigma which rests upon his step-son's name. It would be a great relief to his mind if he could know that it was not deserved. His late wife felt the whole thing very deeply. He feels that he owes it to her to do what he can to clear her son. It was said, I believe, that Alan Thompson had stolen money and a diamond brooch from the Miss Benevents before his disappearance, and what you told Mrs. Kean was that he was innocent."

Mrs. Harbord flushed.

"I told her, and she didn't believe me!"

"You told her that he had never left Underhill."

Mrs. Harbord began to cry.

"I didn't ought to have said that. And I wouldn't, only for her sitting there being so unbelieving. Because it stands to reason he must have gone. Only he didn't take Miss Cara's diamond brooch, for I saw it afterwards, lying there just inside the drawer of Miss Olivia's looking-glass—one of those old-fashioned ones, up on a stand with a lot of little drawers, and she always kept the middle one locked. Only this time it wasn't. The keys were there sticking in it, and my duster caught them and pulled it out. And there was the brooch they said he took—a kind of a spray with diamond flowers and leaves. Miss Cara wore it a lot of an evening, and for best. And there it was in Miss Olivia's drawer, and Mr. Alan's coin that Miss Cara gave him lying there with it."

"What was this coin?"

Mrs. Harbord's voice dropped.

"It was some kind of an old one—gold by the look of it. And it had a hole in it with a ring through it so it could be hung on a chain. He wore it like that round his neck. Miss Cara gave him the chain too. And there they were in the drawer, the two of them. Oh, ma'am—that's what I've got on my mind! He'd never have left them!"

"Why do you say that, Mrs. Harbord?"

"Miss Cara, she told him it was a luck charm. He showed it to me one day when I was up doing his room—pulled it out of the neck of his shirt and told me all about it. Very free and open he was. 'Look at what Miss Cara has given me!' he said. 'Hundreds of years old and a real mascot. I'll have good luck as long as I wear it, and I can't be hurt by wound nor poison. Nice to know that, isn't it, in case anyone ever had the idea of sticking a knife into me or putting something into my tea.' I said, 'Mercy, Mr. Alan! Who would do that!' and he laughed and said, 'Oh, you never can tell.' Well, do you know, not a month after that something broke in the car when he was driving it, and it went smash into a wall at the bottom of Hill Lane. And he come out of it without a scratch. 'What did I tell you, Mrs. Harbord?' he said. 'That charm of Miss Cara's is a mascot all right. I ought to have been killed, and here I am without a scratch. You won't catch me leaving it off in a hurry.' Which was vain superstition, but I could see that he meant it. And not a week later they were saying he had run off with goodness knows how much money and that brooch of Miss Cara's, and I can't say anything about the money except that it's foolishness to keep a lot in the house—just asking for trouble to my way of thinking! But that brooch of Miss Cara's he never took for I saw it with my own eyes in Miss Olivia's drawer a matter of ten days after that, and the coin and the chain was there along with it like I told you. And a week later the two ladies went off abroad. And why would Mr. Alan leave that coin of his behind?"

Miss Silver said in a considering voice,

"If he had been found out in a theft he might have been asked to give it back, and the brooch too. The Miss Benevents might not have wished to prosecute, but they would certainly have required the restitution of the brooch, and if they set a special value on the coin and chain they might have required him to give that back too. It could have happened that way, Mrs. Harbord."

Mrs. Harbord sniffed.

"Well, then, it didn't! Not to Miss Cara's knowledge anyhow, for the very day before they went abroad I was coming along the passage, and there was the two of them in Mr. Alan's room, and the door on the jar. Miss Cara was crying, and Miss Olivia was scolding her. Very harsh she spoke, and I thought it was a shame. 'You ought to have more pride,' she said. 'Crying for a thief and a runaway! A common thief that could steal from those that

79

trusted him!' And Miss Cara said, 'If he wanted the brooch he could have had it. I would have given him anything he wanted.' And Miss Olivia said very sharp, 'Well, you gave him too much. And what did it do but put ideas into his head, and when he saw he'd gone too far he went off with what he could lay his hands on, and you can say good-bye to your brooch and to the lucky charm you set so much store by, for you'll never see them again.' And Miss Cara cried fit to break her heart and said she wouldn't care for anything as long as he would come back."

"And what did Miss Olivia say to that?"

Mrs. Harbord's voice dropped to a solemn whisper.

"She said, 'You'll never see him again.'"

CHAPTER 9

It was when Candida had been at Underhill for a little over a week that she came back from Retley to find Miss Cara Benevent in her room. Something had been said about going to a cinema with Derek, but in the end she lunched with Stephen, and by the time Derek turned up she thought perhaps they had better go home. She didn't really like the way that things were shaping. She told him so as they drove through the rain.

"They'll think I've been lunching with you."

He gave her a charming smile.

"Darling, can I help what they think?"

"Of course you can! You don't say so outright, but

you pull things round so that it looks as if we were going to be together—and I tell you straight out, Derek, it's got to stop."

"Darling, you have only to say, 'Dear Aunts, I cannot tell a lie. I am not lunching with Derek, and he is not lunching with me.'" He made a mock serious recitation of it and ended up with a laugh. "At least that's all you've got to say if what you want is a roof-lifting row. Personally I am all for the quiet life."

"I won't go on helping you to tell lies."

"And who's telling lies, darling? Not me—not you. You hadn't arranged to lunch with Stephen to-day, had you? Well then, how could you have told them you were going to? Upsetting for the old dears, and rather forward of you, don't you think? Because I'm sure you were much too nicely brought up to go running after a young man and asking him to take you out."

Candida looked at him with anger. She liked him— you couldn't help liking him—but she could have boxed his ears half a dozen times a day. She said,

"Don't be silly. I meant what I said."

His shoulder lifted.

"Oh, just as you like. We go home, and we say, 'Dear Aunts, Candida has been lunching with Stephen, and I——' Now I wonder where I was lunching? Do you think there would be any chance of my getting across with a lapse of memory, like the people who disappear into the blue and turn up again smiling after seven years or so to say they can't remember anything about it?"

"I shouldn't think so."

He laughed.

"No, nor should I. Besides, better kept for a major

81

emergency, don't you think? But you know, seriously darling, what is the sense in having rows? It upsets them, it upsets me. And if you had a nice womanly nature, it would upset you."

Candida flushed brightly.

"Peace at any price!"

"And the quiet life. How right you are!"

She looked ahead of them into the pouring rain. Low grey sky and a flat grey road, bare hedgerows and fields with all the colour drained out of them, a monotony of dullness and damp. What was the use of being angry? It had no more effect upon Derek than the rain-water running in streams over the bonnet of the car. Water off a car's bonnet, water off a duck's back. There was something about him which didn't let anything through—a gay shining surface which protected whatever there was underneath. On the impulse she said,

"Derek, are you really fond of them—at all?"

He looked round at her for a moment, his dark eyes smiling.

"Of the old dears? But of course I am! What do you take me for?"

"I don't know—that's the trouble. And I said *really.*"

He burst out laughing.

"Darling, aren't you being a bit intense? Now suppose I was just a scheming villain like the chap they had here before, Alan Thompson. He went off with what cash he could lay hands on and some of the family diamonds. Well, suppose I was like that and you asked me if I was fond of the aunts, what do you suppose I would say? Swear to it every time, wouldn't I? I'd be a fool if I didn't—and it's too much to expect of your luck to let you get away with being both a knave and a fool. So when I tell you that I really am fond of them, you naturally won't believe me any more than I'd believe myself if I were you, and that gets us exactly nowhere."

She said slowly, "I think you are fond of Cara."

He nodded.

"Well, I am, whether you think so or not. They've both been very good to me."

She went on as if he had not spoken.

"You don't like it when Olivia bullies her."

He put up a hand between them.

"Oh, switch off the X-ray! It's not decent to look right through one."

"She does bully her," said Candida. "I don't like it either."

The conversation stopped there, because they had turned in at the gate of Underhill.

Candida passed through the empty hall and ran upstairs. It was three o'clock in the afternoon, and there was no one about. The Miss Benevents would be resting, and the staff would be in their own quarters. She passed along the winding passages to her room. As she approached it she heard the sound of weeping. It was a low sound made up of sighing breaths and a faint sobbing. The door of the room stood ajar, and the sound came from there. After a moment of hesitation she widened the gap and looked in.

Miss Cara stood by the cold hearth, her fingers wrung together and the tears trickling down to her chin. She said, "Alan——" under her breath. And then she must have heard Candida cross the threshold, for she started, turned, and put out her hands. The next moment they were covering her face.

"Aunt Cara—what is it?"

The hands dropped. She peered at Candida.

"I thought—I thought—I was thinking about him—and when you came in—just for a moment I thought——"

It was like seeing a child who has been hurt. Candida put her arms round the little trembling creature.

"Dear Aunt Cara!"

The young warm voice, the words, quite broke Miss Cara down. She began to weep with all a child's lack of restraint. Candida detached herself for long enough to shut and lock the door, and then returned to put Miss Cara into a chair and kneel beside her. There was nothing she could do except to find the handkerchief which was being groped for and to murmur the only half-articulate words and phrases with which she would indeed have tried to comfort a child.

As the weeping stilled, Miss Cara herself began to produce words—snatches of sentences—and the name which had so long been forbidden. She said it over and over again, always on the same note of desolation,

"Alan—Alan—Alan——" And then, "If I only knew—where he was——"

Candida said gently, "You have never heard?"

The word came back to her like a sighing echo,

"Never——"

"You were very fond of him?"

One of the small stiff hands took hold of hers and held it tight.

"So very—fond of him. But he went away . . . This was his room—when you came in I thought——"

"Why did he go?"

Miss Cara shook her head.

"Oh, my dear, I don't know. There was no need—

indeed there wasn't. Olivia said he took money and my diamond spray, but I would have given him anything he wanted. He knew that. You see, Olivia doesn't know everything. I have never told her— I've never told anyone. If I tell you, you won't tell her, or—or laugh at me?'' The clasp on Candida's wrist became desperate.

"Oh, no, of course I won't."

"I've never had a secret from her all my life, but she wouldn't understand. She is so much cleverer than I am, and she has always told me what I ought to do. But clever people don't always understand everything, do they? Olivia doesn't understand about being fond of anyone. When Alan went she just said he was ungrateful and she didn't want to hear any more about him. But you don't stop being fond of anyone because they do something that is wrong. She didn't understand that at all.''

"I'm so sorry, Aunt Cara."

Miss Cara said,

"You are kind. Candida was kind—my sister Candida. She loved your grandfather and she went away with him, and Papa would never allow us to mention her name. I didn't understand then, but I do now. I would have gone anywhere with Alan if he had wanted me to—anywhere." She dropped her voice to a shaking whisper. "Do you know, we were going to be married. I've never told anyone, but you are kind. Of course it wouldn't have been a real marriage—there was too much difference in our ages— more than thirty years. It wouldn't have been right. But if he was my husband, I had what they call a power of appointment and I could leave him quite a lot of the money for his life. I remembered the lawyer telling me so when Papa died. He said, 'If you marry,

Miss Cara, under your grandfather's will you can use this power of appointment and leave your husband a life interest whether there are any children or not.' And Olivia said, 'Then she could use it to leave the life interest to me.' And he said, 'I'm afraid not, Miss Olivia. The power of appointment could only be used in favour of a husband. If Miss Cara were to die unmarried, the will provides for the major part of the estate to pass to your next sister, Mrs. Sayle, or her heirs, your own portion remaining just as it is at present.' I have a very good memory, and I have always remembered just what he said. But Olivia was very angry indeed. She waited until he had gone, and then she said our grandfather hadn't any right to make a will like that, and what was the good of my having the money when I didn't know how to manage it, and she ought to come in before Candida's children. Oh, my dear, she said dreadful things! You see, our sister Candida died before Papa did, and Olivia said she hoped Candida's children would die too, and then she would come into her own. Of course she didn't mean it, but it was a dreadful thing to say."

Candida felt as if something cold had touched her. It didn't come from Miss Cara—her hand was burning hot. It let go of her wrist now and went up to touch the carefully ordered hair, incongruously black above the little ravaged face. She had stopped crying, and though her eyelids were reddened and the smooth powdered surface of her skin had been impaired, she had a relaxed look.

"It's nice to have someone to talk to," she said in quite a pleased voice. "But you won't tell Olivia, will you?"

CHAPTER 10

On the following day when Candida had finished her driving lesson she found Stephen Eversley waiting for her, his car parked outside the garage. He said briefly,

"Get in—we're going for a run."

"But, Stephen—"

"I want to talk to you. Get in!"

He was banging the door and backing out before she had managed to produce any of her reasons for wanting to get back early. By the time she did produce them they were threading one of Retley's narrower streets, and she couldn't very well cavil at his abrupt, "I can't talk in traffic." A sideways glance showed her a frowning profile which she had not seen before. Under a slight surface glow there was the feeling that she rather liked a man who took his own way. Not tiresomely or all the time, but when occasion required. She sat with her hands in her lap and just the beginnings of a smile in her eyes until they ran out upon an open road with fields on either side. When she looked at him again the profile was as before. She said in her sweetest voice,

"May I speak now? Where are we going?"

"Somewhere where we can talk."

"What I was trying to say when you wouldn't let me was that I ought to get back."

"Not yet. I want to talk to you."

"Won't this do?"

"No, it won't. When I say talk, I mean properly—not with a dozen ears flapping in that damned café, or when I ought to have my mind on the road!"

"There doesn't seem to be anything on the road except ourselves, does there?"

He laughed angrily.

"There might be at any moment! I've got a feeling you could be aggravating enough to distract me from three motor-buses abreast!"

"Is that a compliment? And do I say thank you?"

"No, it isn't, and you don't! We're going to park here."

The road had developed those wide grass verges which foreign visitors so justly consider to be wasteful of land which might be growing something of a more edible nature than grass. Stephen drove on to a green level stretch and stopped the car. Then he turned to face her and said,

"All right—now we can get going."

Candida considered him. He had a determined look—determined and purposeful. His hair was ruffled and his eyes were a hard bright blue. She had no idea why she should want to laugh, but she did.

"Well, it's your programme."

"What are you being meek about? I don't like it, and you needn't think it takes me in! Anyhow what is it all about? We can't talk in that café—you know that as well as I do!"

"What do you want to talk about, Stephen?"

He said, "You. How long are you staying at Underhill?"

"I don't really know. Why?"

"I don't want you to stay there."

His brows were a straight line above frowning eyes. Her own brows lifted a little.

"Dear Stephen, you needn't see me if you don't want to."

His hand came down upon her knee.

"Look here, I don't want that sort of thing! I'm serious!"

Something in her shrank. She didn't want to know what he meant. She didn't want to be as serious as all that. She wanted to enjoy the thrust and parry, the advance and retreat, of a surface relationship. She wasn't ready for anything else—not yet. But she had only to look at him to know that what he had brought her here to say he would say. In a way it pleased her, and in a way she was angry with herself for being pleased. The anger tinged her voice.

"All right, go on."

"I want you to go away."

"Why?"

"I don't like your being there."

"Why don't you like it?"

"I think it would be better if you went away."

Her colour had been bright. That is how he saw her, as an angry brightness. She was bare-headed. Her hair shone. Her eyes were darkly blue. And then the brightness went. The carnation left her cheeks and she was pale. She said quite quietly,

"You will have to tell me why."

He had known that all along, and he had not thought that it would be hard. It was the sort of thing that came trippingly from the tongue in one of those conversations which you have in your own mind, and which are amazingly intractable when you try to reproduce them in real life. He had to push the words to get them across.

"I don't like the place. I don't like your being there. I want you to clear out."

"You still haven't told me why."

He said with a sudden jerk in his voice,

"Do you suppose I want you to go away? You know I don't. If you go, I'll come after you—you know that too. Or if you don't you're a lot stupider than I think you are."

He hadn't meant to say anything like that. The things he had meant to say wouldn't come. He was a fool to have touched her. He removed his hand abruptly.

This new pale Candida looked at him and said,

"No, I'm not really stupid. You will just have to tell me why you don't want me to stay at Underhill."

He did get it out then. He said,

"I don't think it's safe."

There was a pause before she said,

"I don't know what you mean."

The trouble was that he didn't know very well himself. If he had had anything in the way of knowledge to put before her he wouldn't be sitting here like a tongue-tied fool. All that he had was an echo from the past, some odds and ends of hear-say, and this steady current of feeling setting away from Underhill. He hadn't liked the place to start with, but it wasn't any of his business to have likes or dislikes about what only came his way professionally. All the same he hadn't liked it. The whole situation of the house there under the hill, those cellars into which he had been conducted—there was something about them which prompted more than a misliking. It might have been Miss Olivia Benevent's cold reluctance to take him there. It might have been partly the feeling that he had not been allowed to make enough of an examination to justify the opinion which was being sought. He had come away angry and frustrated, and had reported that he would have to make a much more detailed inspection before he could advise upon the work to be undertaken. Since when the whole affair appeared to have lapsed. He had two other jobs in the neighbourhood, or he would have had no real pretext for remaining at Retley. He sat there frowning.

She repeated her words with a difference, slight in the arrangement but with a marked deepening of the manner in which they were said.

"Stephen, what do you mean?"

"Don't you ever have a feeling about things?"

"Sometimes."

"I've got a feeling about your being at Underhill."

She was frowning too.

"A feeling—or a prejudice?"

"Why should I have a prejudice?"

"Aunt Olivia could have given you one."

"Why should she?"

"She can be—very—rude."

Stephen laughed.

"To the mere architect? You don't suppose I should worry about that!"

"You might."

"Well, I didn't. Candida, I don't want to say any more. Can't you take it that there are things that won't go into words—and clear out?"

She had a sudden leaping impulse to do just that. She heard her own voice say,

"I haven't got anywhere to go, and they know it."

"How do you mean, you haven't got anywhere to go?"

"Barbara only had her house on a lease. I couldn't afford to pay the rent, and somebody else is moving in. I shall have to find a job."

"Are you looking for one?"

"Not yet. They want me to stay on. There's the family history—I think they're beginning to realise that it won't get very far if it's left to Derek."

Stephen said roughly,

"I suppose you know why they want you to stay?"

"Don't you think it might be because they like having me?"

His roughness was shot with anger.

"They want to marry you off to their precious Derek!"

She had been sitting round to face him. She turned now and looked straight ahead through the driving screen. The long green verge stretched away before eyes that were clouded by an angry mist. She said in a small cold voice,

"I think we had better go back."

He took hold of her and pulled her round again.

"Don't be a fool! I want you to listen to me! You don't care for Derek, and he doesn't care for you. He's got a girl in the town—everyone knows that except the Miss Benevents. But that is their plan. When they find out about Derek things aren't going to be so good for him, or for you. They may find out any day, and when they do there'll be a blow-up. Look here, Candida, you know that your grandmother was the middle one of the three sisters—you told me about finding a photograph with their names and ages. Well, my old cousin Louisa Arnold knew them all very well, and she says your grandmother or her descendants come in for the greater part of the estate if Miss Cara dies unmarried."

"Yes, I knew that. Aunt Cara told me."

Stephen said bluntly,

"Well, that cuts Miss Olivia out. Do you suppose she likes it?"

In her mind Candida heard Miss Cara's little trembling voice— "Oh, my dear, she said dreadful things . . . Our sister Candida died before Papa, and Olivia said she hoped Candida's children would die too, and then she would come into her own. . . . It was a dreadful thing to say." She spoke to drown the sound of it.

"No—no—of course she doesn't like it. But there isn't anything she can do. I mean even if I married Derek it wouldn't really help."

He said grimly,

"She might think it would. He's an easy-going chap and pretty well under her thumb. But if the plan broke down——"

There was something there between them.

She said, "No!" But he was putting it into words. He said,

"Why did she tell you that the tide wasn't high until eleven?"

It was as if she had known what was coming. The shock of saying it was his, the shock of hearing it was hers. The two shocks came together and were one. Everything else went before the impact. She put out her hands, and he took them. The strong clasp hurt her, but she clung to it. She heard herself say,

"No—no—it wasn't."

"If you mean it wasn't the Miss Benevents at the hotel in Eastcliff, you must know perfectly well that it was. I went round there next day, and you had gone, but they hadn't. Their names were in the visitors' book, and they passed through the hall whilst I was looking at it. They were there, and because they told you the tide wouldn't be high until eleven

93

you went walking on the beach and you were nearly drowned. And they knew who you were when they told you that, because they had just seen you write your name. You told me all about it when we were stuck up there on the cliff. They saw you write your name—Candida Sayle—and they remarked on it. And right on the top of that they told you what a nice walk there was along the beach, and that the tide would not be high until eleven."

The outer wall of Candida's defence fell down with a crash. He knew too much, he remembered too well. She said on a quick breath,

"It wasn't Aunt Cara—I'm sure it wasn't Aunt Cara."

"She was there when it was said."

Candida tried to pull away her hands, but he held them.

"She would think anything Aunt Olivia said was right. She is like that—you know she is."

He nodded briefly.

"All right, that goes for her. But it doesn't go for Miss Olivia, does it? What was in her mind when she told you a lie about the tide?"

Candida said in a desperate voice,

"She couldn't have known that it was a lie."

He let go of her and sat back.

"Can you make yourself believe that? You can't make me believe it."

"Stephen!"

"I want you to leave Underhill."

"Stephen, I can't."

"Why can't you?"

"I said I would stay and do this job with Derek."

"You can say you have got to go back and see about a job, or about your Aunt Barbara's business, or anything that comes into your head."

"I won't tell lies just because—just because——
And there's Aunt Cara—she's got fond of me. Stephen, she's pathetic. Olivia bullies her, and she's
grateful if anyone is kind."

He said in a masterful voice,

"I want you to leave Underhill."

CHAPTER 11

Back at his hotel, he rang up his cousin Louisa Arnold. When she answered, there were the sort of
preliminaries in which he had learned to participate.

"You are well, my dear boy?"

"Oh, yes. And you, Cousin Louisa?"

There was some dalliance with Miss Arnold's suspicion, contracted last night, that she might have
taken a slight chill. This had, of course, to be explained in detail, together with the reassuring fact
that by breakfast-time this morning the faint pre-
monitory symptoms had subsided. She would therefore be able to attend a committee meeting of the
Hospital Flower Guild to which she was pledged.

"I really do not like to miss it unless I am absolutely
obliged to do so, and dear Maud says she will not
mind being left. I should be back by six o'clock. The
meeting is at four, but it would be considered rude
if I did not stay to tea. Mrs. Lowry who is our chair-
man is always so hospitable. . . ."

The conversation ended in his being pressed to
drop in at any time.

Miss Silver was enjoying a comfortable cup of tea in the drawing-room when he was announced.

"I am so sorry, Mr. Eversley, I am afraid that Louisa is out."

He made sure that Eliza Peck had closed the door behind her before he replied.

"Yes, she told me she had a meeting. As a matter of fact, I wondered whether you would allow me to have a talk with you. I understand that you do take cases and give advice professionally."

Miss Silver inclined her head.

"Yes, Mr. Eversley."

"Then will you let me talk to you? I—well I'm a good deal worried——"

"About Miss Candida Sayle?"

"How did you know?"

She smiled.

"You were speaking of her the other night. Your concern was evident."

He remembered that he had talked a good deal about Candida. He had not realised that his interest had been so obvious.

Before he could speak the door opened to admit Eliza Peck, bearing a small tray with a second teacup and a supply of hot water. She was a thin, upright old woman with a daunting air of severity. Her eye softened slightly as it rested upon Stephen. She liked to see a young man coming about the house again. Time was when there had been enough of them and to spare, but that was when she and Miss Louisa were young. She put down the teacup and the water-jug and went away with the empty tray.

Stephen heard Miss Silver assure him that the tea had only just been made. He accepted the cup she poured out for him, but almost immediately put it down again upon the edge of the table.

"I don't like her being at Underhill," he said.

"No, Mr. Eversley?"

The lift of her voice made a question of it. He said with emphasis,

"I don't like it at all. I want to get her away."

"And she wishes to stay?"

"I don't believe she does really. Part of the trouble is that she hasn't got anywhere to go. The aunt who brought her up has just died. She has been nursing her for the last three years, so she isn't trained for anything, and there's practically no money, and no relations except the Miss Benevents."

Miss Silver commented mildly,

"An awkward situation."

"Yes, it is. And there doesn't seem to be anything I can do about it. My parents are dead—the uncle with whom I work is a bachelor ——" He broke off with a sound of anger. "Even if I had rows of female relations, I don't suppose it would be of the slightest use. Miss Olivia has got Candida pegged down to a history of the Benevent family, and she is letting herself get fond of Miss Cara. She is sorry for her."

Miss Silver finished her own cup of tea before she said in a thoughtful voice,

"Just why do you think she should leave Underhill, Mr. Eversley?"

He said, "Look here, this is all between ourselves, isn't it?"

She gave a slight reproving cough.

"You have asked for my professional assistance. You can naturally rely upon my professional secrecy."

He found himself making an apology.

"It was just that—well—my Cousin Louisa——"

Miss Silver said graciously,

"You need be in no anxiety. Pray continue."

"I am going to tell you about something that happened more than five years ago. I was staying at a place called Eastcliff, and I had been out in a boat bird-watching—it's a hobby of mine. There's an island with a lot of gulls. I was coming back, making for the mainland, when I saw a girl half-way up the cliffs. She had been caught by the tide, and I could see that she was stuck. I called out and asked her if she could hold on whilst I got help. She said she would try. She was spread-eagled there, with hardly any hold, and I could see that I couldn't risk it. What I could do was to run into the cove I was making for and climb along the cliff to a ledge just over her head. I managed it, and I got her up on the ledge. By that time it was too dark to get her off the cliff by the way I had come, and we had to stay there all night. She was a schoolgirl of about fifteen, and her name was Candida Sayle. She had come to Eastcliff to meet friends who didn't turn up because one of them had been taken ill. And she got cut off by the tide because two old ladies staying in the same private hotel had told her that there was a very nice walk along the beach, and that the tide would not be high until eleven."

"That was a most unfortunate mistake."

He said doggedly,

"I don't believe it was a mistake."

"Mr. Eversley!"

"I can't believe it. The first thing you find out about at any seaside place is the tides. And that tide was high at a quarter to nine. Can you believe that anyone could have been two hours out? And you haven't heard everything. Those two women who told Candida that there was such a nice walk along the beach and that the tide wouldn't be high till eleven were the Miss Benevents. They knew who Candida was, because they had watched her sign her name in the hotel register. They had even commented on its being an unusual one. But they didn't tell her that they were her great-aunts. Oh, no, they just told her what a nice walk there was along the beach, and that she would have plenty of time to take it because the tide would not be high until eleven o'clock."

Miss Silver looked at him gravely.

"Are you suggesting——"

"Yes, I am. I've been over it and over it, and I don't think there is any other explanation. I looked in the register, you know, after Candida had gone home, and I saw the names—Miss Olivia Benevent—Miss Cara Benevent. And they passed through the hall whilst I was there. I didn't know that there was any family connection with Candida, and from first to last they never said anything about it themselves, but when they wrote to my uncle about Underhill I remembered the name, and as soon as I came down here I remembered them. And then Candida turned up, and I found she was their niece. That gave me a jolt, and the whole thing began to come back. And then I found out that Candida's grandmother and her descendants came in for most of the property after Miss Cara. Cousin Louisa was talking about it the other night, do you remember?"

"Yes, I remember."

He went on as if she had not spoken.

"When I told Candida, she said she knew about that. It seems Miss Cara told her. Now why should she have told her?"

Miss Silver had set down her cup and taken up a half-finished stocking. The hard grey yarn had a very schoolboy look, and for a fleeting moment Stephen wondered whom she could be knitting it for. He brushed the thought aside as she said,

"I cannot say, Mr. Eversley."

"But you can see why I want to get Candida away from Underhill——"

She was knitting sedately.

"I can see that the incident which you have described made a deep impression on your mind."

"I suppose it did, but it had practically faded out. Then I met her again, and it all came back, and on the top of it there was all this business about Alan Thompson."

After a short thoughtful pause she said,

"Yes, there was some talk about Alan Thompson the night you were here for supper. Louisa had asked you whether he was spoken of at Underhill, and you replied that you had received the impression he was not to be mentioned there. Have you anything to add to that reply?"

He said,

"Yes, I have. Do you remember Cousin Louisa said there had been gossip about him and Miss Cara— that it had even been said that she might be going to marry him?"

Miss Silver said in a disapproving voice,

"There is often a great deal of gossip in a Cathedral town. The society is formal and the interests restricted. Where such is the case, there is apt to be an undue emphasis on personal relationships. As Lord Tennyson so truly says:

"'And common is the commonplace,
    And vacant chaff well meant for grain.'"

Unaccustomed to her habit of quotation, Stephen felt slightly stunned. After a respectful moment had passed he went on.

"Do you know, I don't think it was just gossip. There is something that came my way last night—I think I had better tell you about it."

"Yes, Mr. Eversley."

Her tone made it a statement of fact.

"Well, it's like this. I was dining with a Colonel Gatling. He has an enormous barrack of a house at Hilton St. John about two miles the other side of Underhill. The original building was one of those small manor houses, but the Gatlings, who came into it in the 1840s, overbuilt it with one of those frightful Victorian monstrosities which are now quite impossible to run. He wants to get it down to its original proportions, retain a very nice walled garden, and develop the rest of the property as a building estate. Hilton is an expanding place with an aircraft factory, and I think the necessary permits will be forthcoming. Well, that won't interest you—it's only to explain how I came to be dining with Colonel Gatling. He's been very friendly—he's a sociable, convivial old boy." He gave an odd half laugh. "Well, there's the key to what I've got for you. He was very friendly and convivial last night. He talked a lot about his neighbours, and after a bit he got round to the Miss Benevents. He told me all about their father, one of the fine crusted Victorian brand, and how he had cut off his daughter Candida because she had married a parson who was probably the only man she had ever met. And then he chuckled and came out with, 'I wonder what he'd have said if he'd known that his daughter Cara had come within an ace of marrying a young waster who might almost have been her grandson!' I said, 'Did she do that?' and he poured himself out another glass of port and told me the whole story.''

"He told you that Miss Cara had actually contemplated marrying Alan Thompson?''

Stephen frowned.

"He put up an extremely circumstantial story. It seems that his brother Cyril was the Rector of the old parish church of Hilton, and that for some reason Underhill falls within that parish.''

Miss Silver exclaimed.

"Dear me! They surely did not put up the banns there!''

"Oh, no. But Alan Thompson came to the Rector about getting a licence—in the strictest confidence.''

Miss Silver looked shocked.

"Then surely he did not tell his brother! It would be a very serious breach!''

"Oh, no, he didn't tell anyone. But he seems to have been a good deal troubled at the idea of such a marriage, and he wrote about it in his diary.''

Miss Silver's disapproval deepened.

"Colonel Gatling should have regarded such a diary as sacred.''

Stephen was inclined to agree with her, but he said,

"Well, he was his brother's executor, and he wasn't just rummaging in the diary. There was some question about rents that had been remitted, and he went to the diary to see whether it backed up what the tenants said. The date was a matter of three years ago, and he stumbled on the Reverend Cyril's heart-searchings over what he called 'this most unnatural marriage'. He appears to have made strong representations to Thompson, and to have entirely failed to impress him. Colonel Gatling quoted him as saying that the young man admitted that the marriage would be a business arrangement, and defended it on the grounds that Miss Cara had always had a bad time and been bullied by her sister, and that if he was her husband he would be in a position to see that she got better treatment. Cyril Gatling seems to have been very unhappy about the whole thing, but both parties being of age and *compos mentis*, he didn't feel justified in refusing his services. And—this is what will interest you particularly—the licence was actually in his possession when he heard that Alan Thompson had gone off into the blue."

Miss Silver turned the stocking on her needles.

"Did Colonel Gatling say whether a date had been fixed for the marriage?"

"Yes, he did. Alan went off on the fourth of March three years ago. The marriage was to have taken place on the tenth."

"And what conclusions did he draw?"

"He seems to have been quite bewildered, saying again and again that he couldn't understand it. Colonel Gatling repeated phrases like 'I simply cannot understand it. He seemed so determined, so set upon this marriage, so lacking in any response to my attempts to deter him.' Colonel Gatling, of course, found the whole thing quite easy of explanation. He just said, 'The fellow got cold feet and bolted.' And that was that."

Miss Silver knitted in silence for a while. Roger's stocking, the second of the pair, was almost finished.

Another half inch and she would have to begin to think about turning the heel. She said,

"That would be a natural but superficial explanation. It is possible that it is the true one, but it does not seem to me to agree with what I have heard of Alan Thompson's character. In all the accounts of him he appears as a good-looking young man with one settled aim in life, to use his good looks and his charm as a substitute for application and industry. He had been two years at Underhill when he disappeared, and from what I have learned from Louisa and others he was during that time steadily increasing his influence over the Miss Benevents, and particularly over Miss Cara. When he found that she could be persuaded into a marriage, and that she would have the power to leave him a life interest in her property——"

Stephen said, *"What!"*

It was an interruption which Miss Silver would not have excused in the days when she presided over a well-ordered schoolroom, yet at this moment she regarded it with indulgence. There is a certain satisfaction in the delivery of a piece of startling news, and it was quite apparent that what she had just imparted was news which startled Stephen Eversley. She contented herself therefore with a slight reproving cough and proceeded,

"Louisa is my informant, and I have no reason to doubt what she says. Under the grandfather's will each daughter who succeeded was to have this power of appointment. As no doubt you know, it is not an unusual provision. It was the knowledge that his daughter Candida would have this power if she ever came into the property which particularly annoyed Mr. Benevent. He used to come here and talk to Canon Arnold about it, and the Canon repeated a good deal of what was said to Louisa. So I feel quite sure that her information is correct. And now, Mr. Eversley, pray consider whether a young man of Alan Thompson's determination to settle himself in life would have thrown away such an opportunity of doing so."

"I suppose he could have got cold feet at the last minute. Look here, what about his letters home? His mother was alive then, wasn't she? Did they give any indication of his state of mind?"

Miss Silver's needles clicked.

"There were no letters, Mr. Eversley."

"Do you mean none at all?"

"From the time that he threw up his clerkship and left Lenton he never communicated with his family. He made it quite clear to his step-father's sister, Mrs. Kean, that he did not want to be associated with trade in any way. He seems to have been unaware that she and her husband had a bookshop in Retley, and when she recognised him he made it quite clear that he did not wish to have anything to do with her. These things are indications of a settled determination to leave his origins behind him and to establish himself in as favourable a manner as possible. I am unable to believe that he would throw away such a chance as this marriage would have offered him."

"Well, you know what was said about his going off. Suppose he had been taking advantage of his opportunities to line his pockets and Olivia had found him out. She is pretty sharp, you know, and if she had found out about the proposed marriage at the same time, do you suppose she would have hesitated to put the screws on him—'Clear out, or we prosecute'? He wouldn't really have had much choice, would he?"

Miss Silver smiled.

"That is quite an ingenious theory, Mr. Eversley, but I believe that it will not bear any closer scrutiny. It does not reckon with the certain fact of Alan Thompson's influence with Miss Cara. When you consider that it had brought her to within six days of marrying him, and that it was strong enough to induce her to keep the fact a complete secret from the sister who had dominated her all her life, it is clear that Alan would only have had to go to Miss Cara and she would have protected him by declaring that she had given him the money. By far the larger part of the income was hers, and she had only to say the missing sum was a gift from herself. Louisa has told me that she saw Miss Cara just once after Alan disappeared. They met by accident in the precincts of the cathedral, and for the moment Miss Cara was alone. She took Louisa by the hand with the tears running down her face and said, 'Oh, why did he go? There was no need—I would have given him anything!' And then Miss Olivia came up and took her away. They went abroad a day or two later."

CHAPTER 12

Derek Burdon looked across the table at Candida. It was a big old-fashioned affair well furnished with drawers, and with such aids to industry as a large blotting-pad, a massive double inkstand, and plenty of pens and pencils. There was also an old-fashioned portfolio full of papers. He said in an exasperated voice,

"It's all very well to say we ought to get on with it, but I ask you!"

"Do you?"

He laughed.

"Well, I suppose I don't really. This sort of thing just isn't my line of country, you know. Well, I mean to say—is it? The old dears don't seem to realise that they might just as well expect me to play the cathedral organ or to fly a plane! As a matter of fact I wouldn't mind learning to fly, but they wouldn't expect me to do it right away without learning how, now would they?"

She could not help laughing.

"I can't think why you took on a secretarial job."

He laughed too, and in a perfectly carefree manner.

"Can't you? I expect you could if you tried. It was a gift-horse, and I couldn't afford to look it in the mouth. You see, the bother about me is that I'm just no use at earning a living. I haven't got any vices, but I haven't got any of the tiresome virtues either.

Industry, application, perseverance—you know the sort of thing. They used to put bits in my reports about them. 'Lacks application'—that one was always cropping up. My father used to get wild about it, but I don't see that it was my fault. You don't have a down on anyone simply because he can't act or hasn't got an ear for music. The things just weren't included in my make-up, that's all. Now my father was a really successful business man until he came a spectacular smash and went off into the blue in his private plane. No one knows whether he got anywhere or not. Personally I feel sure that he did, and that he had parked enough money abroad to see him through. I was eighteen, and as soon as I had done my military service an uncle with an office shoved me into a junior clerkship, a completely repellent job. You see, I really do hate work." He smiled disarmingly.

"Somebody has got to do it," said Candida.

"Yes, darling, but not me—at least not if I can help it. And of course there are two sides to the business— you have to find an employer who will put up with me. The uncle stuck it for two years—I give him marks for that—but he booted me in the end."

"How did you come across the Aunts?"

"Oh, that was easy. I was in a concert party at Eastcliff—they go down there once in a way to take the sea air —and I had a bit of luck. Miss Cara twisted her ankle, and I carried her to their hotel. After that the job just fell into my lap. They've been frightfully good to me, and as a rule I don't get asked to do anything I can't manage. It's this family history business that gets me down."

"Why?"

He rumpled up his hair.

"Well, it's a bit above my head, you know. There are pieces in Latin, and if there was one thing that I was worse at than the other things, it was Latin. I remember a really frightful row after getting 'Doesn't try' in a report. That was a chap called Masterman. He had a down on me, and I fairly loathed him. One of the strenuous, earnest sort."

"I haven't come across any Latin."

"No, darling, but you haven't got very far, have you? Besides, to tell you the truth, the whole thing gives me the pip. Who cares what people did two or three hundred years ago? They're dead and buried, and why not let them be? It's like grubbing into graves and digging up a lot of old bones, and I don't like it. If you ask me, the whole thing stinks."

Candida had an odd feeling that something had startled her, but she didn't know what it was. There was the hint of an uneasy tone in Derek's voice, the hint of an uneasy look behind the smile in his eyes. He looked past her and said,

"What I'd like to know is, why have they got so keen about it again all of a sudden?"

Candida echoed his word

"Again?"

He nodded.

"Yes. It was the chap who was here before me who started on it—Alan Thompson. You've heard about him?"

"Yes."

He waved a hand in the direction of the portfolio.

"Well, all that sort of thing appealed to him, I gather. They don't talk about him, you know. He blotted his copybook—went off with the loose cash and some of Miss Cara's jewellery. A fairly rotten thing to do, don't you think? And stupid too, because—well, they are most awfully generous, don't you know? And according to Anna they were pretty well all over him."

"Was it Anna who told you about him?"

He leaned across the table and dropped his voice.

"Well, she did, and she didn't. She began, and then all of a sudden she dried up, and if there is anything less like Anna than to dry up about a thing before she's got it chewed to a rag, I don't know what it is. But she did tell me that he was dead keen on all this old history stuff, and sometimes I've just wondered whether his going off like that had anything to do with the Benevent Treasure."

There was a pause. The sensation of having been startled became definitely one of shock. Candida found that her breathing had quickened. She said,

"Why?" The word shook a little.

He spoke quickly too.

"Don't you see, it would account for it. Suppose he had laid hands on the treasure and that was what he went off with. Look, I'll show you something."

He opened the portfolio and turned a page or two, took out a folded document, extracted from it a sheet of thin modern paper neatly typewritten, and pushed it across to Candida.

"Here, take a look at that!"

She took it, and would rather have left it alone. There was a heading which took up two lines— "Those things carried out of Italy on his journey to England by Ugo di Benevento in the year 1662." After that there was a list. It began with, "Four dishes richly chased and silver-gilt," and went on all down the page. Candida followed it with extraordinary reluctance. There were things like, "Two salt-cellars with doves—The gold candle-stick reputed to be the

110

work of Messer Benvenuto Cellini—A bracelet with four large emeralds—A set of twelve ruby buttons— A necklace of very large rubies in a border of diamonds," and so forth and so on. The items ran together in a dazzle. She lifted her eyes from them and said,

"What is it?"

"What it sets out to be—a list of the things that Ugo got away with. I wonder how he managed it. The jewels could be tucked away, but all that plate must have weighed a bit. I wonder if the candlesticks really were gold."

Candida said,

"It's really more to the point to wonder whether they were the work of Benvenuto Cellini. They must be enormously valuable if they were. Of course I could see it was a list of what Ugo carried away—it says so. What I meant was, what is this list and where does it come from? It's not old."

He laughed.

"Darling, typewriters weren't invented in sixteen-what-ever-it-was. All I can tell you is that I found the list tucked inside a very dull paper about the lease of a farm. And if I've got to guess, I should say that Alan Thompson copied it off an older list and put it where he didn't think anyone would meddle with it."

"But why?"

"Well, if I've got to go on guessing, I should say that he probably wasn't meant to have seen the other list. He may have just come across it and thought it would be nice to have a copy, or he may have been doing a spot of snooping—I wouldn't know. Or of course it's just possible that Miss Cara showed it to him. You know, she really was most awfully fond of

111

him, poor old dear. Anna said it fairly broke her up, his going off like that. And of course I can't help wondering whether he didn't take the Benevent Treasure or what was left of it along for company."

Candida was looking at him.

"Did Anna ever talk to you about it?"

"In a way. She told me about Miss Cara being so cut-up."

"What did she say?"

He laughed.

"Interested, aren't you!"

"Yes."

"Oh, well, why not? It's your family! Anna came in one day when I had this stuff out and was trying to make head or tail of it. You may have noticed she likes talking. She stood at the other side of the table where you are sitting and she talked quite a lot. She began about the papers—they were all lying about—and she said what did I want with them, they would be better in the kitchen fire, and hadn't they done enough harm already."

"What did she mean by that?"

"Well, I don't know. Your guess is as good as mine. She said, 'Mr. Alan meddled with them, and look what came of it!' And I said, 'What did come of it?' And she said, 'God knows!' and put her hand up to her mouth and went away. I didn't think much about it at the time, but after I found that list I wondered."

Candida was silent. She looked down into her lap and saw the neat typing—"Twelve ruby buttons . . ." She pushed the list across the table and said,

"I think you ought to show it to the Aunts."

He shook his head with vigour.

"Not on your life!"

"All the papers are theirs."

He looked at her with momentary shrewdness.

"You mean they are Miss Cara's. And do you suppose she wants to have the Alan Thompson affair raked up again? I gather it very nearly did for her at the time. Suppose he was up to something he shouldn't have been. We don't know whether he was or whether he wasn't, but that seems to be what Miss Cara believes. Well, it would be frightfully cruel to bring it all back. As I said, she may even have given him the information in this list herself, and that would make her feel pretty bad. As far as I'm concerned it's going back where I found it, and that's that!"

Candida had never liked him so well. She said quickly and warmly,

"Yes, yes, of course—you're right. But, Derek, you don't mean—you don't think the treasure is still somewhere about?"

"Why shouldn't it be? Part of it anyhow."

"Well, I don't know. There aren't such a lot of things of that sort of date knocking about. They get sold, or broken up, or——"

"Stolen?"

Candida said soberly,

"A lot of things can happen in three hundred years without putting any of them on to Alan Thompson."

He rummaged among the papers, pulled one out, and gave it to Candida. It appeared to be an inventory of some kind—linen, curtains, silver of the homelier kind. Nothing like the splendours of the list which Alan had copied—just the ordinary furnishings of a well-to-do household, all set down on old discoloured paper in old discoloured writing. Candida stared at it, wondering why it had been given to her.

"Well?"

He said,

"Turn it round and look at the bottom of the left-hand corner."

There was some writing there, running crossways to the short lines of the inventory, the hand a different one, thin and spidery. There were four lines, not very easy to read, but she made them out:

> "Touch not nor try,
> Sell not nor buy,
> Give not nor take,
> For dear life's sake."

Underneath again there were two words that had been scratched out, the first lightly, but the second with many crossing strokes.

Derek said, "Got it?"

She read the four lines aloud in a slow bewildered voice.

"What does it mean?"

"I think it means the Treasure. The first of those two scratched-out words is a 'the.' That's easy. The second can't be read—whoever did the scratching made a much better job of it. But it's the right length to be 'Treasure,' and that is what I think it is."

"But, Derek, what does it mean?"

He gave an uneasy laugh.

"Well, it might mean that it wasn't a good plan to meddle with the Treasure. Someone, I suppose Alan Thompson, has made a pencil note at the end of this paper, with a date in the eighteenth century and a query after it. Seventeen-forty, I think it is. If that's right, it could mean that the Treasure was still going strong round about that date, and that there was some sort of family belief that it wasn't lucky to

114

meddle with it. It seems to me that Anna might have had the same idea."

The door opened. Joseph stood on the threshold. He said with his usual politeness,

"You are being asked for on the telephone, sir."

CHAPTER 13

It was after dinner the same evening that Miss Olivia began to talk about the Benevent Treasure. Derek was at the piano playing scraps and snatches of whatever came into his head. Miss Cara had said goodnight and drifted aimlessly down the long room to the door. Her feet made no sound on the carpet, the door no sound as it opened and closed again. She left a vaguely unhappy feeling behind her. The thought that came to Candida was that it was the first time she had seen her take the lead in even such a small thing as going to bed. On every evening until now it had been Miss Olivia who gathered up the embroidery or the knitting upon which she was employed and remarked upon the time. But to-night, and before it was quite ten o'clock, Miss Cara had got up, murmured an uncertain good-night, and gone away.

After a short silence Miss Olivia said,

"Cara is not as strong as I am. She has always required a good deal of care. Certain subjects agitate her and are best avoided. I should really have cautioned you on this matter before, but I thought I would wait until we knew you better. One cannot immediately confide in someone who has been brought up as a stranger to the family."

This was rather daunting. Candida wondered what was coming next. Miss Olivia continued.

"You will remember that I mentioned the Benevent Treasure on your first evening here. It would not have been possible to give you even the slightest sketch of the family history without touching on it, however lightly."

Derek was playing the refrain of "Love's Old Sweet Song." There was a pile of these sugary old-fashioned ballads on the music-stand. He made fun of them to Candida, and played them as to the manner born. Miss Cara loved them, and Candida suspected that Derek had a soft corner for them himself. He might jest about them, but there was a lingering fondness in his touch. It came to her that the Aunts had had to make do with what they could get in the way of sentiment, and that it didn't amount to very much.

Miss Olivia said in her clear, precise voice,

"I should have spoken to you before, but no opportunity presented itself. My sister and I are so seldom apart, and the matter did not appear to be pressing. But when Joseph mentioned that he had found you and Derek at work on the family papers I thought it might be as well to touch on the subject. I do not know whether Derek has said anything or not, but we find it better not to discuss the Benevent Treasure in front of Cara. There are some superstitious tales about it, and it is apt to make her nervous."

Miss Olivia was sitting stiffly upright in a Sheraton chair whose brocaded seat was quite hidden by the spread of her black taffeta skirt. She wore a handsome spray of diamond flowers to fasten the fine lace ruffle at her neck. Half a dozen pearl and diamond rings were crowded on to the thin bent fingers which held a tambour frame and an embroidery-needle. The embroidery on the frame was jewel-bright. Candida suspected it of being too fine for comfort. Sometimes half an hour would go by without a stitch being taken. One was taken now as Candida said,

"What tales, Aunt Olivia?"

A second stitch was set beside the first.

"There are stories of the kind in most old families. It was said that the Treasure brought bad luck with it, but that of course was foolish. Ugo did not have bad luck at all. On the contrary. He used part of the Treasure to establish himself in this country. There were some exceedingly valuable jewels. Some of them were sold to build on to this house and to buy the land that went with it. We have no means of knowing how much was disposed of, but it was necessary for your ancestor to make a good appearance and to keep up his rank. He married an heiress, as I think I told you. Her name was Anne Coghill, and she brought him a considerable fortune. There was therefore no need to have further recourse to the Treasure. When from time to time, however, it became necessary to draw upon it, there grew up this idea that some misfortune would follow. James Benevent was known to have withdrawn some of the jewels in 1740. Shortly afterwards he was killed by a fall from his horse, which took fright and threw him at his own front door. He lived long enough to charge his son to have nothing to do with the Treasure, but about fifty years later his grandson, Guy Benevent, having lost heavily at cards, was tempted to sell part of the Treasure to recoup himself. He was set upon by a footpad and received an injury to his

117

head from which he died. He was found quite close to the house and carried in, but he never recovered consciousness."

"How did they know that it was a footpad?"

"There may have been a servant with him—I cannot say. I can only tell you the tale as it was told to me."

"If it was a footpad, I don't see how it could have anything to do with the Treasure."

"You do not believe in things being lucky or unlucky? You modern young people attach no importance to things of that sort?"

"I don't know—I shouldn't like to have anything that had been stolen."

Miss Olivia began to fold up her work.

"I do not care to hear reflections upon our ancestor," she said coldly. "I believe I informed you that he left Italy for political reasons. I imagine that he had every right to take with him his share of the patrimony which would have been his had he remained. I think I will now say good night."

Derek left the piano to open the door for her. When she had gone out he shut it again and came back to the fire with a mischievous expression on his face.

"Feeling snubbed, darling?"

"You were listening?"

"Oh, passionately! She prides herself on her articulation, and you may have noticed that I was playing in a whisper. I'm just wondering why you were treated to those old wives' tales."

"So am I."

He laughed.

"Well, I got the impression that she was a bit disappointed, but I don't know why. She may have wanted to scare you off the horrid unlucky stuff, or she may have wanted to get you all worked up and interested in it."

"Why should she want to scare me off?"

"She might want to protect you, or she might want to stop you laying sacrilegious hands on the Treasure."

"Then why should she want to get me interested?"

"More bits and pieces from Anna! She is quite firm about the Treasure being unlucky, but she says of course if someone who wasn't a Benevent handled it, the curse mightn't act, or it wouldn't matter so much if it did! Old Mr. Benevent went a bit childish before he died. He must have been about a hundred. Anna said he talked quite a lot about the Treasure. He told her the thing to do was to get someone who didn't matter to do the job for you. He said he wouldn't handle it himself and no Benevent ought to, but it could be done by a stranger."

Candida had a horrid cold feeling.

"What did he mean?"

"I don't know. She got rather carried away talking, and when I began to ask questions she was scared and dried up. I had to promise I wouldn't let anyone know that she had talked."

"Derek—you've just told me!"

He waved that away.

"Darling, what she meant was the Aunts! She wouldn't give a damn whether you knew or not as long as you didn't tell them. Anyhow it's all rubbish, only—— Look here, Candida, you keep out of it! Don't get interested in it, don't get scared about it! If she offers to show it to you, say you'd rather not!"

"Why?"

"I can't tell you, because I don't know. I've just got a very strong feeling that it's better left alone.

119

Part of the feeling is that perhaps Alan Thompson didn't leave it alone, and that it would have been better for him if he had. Speaking for myself, I wouldn't go within a mile of the stuff for a million— and I can't put it stronger than that!"

Candida said,

"Where is it?"

She got one of his most charming smiles.

"Darling, I don't know, and I don't want to."

CHAPTER 14

When Candida reached her room she was surprised to find Nellie there. It was no more than half past ten, but that was late for her to be turning down the bed and putting in a hot water-bottle, and when she looked round it was plain to see that she had been crying. Candida shut the door and came towards her.

"Why, Nellie, is anything the matter?"

Tears started again from between the reddened lids. The girl said angrily,

"No, there isn't, nor yet there isn't going to be! I'm clearing out!"

"Clearing out?"

Nellie stamped her foot.

"Yes, I am, and nobody's going to persuade me different! The money is good, and I won't say it isn't, but what's the good of that if you've been scared out of your life or had something happen to you that you're never going to forget?"

Candida said in a half-hearted voice,

"Nellie, what do you mean?"

"I mean I'm catching the 9.25 back to London in the morning, and I don't care what Aunt Anna says, or whether she ever speaks to me again or not!"

Candida came a step nearer.

"Has anything happened?"

"I'm not talking about it!"

"But, Nellie—"

"What you don't say nobody can't bring up against you, and that's flat! I'm not talking and I'm not saying! But I'll go as far as this—what's sauce for one of us is just as well sauce for the other!"

Candida said slowly, "What—do—you—mean?"

Nellie tapped with her foot.

"Can't you take a hint?" Her voice had remained angry. "Here, let me by!"

Candida went back against the door and stood there.

"Not just yet," she said. "There isn't any hurry, and I think you have said too much not to say a little more."

The girl was shaking.

"Let me by!"

"In a minute. Look here, Nellie, don't be silly. Come and sit down and tell me what has upset you. You say you are getting out, and you've as good as told me that I'd better get out too. You can't say things like that and leave them floating in the air."

Nellie tossed her head.

"Well then, I can, and what's more I'm going to! Least said, soonest mended!"

Candida was silent for a minute. Then she said,

"Someone has upset you. Who was it? Was it Derek?"

Nellie laughed.

"Go on! You don't suppose I couldn't look after myself with his kind! Anyhow he's all right is Mr. Derek. I mean he might want to lark about a bit, but—he's all right. 'Smatter of fact he's got a girl in Retley—been going with her steady for quite a long time. Only don't you give him away—there wouldn't half be a row if it came out. He's told me all about her. Showed me her photo, too. Not pretty, you know, but ever so nice. And you could tell he was fond of her, the way he looked. A girl can always tell."

The atmosphere had changed. They were two girls talking about a love affair. Candida laughed and said,

"Oh, I won't give him away." And then, "So it wasn't Derek who upset you. Was it Anna?"

Nellie said in a scornful voice,

"She fusses, and I won't say I haven't cheeked her, but that's all in the family. Up in the air one minute and all right again the next—that's Aunt Anna. Always been like that, she has. I wouldn't take any notice of Aunt Anna."

"Is it Joseph then—your uncle?"

Nellie blazed.

"He's no uncle of mine, thank God! What Aunt Anna wanted to marry him for, I can't think! Twenty years younger than her, and all he thinks about is money! Disgusting I call it! And how Aunt Anna could!"

Candida had a fleeting thought that thumbed its nose and suggested with a giggle that Anna's savings must be considerable and her family would naturally prefer them to come their way. It was the kind of guttersnipe thought which you repress and dismiss. But Nellie appeared to have caught a glimpse of it, for she said on a defiant note,

"And you needn't think we'd have minded if it had been what you could call suitable, and not someone that was young enough to be her son and just to please the Miss Benevents. We all know she's fond of them—do anything for Miss Cara she would. But you're not called on to marry a chap that's after your money just because it suits the people you work for!"

Candida laughed.

"I suppose not, but I expect it's been done before now. Well, you don't like Joseph. Is that why you are going?"

"It's reason enough!"

"But is it *the* reason?"

Nellie looked her straight in the face and said, "No!"

"Then——"

Nellie flushed.

"Why can't you leave it alone? I don't like it here, and I'm clearing out! And if you've got any sense you'll clear out too! Let me go!"

Candida shook her head.

All at once Nellie Brown's resistance broke. She had a temper and it got away with her. She had always hated the place, and now it scared her. It was going to do her quite a lot of good to get some of these feelings off her chest. Her eyes sparkled as she said,

"All right then, here it is—and don't blame me if you don't like it!" She laughed angrily. "How would you like to wake up in the night and hear someone in your room?"

"Nellie!"

"Oh, it wasn't Joseph or Mr. Derek—I'd have known what to do about that! It was something that went crying in the dark, and by the time I'd got a

123

light on it was gone. So I started locking my door, but last night it came again. There was a cold hand that touched my face—it wasn't half horrible. I wasn't properly awake for a minute, and by the time I was, there was the crying thing half across the room. My curtains were back, but all I could see was something white, and it walked right into the wall and wasn't there any more. Well, I put on the light, and the door was locked all right the way I'd left it. It was past two o'clock, and I kept my light on till the morning, and every minute of the time I was making up my mind I wouldn't stay another day. Only when I was up and dressed and the sun was shining it seemed stupid to go away without my money. There'll be a month owing me tomorrow, and I thought I'd get it first." She stopped abruptly and said with a complete change of voice and manner, "Well, I must go."

Candida said,

"Don't you—mind?"

Nellie laughed with an effect of bravado.

"Mind? What about?" Then, as Candida only looked at her, she went into a rush of words, "If you're thinking about my sleeping in that room again, I'm not doing it, and that's flat! I told Aunt Anna I wouldn't, and I won't! I'm going in with her, and she'll be wondering what's keeping me!"

"But—Joseph—"

Nellie tossed her head.

"She's got her own room and always has had! And there's a bolt on the door, what's more! I'll be all right in with Aunt Anna!"

CHAPTER 15

Candida went to bed, but it was some time before she put out her light. When she thought of putting it out there was an echo of what Nellie had said about the cold hand that had touched her face and the thing that went crying in the dark. It was frightfully stupid of course, but she had a horrid feeling that if she told her hand to go out and turn off the bedside light there would be some pretty dogged opposition She went barefoot to the bookshelves which filled the whole of the recess between the fireplace and the window. If she were to read for a little, the pictures in her mind would change and she would be able to sleep.

She took down a book of verse and turned the pages. A couple of lines started to her eye:

> "Alone and warming his five wits,
> The white owl in the belfry sits."

That brought up a picture of cold moonlight and a frosted world. She remembered:

> "The owl for all his feathers was a-cold."

Not just what she wanted at the moment. She turned the leaves, and saw four lines at the bottom of a page:

"I saw their starved lips in the gloom,
    With horrid warning gapëd wide;
    And I awoke, and found me here
    On the cold hill-side."

She clapped the book to and put it back upon the shelf. If all that Tennyson and Keats had got to offer were things about cold owls and horrid warnings, to say nothing of starved lips in the gloom, then they were definitely off.

She found a book of short stories and chanced upon one about a coral island. With a hot water-bottle at her feet and the glow of a reading-lamp at her left shoulder, it was possible to be transported to the tropics and to warm the imagination at a description of blue water, rainbow fish, and exotic blooms. After two or three stories all set amongst surroundings where the temperature never fell below eighty degrees she actually found the bottle too much and pushed it away. A little later on she was so nearly asleep that the book slipped from her hand. The sound that it made as it slid to the floor roused her just enough to make her reach out and turn off the light. She passed at once into one of those indeterminate dreams of which no real impression remains.

A long time afterwards she came back to the place where the dreams that come are remembered. She was in the midst of one, and there was no comfort in it. A wide moor and a blowing wind and the hour before the dawn. There were voices in the wind, but what they said went by. Only if she didn't know what they were saying, how did she know that it was something that she must not, *must* not hear? In her dream she began to run so as to get away from the wind, but she tripped and fell, and the wind went over her and was gone.

It hadn't been dark in the dream—just grey, and the clouds racing. But now when she opened her eyes it was very dark indeed. She was awake and in bed in her own room, and the room was full of darkness. She lay on her back, with the head of the bed against the wall, the door to the right, the windows to the left, and in the opposite wall the bulging chimney-breast and the recess which held the books. She knew where all these things were, but as far as seeing them they might just as well not have been there, except that the shape of the windows showed against the denser blackness of the wall. Outside and away from the hill the darkness would not be absolute. There would be at the very least the remembrance and the promise of light. But it couldn't get into the house. It couldn't get into the room, because the darkness filled it to the very brim.

Candida lay there in the dark and was afraid. Moments went by, each one more dragging than the last, and as they dragged, the fear weighed on her and held her down. She had only to put out her hand to the switch of the reading-lamp and turn it on and a golden light would fill the place. Darkness had no power against light. She had only to put out her hand. But she couldn't move it from where it was clenched upon the other, hard up against the slow beating of her heart.

And then all of a sudden there was a sound and there was light.

The sound was the faintest in the world. Something moved. She could get no nearer to it than that. The sound came first, and afterwards the light—a thin white streak like a silver wire stretched upon the darkness of the recess.

Rows of black books in the shelves which she could not see and a line of light dividing them. Between one heart-beat and the next it came, and was gone. She heard the sound again, and this time she knew it for what it was—the bookshelves masked a door and someone was opening it. And quite suddenly the terror that froze her gave way to the instinct to shield her eyes from the searching light, to cover herself with the semblance of sleep. She turned with one quick movement and lay upon her side with her face turned into the pillow and the bedclothes caught up high about her head.

She was just in time, because the light was in the room. It was the light of a torch. She could see it between her lashes—just the glint of it where the bedclothes fell away and the pillow was pressed down. She could tell that it was a torch by the way it slid and swung. Someone had come through the wall in the recess. Someone was crossing the floor. Someone went out of the door and closed it softly.

Candida was not frightened any more, she was angry. There was someone who was playing tricks— on her, on Nellie. Nellie's room was in the old part of the house too. Secret passages were useful in the seventeenth century. People were persecuted for their religion. There were wars and rumours of wars, conspiracies and plots. A turn of the wheel and you were up, and another turn and you were down. It would be useful to have something to hide yourself or—your treasure. She wondered whether the Benevent Treasure was guarded by one of those secret doors. And she wondered who it was who had come soft-foot through the wall to-night. Nellie's visitor could have been no one more frightening than poor

Miss Cara, wandering in the dark of a dream, looking perhaps for the boy of whom she had been so dearly fond. But she didn't think it was Miss Cara to-night, or if it was, then she wasn't walking in her sleep. Mary Coppinger had walked in her sleep at school, but she didn't need a torch to light her way. Candida had followed her once, and she had gone down-stairs in the dark and into one of the classrooms, walking confidently and without hesitation where she herself had had to grope her way. By the time she caught Mary up there was just enough light from the row of windows to make out that she was sitting at her desk. She had the lid open, and she took out a book, and shut down the lid, and went back by the way that she had come. She didn't remember anything about it in the morning. The book was under her pillow. It was a French grammar, and it turned out that she was worrying about an exam she was taking. Poor Aunt Cara was worried about something much worse than an exam.

But whatever had come through this room with a torch wasn't walking in its sleep. It was when she was confronted with the word *her* in her own mind and found she couldn't be sure it was the right one that she snatched at the non-committal *it*. Because she couldn't be sure, she really couldn't be sure, that it was a woman who had come out of the wall and gone away by the door. It could have been a man. Whichever it was had gone soft-foot and silent.

It could have been Joseph. When had she ever heard him come or go? He walked like a cat—an admirable thing in a butler, but not if he used it to prowl in secret passages and come drifting through one's bedroom at dead of night. It was all in her mind in a flash, and in another she was out of bed and the door open under her hand. There was no light in the passage and no movement, but at the right-hand corner there was, not a glow, but some thinning of the darkness which made the corner visible.

On an angry impulse she ran barefoot down the passage. It turned left-handed and she looked round the turn. There was a faint glow which showed the next bend, and then quite suddenly it was gone. She went towards the place where it had been, her hand stretched out, her foot feeling before her. Even after a fortnight in the house its twists and turns could still play her a trick. There were steps that went up and steps that went down. There were cupboards that were nearly as large as rooms, and rooms that were as small as cupboards. It was easy enough to lose yourself at Underhill. And there were never any lights in the passages at night. One of Miss Olivia's little economies.

The hand that was feeling before her came up against something which rose like a cliff. It barred her way, but it wasn't a wall. Her fingers touched wood, the surface deeply carved. At once she knew where she was. There was a big carved press at the top of the stairway which led from the hall. It was old and black, and most inconveniently placed. The landing was narrow, and the press jutted out and cramped what space there was. There was a choice of three passages here, the one by which she had come, one that went on to the servants' wing, and a wider one which led to Miss Olivia's room and Miss Cara's—twin rooms side by side with a bathroom in between. If it was Joseph whom she had been following, he must be well away—the whole wing was cut off by a connecting door. She skirted the press and looked towards it. There was neither light nor movement. Useless to go any farther. The anger had gone out of her. She went a little way in the direction of the Miss Benevents' rooms. The passage lay dark before her—dark and still. And all at once it came over her that her chance was gone, and here she was in her nightgown a long way from where she had any business to be. She had a horrifying picture of Miss Olivia opening her door and switching on the light. Just what she would say or do was one of those things that don't bear thinking about. And she wasn't going to think about it, because it wasn't going to happen.

She turned, keeping wide of the stairs. Her feet were cold on the carpet and a shiver went down her back. When she had passed another corner she felt for a switch and put on the light. She would have to come back and turn it off, but it would show her the way to her room, and once that was lighted she couldn't lose herself.

When it was all done and she had locked her door, she pushed a chair against the bookshelves in the recess and got back into bed. It was twenty past three, and the hot water-bottle was still faintly warm. As she looked across at the chair she remembered the proverb about locking the stable door after the steed is stolen. She called in another proverb to rout it—"Better late than never."

CHAPTER 16

Stephen was kept very busy for the next two days. He had an urgent summons from Colonel Gatling couched in a somewhat military style. Having made up his mind to the demolition of all except the original seventeenth-century manor house, he was insistent to know how soon the work could be begun, how long it would take, and what it would cost, and whether he would have to have "any of those damned permits." On the top of that there was a telephone call from his uncle to say would he ring up the Castle and make an appointment with Lord Retborough. Following out these instructions, he found himself committed to a long and confidential interview with a worried old man.

"The fact is, Eversley, no one—*no one* is going to be able to keep up this sort of place for another generation. We've been here a long time and we've tried to do our best by the place, but the situation has become impossible. The upkeep of the Castle alone"—he lifted a weary hand and let it fall again—"it just can't be done. Both my sons were killed in the war, but there's a grandson to come after me, and I don't want to hang a millstone round his neck. Now what I had in mind was this. I've had a tentative offer for the Castle—one of these new Colleges. I should have thought it highly unsuitable myself, but my grandfather modernised the plumbing, if you can call Victorian plumbing modern, and my father put in electric light, so I suppose it might be worse. Jonathan will join me in breaking the entail. He is prepared to go in for farming in a big way and on the latest scientific lines. He is in his last year at an agricultural college and as keen as mustard. What I want you to do is to get out plans for the sort of house one can live in and run without landing in the bankruptcy court. We've picked the site, and I'd like you to come over and look at it."

With the two other small jobs which he had on his hands, Stephen had plenty to occupy him. He was full of enthusiasm when he rang his uncle up that evening. Yet he had hardly cradled the receiver before he was aware that the dead weight upon his mind had not really lifted. He had been able to ignore it in the interest of his work, but with the first moment of relaxation the old burden was back again— the heaviest and least bearable burden in the world, the fear which will not come out into the open to be proved or disproved, accepted or destroyed.

His room at the Castle Inn had a comfortable chair and, specially imported for his benefit, a good-sized table at which he could work, but neither the chair nor the table attracted him now. He got to his feet, picked up a book and threw it down again, walked to the window, looked out upon the market place, and watched the lights go by. Shocking for one's tyres these old cobbles, and as noisy as a riveting yard.

The telephone rang in the room behind him, and he turned with a quickened pulse. There was no reason on earth why Candida should ring him up, and probably every reason why she should not. She had been angry when they parted, and they had made no plan to meet again. He had a sense of immeasurable loss as it came to him that he would pay forfeit with every treasure of his heart if he never saw her again. He lifted the receiver, and was aware of a woman's voice that was not Candida's. His Cousin Louisa said,

"Oh, is that you? I mean, is it Mr. Eversley?"

"It is."

"Oh, my dear boy—how nice to hear your voice! Ringing up an hotel is always so tiresome, don't you think? You can never be sure that you have really got the person you want!"

"And did you want me, or am I just another wrong number?"

She had one of those rather high, sweet voices. It sounded quite shocked as she said,

"Oh, *no*. It was you whom I wanted—and most particularly. I was afraid that you might be out. You see, Mrs. Mayhew is having one of her musical evenings at the Deanery to-morrow. They are really very agreeable, and it is such a beautiful old house. She had asked me to bring Maud Silver, and this afternoon she rang up and said she heard I had a young cousin staying with me, and why had I not let her know, because she would be so glad if you could find time to come too."

"But Cousin Louisa——"

"My dear boy, not a word! Of course I explained that you were not really staying with me, but she was most kind, and she hoped I would bring you all the same. Lord Retborough will be there. He plays the violin. Not in public of course, but it makes him take an interest. And it seems he has spoken of you in very high terms."

Stephen said,

134

"Very nice of him—but you know, I am most awfully busy."

Louisa dropped to a confidential note.

"Too busy to meet some friends? The Miss Benevents will be there, and I am so much looking forward to meeting Candida Sayle. I really was very fond of her grandmother."

What good was it going to do him to sit in a packed room, or even quite possibly to stand, and look at Candida across a sea of strangers whilst the amateur talent of Retley displayed itself? Candida on the other side of a gulf, and Miss Blank not quite hitting a high note or Mr. Dash scooping lugubriously upon the cello! None that he could see, but he knew that he would be fool enough to chance it. He had, in fact, arrived at the point where he could no longer keep away from her. If she was still angry, he had to know it and rekindle his own anger at the glow. At the first moment of their meeting, at the briefest encounter of their eyes, he would know what it had become imperative for him to know. He said,

"Well, it's very kind of you, Cousin Louisa—and of Mrs. Mayhew."

When it came to the point, the Deanery was not so crowded as Stephen had feared. Mrs. Mayhew was a woman of taste and discretion whose aim in entertaining was to give pleasure to her friends. She did not, therefore, pack them like sardines or oblige them to shout themselves hoarse in order to be heard above the competing voices of a crowd. He found her an agreeable woman with an air of breeding and competence.

"Lord Retborough has told me about you, Mr. Eversley. You cannot think how much he is looking forward to the house which he tells me you are to

135

design for him. Old places may be interesting, but one cannot pretend that they are easy to run."

He passed on, Louisa Arnold introducing him here and there, until she and Miss Silver became absorbed into one of the groups already provided with seats. There would be no music until everyone was settled and the first flow of conversation had had its way. Stephen was listening to a tall, thin old man who was one of the Canons, and who might have been interesting enough if it had been possible to hear what he said. He appeared to be imparting architectural information about the Cathedral, but as a naturally soft manner of speech was impeded by the kind of dentures which produce a lisp, all that was possible was to maintain an attentive attitude and be on the alert for a chance to get away.

It came at the moment when the Miss Benevents were shaking hands with Mrs. Mayhew and the Dean and introducing their great-niece. For once they were not dressed alike. Miss Olivia was in violet brocade with a stole of Brussels point. A necklace of very large amethysts came up tight about her throat. The matching bracelets clasped her wrists. A massive corsage ornament reposed upon her chest. Stephen was reminded of the pictures in a book of old French fairy tales, but he couldn't be sure whether she was the Beneficent Godmother or the Wicked Fairy. He thought it was the Godmother, because now he came to consider it the Wicked Fairy had a retinue of toads and bats. Miss Cara, behind her, was small and shrunken in black velvet and a scarf of heavy Spanish lace. She wore one of those early Victorian necklaces of seed pearls fashioned into little flat roses.

Candida was in white. It was a new dress, a present from the Aunts. Stephen wasn't to know that.

He only saw that she was beautiful, and that she looked at him and smiled. There was a bright, pure colour in her cheeks and her hair shone under the lights. All the drag and strain of their quarrel was gone. She carried beauty with her. The look between them was a long one, but he would have to wait before he could speak to her. Miss Olivia was making a procession of their advance, Cara a little behind her on the left, Candida on the right, and Derek bringing up the rear. There were gracious bows and an occasional pause for the appropriate courtesies—"How nice to see you, Lady Caradoc! May I introduce our great-niece, Candida Sayle?...Canon Verschoyle, it is far too long since we met! This is our great-niece." And so forth and so on.

Candida was smiled upon by the Bishop, a large old man with a kindly face and a comfortable figure, and by the Bishop's wife, who had seventeen grandchildren and an air of placid indulgence. Everyone to whom she was introduced was kind, and there were one or two who remembered Candida Benevent and the stir it had made when she married John Sayle. Candida had been to a small dance or two, but never before to a large formal party in a beautiful old house like this. And she had a new dress for it. The Aunts had really been noble about the dress. They had escorted her in state to a small exclusive shop, where Miss Olivia handed her over to Mme. Laurier—"who will know just what you ought to wear." A rather intimidating opening, but fully justified by the result. The white dress was produced, tried on, and acclaimed, Miss Olivia's "Very suitable" being followed by Aunt Cara's "Oh, my dear—how pretty!" Candida had no words. If she had tried for any, they would have failed her. The dress did everything that a dress can do. She flushed and turned a swimming look of gratitude upon the Aunts, only to be shocked into dismay at the sound of the price.

The Miss Benevents did not turn a hair. They nodded, and Miss Olivia said,

"It will do very nicely. You will put it down to my account, madame."

It was not until the last of the guests had arrived that Stephen and Candida met. The first item on the programme was about to begin. The Miss Benevents were already seated. Just behind them Louisa Arnold leaned forward and introduced "My cousin, Maud Silver." There was a moment when everyone's attention was taken up, and in that moment Stephen slipped a hand inside Candida's arm and drew her away. It really was very skilfully done. He had two chairs marked down, set back against one of the recessed windows and well away behind the Aunts and Cousin Louisa. They reached them just in time and with the sense of adventure achieved. And then a tall young cleric with a fine carrying voice was announcing that Mr. and Mrs. Hayward and Miss Storey would play Mr. Hayward's own trio in A major. Everyone clapped politely. All those passionately addicted to chamber music settled down to enjoyment, while those who did not care for it resigned themselves to some twenty minutes of boredom.

Mr. Hayward's trio was not unknown. A good deal to his own suprise, Stephen found it to his taste. There was vigour and melody, there was a triumphing note. It went well with his mood. The three executants played remarkably well. He had felt obliged to drop his hand from Candida's arm, but their chairs were so close together that her shoulder touched his sleeve. It was tantalising, but they were together and she wasn't angry any more. They sat in silence side by side and the music filled the room. There was an enthusiastic burst of clapping at the end.

Stephen said, "Candida," and she turned her head and looked at him. The people in front of them were standing up. There was, for the moment, a small private place where they were alone. He touched her hand and said,

"You've finished being angry?"

"Yes."

His voice came low and abrupt.

"You mustn't do it again. It does things to me."

"What sort of things?"

"Damnable."

"Why?"

"You know why."

"How can I—if you don't tell me?"

"I have told you. It does things. Candida, you know—don't you—don't you?"

She looked away. Her lips trembled into a smile.

"You'll have to say it, Stephen."

The people in front of them were moving—their moment was almost gone. He said in an angry whisper,

"I can't—not here. Candida, you know I love you horribly!"

"How can I know—when you don't tell me?"

He could hardly catch the words. The hand he was touching shook.

"Did you want me to tell you?"

"Of course."

Their privacy was gone. There would be a quarter of an hour's interval. People were walking about, talking to their friends. He pulled her to her feet and

139

held aside the curtain from the recess behind them.

"Come and look at the Cathedral by moonlight. It ought to be worth seeing."

And all in a moment they were there alone together, the curtain dropped and all the world shut out. Neither the moon nor the Cathedral received any attention. Both had been deemed worthy of a good deal of it in the past, but this was not their hour. The moon shone coldly down upon the stone, and the cold stone took the light in all the beauty that men's hands had given it, but Stephen and Candida had no eyes for them.

Miss Louisa Arnold and Miss Silver had kept their seats, and so had the Miss Benevents. Louisa desired nothing better than an opportunity of conversing with her old friends. As soon as it was politely possible she stopped trying to applaud and leaned forward to touch Miss Cara's arm.

"My dear Cara! How long is it since I have seen you? Have you been ill?"

Cara Benevent turned round with a rather too hurried, "Oh, no, Louisa—I am very well."

"You don't look it," said Miss Arnold without any tact.

She was, in fact, a good deal startled. No one would have taken Miss Cara for the younger sister now. She had always been small and slight, but she looked as if she had shrunk. The bones of the face showed through the sallow skin. And all that unrelieved black! Neither black velvet nor black lace had been considered mourning in the days when such observances were more strictly regulated, but the plain, solemn folds of the gown and all that heavy Spanish lace presented quite a funerary appearance.

She began to talk about Candida.

"How pretty she is—really quite charming! And how nice for you and Olivia! Young people do make such a difference in the house, do they not?"

It was not possible for Miss Cara to lose colour. A tremor went over her. Louisa Arnold became aware that she had said the wrong thing. She had for the moment forgotten about Alan Thompson. She hurried on, her voice a little higher and more flute-like than usual.

"It has been such a pleasure for me to have the opportunity of seeing something of my young cousin, Stephen Eversley. I believe you have met him."

Miss Cara became noticeably embarrassed.

"Oh, yes—yes——"

"His mother was the daughter of Papa's first cousin, the Bishop of Branchester. Such an eloquent preacher, and an authority on the Early Fathers. I believe he was considered for the Archbishopric. Papa used often to talk about it. He married a daughter of Lord Danesborough, a very quiet, religious kind of person and extremely dowdy in her dress. But the daughter who was Stephen's mother was by way of being a beauty. Of course the Bishop was a very good-looking man—really quite a commanding presence."

Miss Silver pursued an equable conversation with Miss Olivia Benevent. She was aware that she was being condescended to as an unknown and probably distant relative of Louisa's. She was, however, perfectly able to sustain her part in a tactful and dignified manner, choosing such subjects as the beauty of the Cathedral and the remarkable number of old and historic buildings in Retley and the neighbourhood.

"Louisa tells me that you yourself own a very interesting old house."

141

Miss Olivia did not disclaim the ownership.

"It has been a long time in the family."

"That, of course, adds very much to the interest. There must be so many associations."

Miss Olivia was not displeased at being afforded an opportunity of talking about the Benevents. Miss Silver listened with the attention which family history does not always command.

"Then it was your ancestor who actually built the house? Louisa tells me that it really does stand, as the name would suggest, under the hill. Was the site chosen, do you know, in order to provide shelter from a prevailing wind?"

Her interest was so unaffected that Miss Olivia found herself imparting the fact that the site had actually been determined by the presence of the small Tudor house in which Ugo di Benevento had resided prior to his marriage with the daughter of a neighbouring landowner.

"She was a considerable heiress, and it was of course desirable that a more suitable residence should be provided. We have no means of knowing what decided them to build on to the existing house, but that is what they did. A good deal of it was not touched, and remains very much as it was in the sixteenth century."

It was at this point that the name of Stephen Eversley reached her. It was pronounced by Louisa Arnold in a tone which Miss Olivia mentally stigmatised as shrill, and it was followed by what she considered to be an unwarrantable assumption.

"You are giving him a commission to restore Underhill, are you not?"

Miss Olivia entered the conversation with an air of authority.

"My dear Louisa, Underhill is not in need of being restored. If Mr. Eversley gave you that impression he must have been under a grave misapprehension. It is not, I believe, for a professional man to discuss an employer's business, and I am surprised that Mr. Eversley should have done so. It was his uncle to whom we applied for an opinion as to whether some structural repairs were necessary, but instead of coming himself he sent his nephew, a young and inexperienced person in whose judgment we cannot feel the same confidence. We have therefore informed Mr. Stephen Eversley that we shall not require his services."

There is no knowing what Louisa Arnold might have said in reply. Her colour rose sharply. It was perhaps fortunate that Mrs. Warburton should at that moment have evinced the intention of returning to her seat. Since she was an extremely large person, this necessitated everyone else in the row getting up and making room for her to pass. Louisa had therefore to refrain from the no doubt well chosen words in which she might have reminded Olivia of Stephen's unexceptionable connections and deprecated her use of the word employer.

All the places were filling up again. Stephen and Candida emerged from the curtained recess and resumed their seats. To an attentive eye it would have been obvious that they were not really there at all. They walked in some Cloud-Cuckoo-land and listened to an older song than that which a Minor Canon's niece now warbled. There was a piano accompaniment by a stout lady in puce and a violin obligato by the Minor Canon—altogether a charming performance, and a voice as clear as running water. But the other song was the sweeter.

CHAPTER 17

Derek had penetrated to the farthest corner of the room and the one least commanded by Miss Olivia's eye. He seemed to have quite a number of friends, and had been graciously received by Mrs. Mayhew, who was wont to deplore the fact that he had never really cultivated his musical talent—"Such a charming touch."

During the next interval he was found to be at Jenny Rainsford's side, and it was there that Miss Olivia discovered him. Her sight being excellent, the distance did not prevent her being struck by something in his manner. It was usual enough for him to turn that charming smile upon all and sundry. He possessed an amiable nature and a strong desire to please. He could have smiled upon fifty girls without causing her the least uneasiness. It was because he did not smile at Jenny Rainsford that she felt disturbed. Whoever the girl was, Derek was looking and listening in a deeply serious way. And the girl was doing most of the talking.

She regarded her with some attention. There was nothing particular about her looks. She was not very tall, and she had nothing very special in the way of features—brown curls, blue eyes, and rather a round-shaped face. Her dress was one of those modern high-necked affairs, the top in blue and black brocade coming down over the hips and worn with a tight black satin skirt. Frowning, Miss Olivia accorded it a certain distinction. She turned to ask Louisa Arnold who the girl might be—"Over there at the far end, talking to Derek."

Louisa had plenty to impart.

"Oh, that is Jenny Rainsford."

"And who is Jenny Rainsford?"

"My dear Olivia, you must remember her father, poor Ambrose Rainsford. Such an eloquent preacher. He was the Vicar of St. Luke's. But first his wife died leaving him with three little girls, and then he did. I don't think he had the heart to go on alone."

"I suppose the girls had to," said Miss Olivia drily.

"Yes, indeed. Jenny was seventeen, and the other two were younger. There wasn't any money at all, and she went into Adamson's garage. If you have ever been there you must have seen her. She answers the telephone, and takes the orders, and rings up about theatre tickets. Mr. Adamson says she is most business-like and efficient and he doesn't know what he would do without her."

Miss Olivia could not have disapproved more. What an occupation for a girl whose father seemed to have been a gentleman! She said in her curtest manner,

"She looks a good deal more than seventeen to me."

"Oh, yes—she must be twenty-three or twenty-four now. The second girl is married, and Linda who is the clever one has got a very good secretarial post, so they are off Jenny's hands."

Miss Olivia broke off the conversation abruptly. She had no wish to hear any more about Miss Jenny Rainsford. If she could have overheard what was being said between her and Derek Burdon, the uneasiness which had led her to drop the subject would have been very seriously increased. Every word, every tone would have betrayed them. At the moment when she attracted Miss Olivia's notice Jenny was saying, "He only told me this afternoon, but I think he has quite made up his mind—"

"To retire?"

"Well, that's just it—he doesn't want to go on working, but he doesn't really want to retire."

"Darling, he can't have it both ways."

"Well, he thinks he can. He has got it all worked out. He would like to take a partner who would run the show and pay him over say two-thirds of the profits. He wouldn't ask him to put in more than a thousand if he felt it was someone he could get on with."

"Oh, he wants to go on working?"

"Well, not to say working. He'd just like to come in and potter round when he felt like it. You know, he hasn't really been up to it for some time, and the place has gone down, but it could soon be worked up again. It would be a wonderful chance for some-one—Derek, it would be a wonderful chance for us."

"Us!"

"Yes, darling. I didn't mean to talk about it here, but I just can't keep it back."

"I couldn't do it. I don't know the first thing about running a business."

"But you know about cars. Mr. Adamson always says you're a first-class mechanic—the Army did that for you. And you're a very good driver. As for the business side, I've got it all at my fingers' ends. There's nothing you wouldn't learn easily enough as soon as you got going on it."

"And where do we get the thousand pounds, dar-ling?"

She looked up at him, her eyes very blue, very serious.

"How much have you saved?"

"Nothing like that."

"How much?"

"I only started just over a year ago. I'm not much good at saving."

"I said, 'How much?'"

"Well, about four hundred."

She let the blue eyes smile.

"But that's very good. I didn't think it would be as much as that. You've done frightfully well."

Jenny didn't praise very often. He considered ruefully that she hadn't had much reason to praise him, but when she did, it was worth having. He felt abashed and humble.

"I've been able to put away most of my salary, and they gave me another hundred for Christmas."

Jenny stopped looking at him. She hated the salary for which he didn't work. She hated the cushioned life with the two old ladies. She hated the things that people said, or that she thought they might be saying. But she loved Derek. And she believed that Derek loved her. And if he loved her, he had got to work for her and for their life together. The salary and the cushions must be given up. They must live on their own hard work. She said,

"I think we can do it."

"Darling, four from ten leaves six."

She nodded gravely.

"Derek, I didn't tell you that old Cousin Robert Rainsford left me a thousand pounds. Peg had two hundred out of it when she married, and Linda had two hundred and fifty to help her through college and get her started."

147

"Then we are only fifty pounds short. Would Mr. Adamson wait for that?"

She said, "I've got fifty saved."

He gazed at her with genuine pride.

"Darling, you're a wonder! If it wouldn't send the balloon up like a rocket, I'd kiss you!"

She let her eyes smile back into his for a moment, then was serious again.

"Mr. Adamson is going to live with his married daughter. They've got that nice cottage a couple of miles out, and he loves the children, so he won't be wanting the house any more. There are six rooms and it would suit us down to the ground. It was bombed in the war and rebuilt a couple of years afterwards, so it's all modern—built-in cupboards— frightfully labour-saving. We can have the curtains and the floor-coverings for a song. I chose them for him, so they're all right. And if we want any of the furniture, he'll let us have it cheap. It really is the most marvellous chance."

It was. He knew that well enough. Opportunity doesn't knock a second time upon the door that will not open. He saw that quite clearly. And he saw the things that would come in if he opened the door. There would be a lot of hard work, and he hated work. There would be Jenny. He didn't mind messing about with cars. It was one thing to do it now and again with a car of your own, and quite another to do it all day and every day with strange crocks whose owners wanted them made over new whilst they waited and got terse with you when you said it couldn't be done.

Jenny's steady blue eyes looked up at him. He had a feeling that they looked right through him and

148

could see just what he was thinking. He was ashamed of some of the things. He didn't want Jenny to be ashamed. He said quite simply and humbly,

"Do you think I could make a go of it?"

Jenny said, "Yes, darling."

CHAPTER 18

The Deanery party broke up in due course. Everyone told Mrs. Mayhew how much they had enjoyed it, and in most cases they spoke no more than the truth. Louisa Arnold, coming back into her own house with her cousin, was really quite reluctant to admit that the evening was over and to say good-night. It was so very pleasant to linger by what was left of the drawing-room fire and gossip for a while.

"I am really quite charmed with Candida Sayle, but, my dear, did it not strike you that Stephen was too?"

Miss Silver smiled. She could have expressed it a good deal more strongly than that, but she refrained.

"And, my dear Maud, did you notice Derek Burdon and that nice girl I was telling you about, Jenny Rainsford? They seemed to be having quite a serious talk, and I don't think I have ever seen Derek look serious before."

"He is very good-looking."

"Oh, quite charming. And he really plays delightfully. Not highbrow enough for Mrs. Mayhew, but she can't help liking him—no one can. He has been dangling after Jenny for months. Olivia Benevent was watching them to-night, and she didn't look at all pleased—not at all. It's a shocking life for him, being spoiled and pampered at Underhill, but I don't see how he could get out of it now. I fancy Olivia would like to get him married to Candida."

Miss Silver was wearing the dark blue crêpe-dechine. With the gold locket which bore her parents' initials in high relief and contained locks of their hair, it supplied her modest needs. For the party at the Deanery she had substituted light silk stockings for her usual wool, changed during the summer months for lisle thread. With an almost new pair of glacé shoes, she had felt very well equipped. She said a little primly,

"I do not fancy that Miss Olivia has any chance of seeing her wishes fulfilled. Young people have a way of taking these matters into their own hands."

"Oh, yes, *indeed!* But Olivia always has to have things her way. She was like that as a child, and she could be very nasty indeed if she was crossed."

"No one can expect to have his own way all the time."

"Well, Olivia does. And she bullies Cara shockingly—she always has. Maud, didn't you think she was looking terribly ill? I really felt quite concerned."

"Miss Cara?"

Louisa Arnold nodded.

"I thought she looked terrible. And all that black— so unbecoming." She looked down complacently at her own full skirt of mauve and blue brocade. "But of course it is just about three years since Alan Thompson went off in that extraordinary way. Cara was always one for keeping anniversaries. A *great* mistake. I remember Papa saying so—'dragging things back to be miserable over, when Heaven in

150

its mercy has lightened the load of grief!' "

Miss Silver smiled benignly.

"Your father was not only a sensible man, he was a Christian."

Louisa Arnold's eyes were suddenly moist.

"Oh, *yes!*"

The Miss Benevents drove home in silence. Miss Cara was exhausted, but in Miss Olivia's case it was the silence of displeasure. Derek and Candida, in front, had their own thoughts. If they had been alone they might have found quite a lot to say, but since everything must be overheard, they kept their warm and happy counsel.

Arrived at Underhill, the three ladies entered the hall, and Derek took the car round to the garage. Miss Cara's ascent of the stairs was so slow and so halting that Candida put an arm round her and went with her to her room.

"Can I help you, Aunt Cara?"

"Oh, no, my dear—no. I will just sit in my chair until Anna comes—if you will ring the bell—I am only a little tired—so many people all talking at once." She leaned back and closed her eyes.

Candida went out into the passage and looked along it. She wouldn't go until Anna was in sight.

But it was Miss Olivia who came towards her in her purple dress, her gold and amethyst ornaments catching the light. Not for the first time Candida found herself wondering whether the black hair was a wig. It was so incredibly shiny and so very, very black. There was never a break in the even waves, or a hair that was out of place. The dark eyes looked coldly at Candida.

"What are you doing here? It is time we were all in bed."

There was nothing to soften the words. Candida coloured high.

"It was Aunt Cara," she said.

"What about her?"

"She seems so tired. She said Anna would come—"

"Anna will assist us both. She always does."

A little spark of anger kindled in Candida. She said quickly and warmly,

"I don't think Aunt Cara is well—I don't really. People kept saying to-night how ill she looked."

"They should mind their own business."

Candida said,

"I nursed Barbara for three years. I think Aunt Cara is ill."

Miss Olivia's face changed suddenly. The features went sharp. There was a cold fury in the eyes. Her hand came up and struck. A quick blow took Candida on the cheek-bone. The heavy amethyst bracelet tore a long scratch across her chin.

She stepped back, too much shocked for anger. Miss Olivia said in a voice edged with rage,

"Hold your tongue!"

Neither of them saw Anna until she was there between them, her face twitching, her hand shaking on Candida's arm.

"What is this! No, no—there is nothing—I am stupid! It is late, and Miss Cara will be tired! We shall all be tired in the morning!"

Candida said in a level voice,

"Yes, Aunt Cara is tired. You had better go to her."

Miss Olivia Benevent walked past them into her room and shut the door.

CHAPTER 19

Candida walked away. She had nothing to say to Anna. She had nothing to say to anyone. She was too horrified to be angry. The sudden violence appalled her. It seemed so completely without reason—in such unexplained conflict with Olivia Benevent's dignity and self-control.

When she reached her room she took off the white dress and hung it up in the gloomy Victorian wardrobe on the right of the door. She wondered if she would ever want to wear it again, because Miss Olivia had chosen it and given it to her. And then it came to her that she would forget that and only remember that she had worn it when Stephen held her in his arms. The shocked feeling began to pass. She began to wonder why the thing had happened. She had said that Miss Cara seemed ill, and Olivia had struck her. There didn't seem to be any sense in it. Perhaps there wasn't ever any sense about people getting angry, but as a rule you did know why.

She put up her hand to her face and brought it away with a smear of blood on the forefinger. If there was blood on the dress, she couldn't wear it again. They said blood never came out, but that was nonsense. But she didn't want to look and see whether the dress was stained. If it was, let it stay in the dark—she didn't want to see it. It was the amethyst bracelet that had broken the skin. The stones were

153

large and the gold setting heavy. She held a cloth steeped in cold water to the scratch, but the blood went on starting. It took her some time to stop it.

She put on her dressing-gown and sat down by the fire. There was so much to think about. There was Stephen. She remembered with astonishment that there had been anger between them, that they had quarrelled. It didn't seem possible that their bond had ever been broken. She could see it bright and strong, always there even from the very first moment when he had called to her from the sea. Perseus coming to rescue Andromeda chained to the cliff. But it wasn't he who had the Gorgon's head. It was Olivia Benevent who was Medusa with the eyes which turned to stone. Only instead of the wreath of twining snakes there were the black waves of her hair.

Her thoughts had begun to slip into fantasy, when there was a tapping at the door and without waiting for an answer Anna came in, her hands outstretched, her eyes full of tears.

"Oh, Miss Candida, what do I say—I am so sorry, so sorry! I would have come before, but I have to put my poor Miss Cara into her bed. She is tired, she is exhausted, she is ill. And she is cold, my poor Miss Cara—she is so cold! There are two hot water-bottles in her bed. I wrap her in a soft, warm shawl, and I bring her hot milk with brandy in it. Now she sleeps. And all this time Miss Olivia shuts her door. I knock upon it and there is no answer. I try the handle and it will not turn—the door is locked. So then I come here to you." She drew in her breath with a sound of sharp distress. "Oh, there is blood on your face! My poor Miss Candida!"

Candida said, "It isn't anything." There was a little

154

bead of blood upon her chin, but it had begun to dry.

Anna clucked over her like a distressed hen.

"It was the heavy bracelet. She did not mean to do that. It will not leave a scar."

"Oh, no—it's nothing."

"She will be so distressed when she sees it. And your cheek—there will be a bruise!"

"It will soon go. Anna, why did she do it?"

Anna made a wringing motion with her hands.

"You said something about Miss Cara—I should have warned you. But what is one to do? One says too much, or one says too little. How is one to know what is right? I say nothing, and this happens! I have served them for forty years, and still I do not know what is best."

Candida looked at her gravely.

"Why was she so angry?"

Anna threw up her hands.

"How do I know? You do not tell me what you say. It is something about Miss Cara?"

"I said that she was tired—I had to help her up the stairs. I said that she was ill."

"But that is what no one must ever say. No one—no one must say it. I should have told you. Even I, after all these years—I tell you, you are not the only one. She has struck me before now. No one must ever say that Miss Cara is ill—she will not bear it."

"Why?"

"Do you not know?"

"How can I? It doesn't make sense."

Anna closed her lips and turned away. She moved towards the door. And then very suddenly she came back again, her white hair sticking up in a fuzz and her face working.

"Miss Candida, do you not know what is on her mind? If Miss Cara is ill—she thinks suppose it were that Miss Cara should die. She is not strong—she has never been strong. If she dies, what happens then—what will there be left for Miss Olivia? Everything belongs to Miss Cara, but only for her life. She cannot leave it to her sister—not one penny of it! Miss Olivia will have enough to live on—in a little house in Retley! What would that be like for her? Do you think she would bear it? But this house and everything in it, and the money, and the Treasure— if there is any of it left, and how do I know if there is or not—all these things will be yours! And you tell her that Miss Cara is ill! Do you ask why she strikes you!"

She turned round and went out of the room.

CHAPTER 20

Since Nellie had gone, it was Anna who brought in the morning tea. Candida, who had not thought that she would sleep, lost herself almost from the moment that her head touched the pillow. There were no dreams, there was not anything, but she awoke with the feeling that she had been a long way off. Anna stood beside her, smiling and solicitous.

"You slept? There is nothing like sleep and another day. Last night everyone is tired, everything goes wrong. We are gloomy, we quarrel. It is all very bad. But this morning we forget about it—it is gone."

Candida pulled herself up in the bed, her nightgown slipping from one shoulder. She blinked at Anna and said,

"I don't think it's as easy as that."

Anna laughed.

"Oh, yes, yes! Why, the rain is over, the sun shines and the birds sing! What is the use of thinking about yesterday's weather? We are not there any more. If it rained yesterday, there is no need for us to wet our feet to-day. Come, you did not tell me about the party. Did you like the music? Did you see Mr. Eversley? Well, I think you did, and I think that was one of the things that made Miss Olivia cross. She does not think he is good enough for you. She would like you to be fond of Mr. Derek, and she would like him to be fond of you."

Candida laughed.

"But I am very fond of Derek, and I hope he is fond of me."

Anna tossed her head, the white hair flew up.

"If it were like that, you would not say so! When you say of someone, 'I am so fond of him,' that means nothing at all! But if you say, 'I hate him,' or 'I don't think about him,' that is the one I would look out for! Now drink your tea, or it will be cold. And let me see your face . . . *Dio Mio*! What it is to have a skin that heals like that! There is hardly anything to show! If you will put a little cream and powder on it, there will be nothing for anyone to talk about."

Candida drank her tea and set down the cup. Then she said,

"Anna, I can't stay here."

Anna threw up her hands.

"Because Miss Olivia loses her temper? In forty years how many times do you think she has lost it with me? And for you it is all in the family. You are

157

the child of the house, the little niece of whom everyone is fond, and you get sometimes a present and sometimes a slap. Would you make any more of it than that? If you do, you will be making much trouble about a very little thing. And Miss Cara will be sad, and that is not good for her. My poor Miss Cara, she has had enough!"

And that was true. Remembering how small and frail the little creature had looked, Candida's heart misgave her. You can't just ride your high horse down the middle of the road and not care whether you knock someone else over, especially if they are poor little things like Aunt Cara.

Anna's large dark eyes were fixed on her with a melting expression. Candida was reminded of a spaniel pleading for cake. She thought, "Oh, well, let her have it," and broke into a smile.

"All right, Anna. But what do I do next—walk into the dining-room and say good-morning as if nothing had happened?"

Anna nodded vigorously.

"That will be the best thing. Yes, that will be much the best. I do not think that Miss Olivia will say anything. And if you say nothing and she says nothing"—she brought her hands together with a clapping sound— "well, then there is nothing to be said. You have your breakfast in peace, you eat in peace. There is nothing at all that is so bad for the digestion as to quarrel when you are eating. No, no, no, for the good digestion there should be pleasant talk with friends, there should be smiles, there should be laughter. And that will do my poor Miss Cara good."

Candida laughed.

"A little optimistic, aren't you, Anna? But I'll do what I can for Aunt Cara's sake."

Anna smiled, nodded, and then turned suddenly grave again.

"Oh, my poor Miss Cara!" she said, and was in a hurry to go.

Seen by daylight the mark on Candida's cheek really did show very little. Still it did show, and so did the scratch on her chin. She did what she could, yet when she met Derek on the stairs his eyebrows went up.

"Hullo, what have you been doing to yourself? Had a rough house?"

She put her finger to her lip. There were footsteps on the landing above. As they glanced round, Miss Olivia came into sight. She wore a straight black woollen gown buttoned down the front, and a short coat of grey and violet stuff. Her hair shone. Her smooth sallow skin showed no trace of an emotional upset. She came down slowly and with her accustomed dignity to where they were waiting at the foot of the stairs. Arrived, she said good-morning first to Candida and then to Derek, and offered a cool cheek to each of them in turn.

Candida had not known that she would feel so much revulsion. The brief touch of that cold skin was horrible. It took her all she knew not to recoil from it.

Whatever Derek knew or didn't know, he could always be counted on for a pleasant flow of words. He opined that it was going to be a fine day, and he talked about the party in a very lively manner. It did just occur to Candida that it wasn't perhaps the safest subject in the world. Miss Olivia didn't miss much, and she might have seen her step behind the curtain with Stephen. Perhaps she had. Perhaps that was at the back of her anger. Or if she had not actually seen

159

them go, she might have missed them both and guessed that they were together. Impossible to say.

Miss Cara came down, shadowy in a replica of her sister's clothes. And that was a mistake, for they made her look as if she had shrunk, or as if they really belonged to someone else.

When the little bustle of serving was over the talk went on again. Miss Cara said that it had been a nice evening, and that she had enjoyed seeing Louisa Arnold, but all in a little flat voice and without conviction.

Olivia Benevent sat up very straight.

"Louisa is just as foolish and as voluble as she always was. She must have been a great trial to the Canon. But then Cathedral circles are always very gossipy, and I suppose he had become used to it."

"I always liked Louisa," said Miss Cara in a faint, obstinate voice. "I was very pleased to see her again. She was telling me that the cousin who is staying with her is really a very clever detective but she does not care about having it known."

Miss Olivia gave a short scornful laugh.

"Then how like Louisa to talk about it!"

Miss Cara persevered.

"Her name is Maud Silver. Louisa says she has solved many difficult cases besides being an extremely expert knitter."

It was when breakfast was over that Derek found himself summoned to the study. When the ladies had seated themselves Miss Olivia spoke in gracious tones.

"We are very much pleased that you and Candida are now beginning to work at the family history."

"Well, she's a lot better at it than I am."

She smiled.

160

"You will help each other, I have no doubt. It is not necessary to say who contributes the most. It is enough that you should be able to work pleasantly together. We have been very glad to see that you are making friends."

Miss Cara echoed her.

"We are so very glad."

His attractive smile flashed out.

"Well, I suppose you can say that we are both friendly people."

Miss Olivia looked at him.

"You would call Candida friendly?"

"Oh, yes."

"And attractive?"

He said, "Oh, very," and wondered where this was getting them.

"She seemed to be a good deal admired last night. May I ask what terms you are on?"

"Oh, the very best."

Just as well to be hearty about it, but he did wish that she would stop.

She said in an alarmingly deliberate manner,

"You would do well to consider whether they might not be even better." Then, after a pause, "Better—and closer."

There didn't seem to be any way out of asking her what she meant.

Miss Cara's eyes went from one to the other, but she did not speak. He said,

"I don't think I know what you mean. We are very good friends."

"I mean that you might be something more."

His "I don't think so" set her frowning. She said very deliberately,

"Candida is a Benevent. She is considered both

161

pretty and charming. She will have a good deal of money." She forced her voice and made it say, "She will have Underhill."

There was another pause. He would have to speak now, but just what was he going to say? Enough, but not too much. There was no sense in pulling the roof down over his head—nasty for him, nasty for Jenny, and nasty for Candida. He met Miss Cara's anxious eyes. Her hands fluttered out a little way towards him and drew back. Her "Don't make Olivia angry" was as plain as if the words had been spoken. He said,

"Yes—"

The frown deepened. Olivia Benevent spoke sharply.

"My dear Derek, you are not really stupid, so why pretend that you are? You have already agreed with me that Candida is a charming girl, that she is much admired, and that you are very good friends. She comes of a family to which, I think we may say, you are already bound by ties of affection, and she will be a very considerable heiress. You are our adopted nephew. Owing to the terms of my grandfather's will we are not in a position to make the provision for you which we should have wished. In an earlier and more practical age we should simply have arranged a marriage between you and our niece, and I have no doubt that it would have turned out very happily. As it is, all I can do is to point out the advantages of such a marriage."

It was impossible to let her go on. He said in a protesting voice,

"But my dears, she doesn't care for me like that— she doesn't really."

Miss Olivia said, "Nonsense! You are here in the

162

house with her—you have every opportunity of making love to her. But you are just throwing them away. I have been watching you, and you have simply been wasting your time. It cannot go on."

He had remained standing. He backed away now towards the window.

"You know, you have got this all wrong—you really have. Candida wouldn't have me if I asked her."

"You cannot know that unless you do ask her. She naturally would not make the first advances. She would expect you to let her see that you care for her."

"But I don't. At least not like that."

Miss Cara pressed a handkerchief to her eyes and spoke in a trembling voice.

"She would make you very happy, my dear. She has a very kind heart."

"Dear Aunt Cara—"

"I have grown very fond of her. It would make me very happy."

Well, there was nothing for it. He put out a hand towards them and said,

"You know there is nothing I would like better than to please you, but it isn't any good, because, you see, I am fond of somebody else."

They sat and stared at him, a tear just trickling down Miss Cara's cheek, Miss Olivia with a hard blank look. For once it was the elder sister who spoke first.

"Oh, my dear boy!"

Olivia Benevent just went on looking at him. The silence had grown heavy before she said,

"Indeed?" Just the one word. And then, after a glacial pause, "Who is she?"

He was burning his boats, but he didn't care. It was going to be worth everything to be able to say Jenny's name out loud and have done with all the secrecy. You slip into it, and before you know where you are it is sliming you all over.

He said, "Jenny Rainsford," and Miss Olivia came back at him like the crack of a whip.

"A young woman in a second-rate garage!"

"You don't know anything about her."

"I know what Louisa Arnold told me."

"No one could have told you anything that wasn't good about Jenny—there isn't anything else to tell! Her father died, and she worked for her sisters. If Miss Arnold told you anything, she told you that."

"She mentioned it. I am afraid it didn't interest me. A girl who is left penniless would naturally have to work. I see nothing remarkable about that. And I am afraid that I do not admire her choice of what she would no doubt call a job. Louisa mentioned that her father was a gentleman. I should think he would have been a good deal distressed at his daughter's deliberate descent into quite another class."

Derek bit his lip. There was no sense in having a quarrel about it. It wouldn't help Jenny, and they had been very good to him. He took a step towards the door, and all at once Olivia Benevent blazed.

"Is this your gratitude? Is this the return you make for all we have done for you? Don't you realise what you are throwing away? Do you think we shall still take an interest in you when you have gone down into the gutter? Do you imagine for one moment—"

Her voice had risen to a scream, but he heard Miss Cara's piteous "No, no!" She put a hand on the arm of her chair and tried to rise, but before she had steadied herself to take even one step she gave a gasp and fell forward. If Derek had not been moving already he would not have been in time to catch her, but as it was, he did just manage to break her fall. It all went faster than it can be told. Derek exclaimed, Miss Olivia cried out sharply, and the door was opened. It disclosed Joseph standing just beyond the threshold. As he was afterwards to testify, what he saw was Miss Cara lying on the floor with Derek Burdon standing over her, and what he heard was Miss Olivia saying on a note of mounting hysteria,

"You've killed her—you've killed her—you've killed her!"

CHAPTER 21

It having been ascertained that Miss Cara was not dead but merely in a swoon, she was lifted and laid on a massive Victorian couch. Miss Olivia went down on her knees beside her, and Joseph went for Anna. Presently, when she had recovered consciousness, Derek carried her up to her room. As far as Olivia was concerned he might not have been there at all. She had words for Anna and for Joseph, but not for him. Her glance passed over him as if he were not there.

Since Candida was having the last of her driving lessons, he had a good excuse for getting out of the way for some hours. He told her about the scene.

"Darling, it was completely shattering. I've seen her a bit on the high horse before now, but nothing like this, I give you my word. I can't imagine what has happened to her."

"She doesn't like being crossed," said Candida. "Aunt Cara doesn't do it ever, and you haven't much. And then I come here, and she doesn't like me a lot anyhow, so when I start crossing her it gets her back up."

"Why did you start crossing her?"

"I couldn't help it—not if I didn't want to be a trodden slave! She started on about Stephen being an architect and so I couldn't have lunch with him or anything like that, and I couldn't let her get away with that sort of thing—now could I?"

"Well——"

"I wasn't going to anyhow! That is the way poor little Aunt Cara has been ground down until she hasn't got a will of her own or enough courage for anything except to say yes when Aunt Olivia says yes, and no when Aunt Olivia says no."

Derek looked at her, half laughing, half serious.

"If Stephen is the bone of contention, you paraded it a bit last night, didn't you?"

She coloured brightly.

"I suppose I did."

"Anything in it?"

"Oh, Derek, yes!"

"Have you fixed it up?"

She nodded.

"Last night."

He took his left hand off the wheel and patted her shoulder.

"He's a good chap. Jenny and I are fixing things up too."

He told her about Jenny and the garage, slowing the car down and even stopping on the grass verge

before they came to the straggle of bungalows outside the town. At the end he said,

"I don't know what's going to happen now. She
may shoot me out straight away, or she may have a
stab at rescuing me. I didn't get as far as telling her
that Jenny and I are going to take over the garage,
so she doesn't know the worst."

"But you'll have to tell her now."

"I don't want to upset Aunt Cara."

Candida reflected that this was Jenny's business.
She could have said plenty of things herself, but she
had enough on her hands without Derek's affairs.
She said,

"I'll be late for my lesson!"

He put out his hand to the switch and drew it back
again.

"I'm not the only one who has put a foot wrong,
am I?" he said with a hint of malice.

"What do you mean?"

"Well, you've got rather a lot of make-up on this
morning, haven't you, darling?"

"I don't think so."

"Well, I do. And it doesn't quite prevent me from
seeing that you've got a bruise on your cheek and a
scratch on your chin. Being the soul of tact, you will
notice that I haven't asked, 'How come?'"

She flushed to the roots of her hair, but she did
not speak.

His eyebrows rose.

"She hit you? I could have told you that girlish
confidences would be out of place."

"There weren't any—you needn't be horrid about
it. And it wasn't about Stephen at all. It was because
I said I thought Aunt Cara was ill. And she is. I had
to help her upstairs last night."

167

He whistled softly.

"Darling, I could have told you that too—it's quite fatal. I did it once when I first came, and had my nose more or less bitten to the bone. I suppose it was one of those heavy bracelets that scratched your chin. They are practically fetters, but she always wears them when she wants to be grand. Well, we had better be going. Are you seeing Stephen?"

"I'm lunching with him."

He laughed.

"I'm having a heart to heart with Mr. Adamson at the garage. Burning the boats, you know. He's in a hurry to get everything fixed up. He wants to hand over the house and a lot of the business and take a bit of an easy."

It was odd to meet Stephen with everything changed between them. He brought a picnic lunch, and they drove out to the place where they had quarrelled and ate it there. It was one of those early days of spring when the sun shines sweetly for perhaps half an hour, and then without a warning the sky clouds up and the rain comes plumping down.

They sat in the car and talked. It was past hoping for that at such close quarters Stephen would not see what Derek had seen—the slight change in the contour of the cheek, the faint dulling of the skin, and the line where the bracelet had scratched her chin. At a little distance and to the casual eye there was not so much to be seen, but where there was no distance at all and the eye was that of a lover, concealment could hardly be hoped for. Stephen exclaimed, questioned, cross-examined—and went up in smoke.

"That settles it! You must get away at once!"

"Oh, no, we have an amnesty."

"Nonsense! Did she beg your pardon?"

Candida laughed.

"Of course she didn't! I don't suppose she has ever begged anyone's pardon in her life. We just ignore the whole thing."

"All very well for her, but where do you come in?"

"Darling, come down off the high horse! She lost her temper, and that was all there was to it. You can't have a brawl with a great-aunt—it isn't done. Besides, there is Aunt Cara. She is ill, and I think she is very unhappy, and she does rather cling to me. No, Stephen, listen—you really must! I can't just rush away in a temper and leave the bits lying about all over the place. What I thought I would do was to let a day or two go by, and then say I must begin to look for a job in earnest."

He put his arms round her.

"You don't need to look for a job—you've got one. I rang up my uncle this morning and told him you were taking me on."

"You didn't!"

"Why shouldn't I? I don't have to walk round my relations like a cat on hot bricks. He was thrilled, and suggested I should bring you over for the next weekend. And then, I think, it would be a good plan if you came and stayed with Cousin Louisa for a bit while I am getting on with the jobs round here."

"But she hasn't asked me."

Stephen said in a purposeful voice,

"She will."

CHAPTER 22

However much Miss Cara might have wanted to stay quietly in her bed, cosseted by Anna and visited by Candida and Derek, she was not permitted to do so. She could stay where she was for the morning, and she could have her afternoon nap, but she must get up and come down for tea. Candida, who had come to enquire, stood unnoticed by the half open door and heard Miss Olivia dealing with her reluctance.

"If you do not feel able to get up, I shall be obliged to send for Dr. Stokes."

Miss Cara said in her mousy voice,

"He is away."

"How do you know?" said Miss Olivia sharply.

"Louisa mentioned it."

"Then I shall send for his partner. We haven't met him yet, but I suppose he is competent, and I have no doubt that Louisa has supplied you with his name."

"It is Gardiner. She says he is very clever. But there is no need to send for him—I am quite all right."

"Then you can come down to tea. I will ring for Anna."

As she had not been seen, Candida thought it best to slip away.

Derek did not return until it was time to change. The evening dragged. It was Miss Cara who saved the situation by asking for music.

"Some of those nice old waltzes, and the duets

you and Candida were practising."

Once at the piano, it was easy to stay there. Miss Cara, pleased and relaxed, leaned back in her chair, fingering out the tunes upon her knee or humming a bar or two in a kind of toneless whisper. With yesterday's late evening for an excuse, she was able to make a move before ten o'clock, and Miss Olivia went with her.

Derek and Candida looked at each other.

"You got home all right?"

She nodded.

"Stephen dropped me at the gate. Did you get anything fixed?"

"I'm practically a garage proprietor. I've been going through the books with Mr. Adamson. If he'd any tact he'd have turned me over to Jenny, but not a bit of it! And in between showing me the ropes he told me all about everything that had ever happened from the word go."

Candida laughed.

"Where was Jenny?"

"Sitting behind the counter, and coming backwards and forwards with ledgers and those spiky things you stick bills on, and reminding him about anything he happened to leave out. You know, she really is a marvel. I shall never know half as much about it all as she does."

They put away the music and went up together with so much friendly feeling that it seemed natural enough when he put an arm about her and kissed her good-night at the top of the stairs.

She was just going to get into bed, when Anna came in.

"Perhaps if you will come and say good-night to Miss Cara——"

"Is anything the matter?"

Anna flung out her hands.

"She is sad—she cries all the time!"

"But why? She was all right downstairs. Derek played, and we sang——"

"Yes, yes—it is because of that—it reminds her of the old days! And then she thinks that Mr. Derek will be going away and there will be no one to play and sing any more—and she thinks that you will go away too! And she thinks that when she loves anyone it is always the same thing—they go away and they do not come back! She thinks about Mr. Alan and she weeps for him!"

Candida said, "I'll come."

But when they reached Miss Cara's door it was opened with great suddenness by Miss Olivia in a black velvet wrap. Candida thought she looked like an angry raven. Her foot stamped the floor and she said, whispering fiercely,

"She is not to be disturbed! I do not know what Anna is thinking of to bring you here! Go to your room and stay there!"

She stepped back as she spoke, and the door was shut. There was the sound of a turning key.

Anna said "*Dio mio!*" And then she had Candida by the sleeve, pulling her away. When they were round the turn where the stairs went down she stopped. Her hand shook on Candida's arm. She said in a stumbling voice,

"After forty years—still I am afraid of her——"

CHAPTER 23

The last thing Candida heard before she slept was the rain dashing against the windows. It went through her mind that it must be driving in, and then she slid away into a dream in which the sound was changed to the voice of someone weeping bitterly and comfortless. She didn't know who it was, and she didn't know how long it went on, but she waked suddenly with the wind swirling into the room and the curtains wet and flapping. It was quite difficult to get the windows shut. There was a gale blowing, and the casements strained against it. After she had got them fastened there was quite a lot of water on the floor. There were cloths on a pail in the housemaid's cupboard just across the passage. She fetched them, got the water mopped up, and then found she had to change her nightgown.

When she and the floor were both dry she stood a minute and listened to the wind. It came against the house in great roaring waves and went howling through the gap between the old back wall and the hill. It came to her that Miss Cara might be frightened. She remembered hearing her say that the wind at night was a sound that frightened her, and Miss Olivia had said "Nonsense!" very sharply. She wondered whether Aunt Cara was awake in the dark and afraid. There was only a bathroom between the sisters' rooms, but she didn't think Cara would call for help, or that Olivia would come to her if she did.

She wondered if the door would still be locked.

And then, without any conscious decision on her part, she had her own door open and was feeling her way to the end of the passage. When she turned the corner she had the light behind her, and so came to the head of the stairs. The hall below was a black pit. She skirted it and went softly down the corridor to Miss Cara's room. When she came to the door she stood there listening. Here in the middle of the house the sound of the wind was heavy and dull. No other sound came through it. If she had called aloud, no one would have heard her. She could try the handle and have no fear that anyone would wake. She turned it, and felt the door give under her hand. The room was perfectly dark—no shape of the windows, no faintest glimmer of light, the wind shut out, the curtains closely drawn. She could hear no sound of breathing. She could not even distinguish the position of the bed. There was only darkness and the heavy droning of the wind.

She stood like that and let the minutes go by. If Miss Cara was awake and afraid, surely she would have put on the light. She wouldn't just lie in the dark and do nothing about it. After what seemed quite a long time Candida drew back and closed the door. She did not know, she could not have known, how bitterly she was going to regret this most reasonable action. Go over it as she would, she did not see how she could have done anything but what she did. And yet it hurt her at her heart, and always would.

It may have been the faint jar of the closing door that touched Miss Cara's sleeping thought. It may have been the next wild gust that shook the house, or it may have been an earlier one. It may have been the sense of Candida's presence. No one was ever to know. Sometimes a very small thing slips into a dream and troubles it, or the utmost raging of a storm may leave it untroubled and apart. At some time during that night of wind and rain Cara Benevent rose up out of her bed, put slippers on her feet, and wrapped a dressing-gown about her. There was no means of telling whether she had a light to see by. It was certain that she left her room, but whether she went waking or sleeping no one could know. She went, and she did not return.

Candida went back to her room and slept until the cold grey dawn came up. She was awake when Anna burst into the room. She was dressed, but she carried no tray. The tears ran down her cheeks and her eyes were wild. She fell down on her knees by the bed, her arms flung out and the breath catching in her throat.

"My Miss Cara—oh, my Miss Cara! Why did I leave her—why did I not stay with her!"

Candida pulled herself up in the bed.

"Anna, what is it? Is Aunt Cara ill?"

Anna gave a long wailing cry.

"If she were ill, I would nurse her, I would stay with her—I would not come running to anyone else! She is dead! My Miss Cara is dead!"

Candida felt a coldness creep over her. It slowed her movements, her words. Her tongue stumbled as she said, "Are—you—sure?"

"Would I say it if I were not sure? Would I not be with her? I leave her because there is nothing we can do any more! She lies there at the foot of the stairs and she is dead! The storm frightens her—she walks in her sleep—she falls and strikes her head! The old houses—the stairs are not safe—they are so narrow

175

and so steep! She falls, my poor Miss Cara, and she is dead! And will you tell me how I am to tell Miss Olivia?"

"She doesn't know?"

"How should she know? She is expecting me to bring the tea! How can I go in to her and tell her, 'Your tea is here, and Miss Cara is dead'? The hardest heart in the world could not do it—I cannot do it!"

Candida was out of bed, slipping into her clothes, running a comb through her hair, putting on a grey and white pullover and a grey tweed skirt because they were warm and everything in her seemed to have turned to ice. They went down the stairs to the hall. Miss Cara lay in a twisted heap where the left-hand newel met the floor. One arm was doubled up under her and she was cold and stiff. There could not be any doubt at all that she was dead.

Candida, on her knees by the body, found herself whispering, "Did you move her?"

Anna had sunk down upon the bottom step. She sat bowed forward, her head in her hands. She said on a low sobbing breath,

"No—no—I only touch her cheek, her hand. I know that she is dead——"

"Yes, she is dead. We mustn't move her."

"I know—it is the law."

"We must send for the doctor."

Anna caught her breath.

"He is away—only yesterday Miss Cara said so. It is his partner who will come, Dr. Gardiner—but what can anyone do now?"

Candida said, "Fetch Mr. Derek!"

He came, as shocked as she was herself. They knelt on either side of Miss Cara and spoke low, as if she

176

were asleep and must not be disturbed.

"You must ring up the doctor. You had better go and do it now."

"Has anyone told—*her*?"

"No, not yet."

"Someone must."

"And who is to do it?" said Anna on a sobbing breath. "It should be you who are of the family, Miss Candida."

Candida steadied herself. If she must she must, but it would come better from Anna—perhaps even from this weeping, shaken Anna who had gone back to her crouched position on the bottom step—not from the girl who came between Olivia Benevent and all that she was accustomed to look upon as her own. She said, "Anna, you have been with her forty years," and Anna wailed, "Do not ask me—I cannot!"

There was a silence, and then a sound. It came from the stairs above them, and it was made by the heavy tassel of Miss Olivia's dressing-gown dropping from step to step as she came slowly down. It was a purple tassel on a cord of purple and black, and the gown was purple too.

Olivia Benevent came down at a measured pace, her hand on the balustrade. Not a hair of her smooth waves was out of place. There was no expression in her face or in her eyes, but Candida, looking up, could see where a muscle jerked in the side of the throat. She came right down to the floor of the hall and stood there staring at her sister's body. Then she said,

"Which of you killed her?"

CHAPTER 24

Dr. Gardiner sat looking at Inspector Rock. They made a sharp contrast—Gardiner thin, dark, alert, and the Inspector a big fair man who would be massive by the time he was fifty. At present he was a likeable thirty-six with a pleasant blue eye and a humorous mouth. They were in the study, and somehow they made it seem crowded. Too many pictures on the walls, too much china, too many nicknacks. Gardiner said,

"Well, I can only go on saying what I have said all along. If she fell down the stairs and was killed, then someone arranged the body in the position in which we found it. The back of her head—well, you saw it for yourself—completely crushed. But she was found lying on her face, and everyone swears they didn't turn her over. And why should they? The other way round and there would have been some sense in it. If you find a woman lying on her face, you might turn her over, but if she's lying on her back, why should you? No sense in it at all."

He had pulled a chair sideways to one of the windows and sat there, one knee over the other—Rock conventionally at Miss Olivia's writing-table, but with his chair slewed about to face the doctor. He made one of those non-committal sounds, and Gardiner went on.

"I won't dogmatise about the time she died. Your man will be able to tell you more about that after the

178

post-mortem, but if Burdon and Miss Sayle and the maid are all telling the truth about when they found her, then they couldn't have had any hand in arranging the position. To have been done with any chance of deceiving anyone it must have been done soon. It wasn't much after half past seven when they rang me, and I was here by ten minutes after eight, and she had certainly been dead a good many hours then. As you know, I rang you up at once, and here we are. I take it the rest of your gang will be along at any time. You won't want me any more."

"I thought you might stay until Black gets here. I thought he might like to see you."

Gardiner's shoulder lifted.

"Nothing I can do," he said.

"Well, you were the first on the spot. I was going to ask you what you thought of it all."

The shoulder jerked again.

"Not my business."

"Oh, just for my own private consideration and strictly off the record."

Gardiner had a twisted smile for that.

"Oh, well, plenty of animus knocking about. Miss Olivia very determined about someone having killed her sister. Miss Sayle very quiet and shocked. Burdon a good deal distressed. And the maid Anna as temperamental as they come. She's been with them for forty years, so I suppose she has a right to be upset. The butler is her husband—a whole lot younger, and not so long in their service—a mere fifteen or twenty years. He appears to be normally affected. That's the best I can do."

"No one else in the house?"

"Not living in. The daily woman showed up and had hysterics. She comes out from Retley."

He had got to his feet and was stretching, when the door opened and Olivia Benevent came in. She was now fully dressed in the black buttoned-up garment which was her usual morning wear, only instead of the grey and mauve coatee which she had worn yesterday she had thrown about her shoulders a plain black shawl. The whole effect was that of the deepest mourning. Dr. Gardiner had the ironic thought that whatever happened, women must still be thinking of their clothes.

She came up to her writing-table in a very composed manner and addressed the Superintendent with chill formality.

"May I enquire how long you intend to leave my sister's body lying on the floor in the hall?"

The Inspector rose to his feet.

"I am very sorry, Miss Benevent, but you yourself have suggested that this may be a case of murder. It is my duty to see that nothing is moved until measurements and photographs have been taken. The necessary apparatus is on its way. If you will retire to your own sitting-room, I will let you know as soon as we have finished."

She stood there without moving.

"And when do you propose to arrest the person who killed my sister?"

"Miss Benevent——"

"Do you need me to tell you who it was? There is only one person who had any interest in her death, her great-niece Candida Sayle—a girl whom we invited here in the kindness of our hearts, a girl who had been left penniless, but who now inherits Underhill and everything that belonged to my sister. Perhaps you did not know that."

"Miss Benevent——"

She interrupted him in the same cold manner as before.

"I assure you that that is the case. You may, if you please, refer to our solicitor, Mr. Tampling, for corroboration. So you see, there is quite a strong motive."

"This is a very serious accusation. Have you any evidence to support it?"

"There is the motive."

"Is there any evidence?"

She pressed her lips together for a moment, and then said,

"We were at a reception at the Deanery the night before last. Candida made herself conspicuous with a young man of whom we do not approve. On our return home she went upstairs with my sister, accompanying her to the door of her room. It is possible that my sister reproved her for her conduct—I do not know. But as I came up behind them I was aware that there was something wrong—my sister seemed to be much distressed. When she had gone into her room I spoke to Candida. I told her that her aunt was not strong and must not be upset. She said, 'What does it matter when you are as old as that? She will die soon anyhow.'"

"She used those words? You are certain?"

"I am perfectly certain."

"They were spoken in anger?"

"They were spoken coolly, impudently—and I struck her."

He made no comment. Perhaps that stung her. She tapped with her foot.

"No doubt she will tell you about it herself, but you need not suppose that she will tell you the truth. You can ask Anna. My sister had rung for her, and she was coming along the passage. I do not know how much she heard, but she saw what I was provoked into doing. I am not accustomed to having my word doubted, but in a case of murder I understand that the testimony of a second person is desirable. Anna is such a person."

"Certainly. But I would ask you again what reason you have to suppose that your sister was murdered."

She stood there straight and motionless, the black shawl falling almost to her feet.

"My sister was greatly fatigued—she went up early. Anna left her in her bed. Why should she have got up again. She would not have done so unless she had been persuaded, and who was there to persuade her except that girl? I know that she had already tried to see my sister, because I heard a sound in the passage and I opened my door. Candida was about to enter my sister's room. Anna can confirm this if she chooses. She was there, but Candida seems to have bewitched her—she may not tell the truth. I have not discussed the matter with her. When I said that my sister was not to be disturbed, they went away. Do you think it surprising if I believe that Candida came back later? I do not know how she persuaded my sister to leave her room, but it is clear that she was persuaded, and that when she came to the head of the stairs she was pushed. She was in frail health, and it would not have been difficult. That is all I have to say." She turned round and walked out of the room.

Dr. Gardiner whistled.

"And where do we go from there?" he said.

Since it was just then that the police surgeon, the photographer, and other police reinforcements arrived, Rock had no occasion to reply. There is a routine that waits on violent death. Photographs and fingerprints must be taken before the body can be moved or decent privacy be accorded it. A postmortem lies ahead. It was some time before Rock was at leisure for an interview. He had in a young detective to take shorthand notes and sent for Anna.

The resulting interview was both confused and confusing. Anna had had time to weep herself stupid. Yes, she remembered the ladies coming back from the Deanery party. Her poor Miss Cara had gone upstairs with Miss Candida. Miss Olivia came up afterwards. No, she didn't see them come home, she didn't see them go up. She came when the bell rang from Miss Cara's room.

"When you came along the passage, what did you see?"

"Nothing—nothing. Why should there be anything to see?"

"Miss Olivia says there was. She says that she struck Miss Sayle. She says you must have seen it."

Anna gave a convulsive sob.

"Why does she say that? It is better that we all forget!"

"But she did strike her?"

Anna threw up her hands.

"She has a quick temper. She has struck me before now. If anything is said about Miss Cara, she cannot bear it."

"Something was said about Miss Cara?"

"Yes—yes! She will not bear it—ever!"

"Miss Sayle said something about Miss Cara. What did she say?"

"It was something about her being ill."

"Was there anything said about her dying?"

Anna cried out.

"Oh, no, no—I do not know—I do not know! If one is ill one can always die! And she will not bear it—that is the thing she will not bear! No one must say that Miss Cara is ill, that she is tired, that she is old—no one may say it ever!"

"Did Miss Sayle say that she was old?"

Anna looked at him in a bewildered way.

"How do I know?"

"Did you hear her say it?"

"I do not know what I heard. It was all so quick, and Miss Olivia was angry."

"Did you hear Miss Sayle say that Miss Cara was old and would die soon?"

Anna put her hands over her face.

"No—no—no! I tell you I do not know what they say! When Miss Olivia is like that I shake all over! Yes, after forty years!" Her hands dropped. She looked at him with streaming eyes. "Miss Candida says something about Miss Cara—that she is ill, she is tired—I do not know what! And Miss Olivia strikes her in the face!"

Try as he would, he got no more from her than that.

When he came to the previous evening, she was still very much agitated, but not nearly so confused. Miss Cara would not settle down. She was tired, she wept. Anna went to fetch Miss Candida.

"Why?"

"Miss Cara loves her. I think it will comfort her if Miss Candida comes to say good night. But Miss Olivia is angry. She sends us away, and she locks the door."

"She locked Miss Cara's door?"

Anna nodded vigorously.

"There is a bathroom between their two rooms.

184

She locks Miss Cara's door and she goes through into her own room."

"And after that did you go back to Miss Cara at all?"

"No—no—I do not see her again—until this morning—and she is dead!"

He picked up a pencil and balanced it.

"Yes, you found her, didn't you? Tell me about it."

He had had it all poured out to him when he came, but he wanted to hear it again. A tale repeated word for word could suggest that it had been learned by heart, yet sometimes that was how an uneducated witness would repeat it. On the other hand, a frightened woman telling lies could easily forget just what lies she had told and slip into a revealing difference.

Anna's tale remained as she had sobbed it out over Miss Cara's body.

"I come to wake her. It is seven o'clock. I bring with me the tray with the tea things and I go to her room. I go to her first because I want to know how she has slept. She is not in her bed, and I think perhaps she is in the bathroom. I put down the tray and I go to look, but she is not there. I listen at Miss Olivia's door, but there is no sound. Then I think she has gone to Miss Candida, and I go back along the passage and past the stairs, and when I am there I look down into the hall and I see my Miss Cara lying there, and she is dead!"

The tears were streaming down her face.

"You went down to her?"

She spread out her hands.

"Oh, yes, yes—how can I not go down!"

"Did you touch her—move her?"

"I touch her hand, her cheek, and I know that she

is dead! I see her poor head—oh, *Dio Mio!* But I do not move her—I know I must not do that! I go to fetch Miss Candida!"

Rock said quickly,

"Was Miss Cara's door still locked this morning?"

"No—*no!*" Anna was emphatic.

"Then she must have unlocked it herself."

Anna looked down into her lap.

"Or Miss Olivia," she said.

CHAPTER 25

Candida came into the room and took a chair at the side of the writing-table. She had seen the Inspector when he arrived, but the young man with his writing-pad on his knee was new to her. They were both part of the horrid dream which had taken the place of normal everyday life. She felt giddy and a little sick. Things seemed to be a long way off. She was glad to sit down.

The Inspector had a pleasant voice. He asked her to tell him about what had happened when they came back from the party at the Deanery. She answered with simplicity.

"I went up with Aunt Cara. She was very tired. I had to help her up the stairs. When we got to her room she sat down, and I rang for Anna. She didn't want to talk, so I went out into the passage. I thought I would wait there till I saw Anna coming, but Aunt Olivia came first. She asked what I was doing there, and I said Aunt Cara wasn't feeling well and I was waiting for Anna. She wasn't pleased." She paused, and added in a hesitating voice, "Then Anna came, and I went to my room."

Rock said, "Are you not leaving something out, Miss Sayle?"

She was pale, but a momentary colour sprang up and then ebbed again.

"What do you mean?"

"There is some evidence of a quarrel between you and Miss Benevent outside Miss Cara's door. I would like to have your account of what took place."

Candida bit her lip.

"I didn't want to speak about it. It hadn't anything to do with—with what has happened."

"I'm afraid I must ask you to tell me about it."

She said in a distressed voice,

"It seems so horrid—now. I was feeling worried about Aunt Cara. She was very tired, and I thought that she was ill, and that Aunt Olivia didn't realise it. So I said what I thought, and—she was angry."

"Will you tell me just what you said?"

"I don't know—I think I said that Aunt Cara seemed so tired, and that I thought she was ill. And—oh, yes, I said that people at the Deanery party had noticed it. Aunt Olivia said they ought to mind their own business. She told me to hold my tongue——" Her voice faltered.

Looking at her sharply, Rock could see the faint mark on her cheek and the line of the scratch on her chin. He spoke very directly.

"That is what she said. You haven't told me what she did. I think she did do something. Didn't she?"

There were tears in Candida's eyes, deepening and darkening the blue.

"She couldn't bear to hear about Aunt Cara being

ill—Anna told me afterwards.''

"She struck you?"

"Please—''

"Well, she did, didn't she? She says so herself, so you needn't mind admitting it. Now, Miss Sayle, I want to know just what you said to provoke her into doing that."

Candida's head lifted a little.

"I said Aunt Cara was ill."

"Did you say that she was old?"

"No—no—I wouldn't say that!"

"Or that she would die, or that she would soon be dead?"

"Of course not!" Her voice rang on the words.

"You are quite certain about that?"

She used the very words that Miss Olivia had used.

"I am perfectly certain."

He left it there and took her through the previous evening. Her story fitted in well enough with Anna's. She had gone to her room. Anna had come to fetch her because Miss Cara was unhappy, but Miss Olivia had sent them away and locked the door. When she had done, Rock said,

"Was there any reason why Miss Cara should have been sad? Was something troubling her?"

Candida hesitated. How much had one to tell?

He said quickly, "Was she upset about the quarrel between you and Miss Olivia?"

"There wasn't any quarrel."

"Really, Miss Sayle—when she had struck you in the face only the evening before!"

She had an impulse to be frank.

"I know. But there wasn't any quarrel. Anna told me Aunt Olivia would never mention it again, and she didn't. We met in the morning as if nothing had happened. Derek and I were together when she came down. She kissed us both. And I'm sure Aunt Cara never knew anything about it at all.''

"Then what reason had she for being unhappy?''

It was better to tell him than to have him imagining things. She said,

"There was someone who used to be their secretary before Derek Burdon. They were very fond of him. He went off suddenly about three years ago.''

Rock nodded.

"Thompson,'' he said, "Alan Thompson. There was a lot of talk about it when I first came here.''

"He is supposed to have gone off with a diamond brooch and a good deal of money. Aunt Cara cared for him a lot, and it nearly broke her heart. She was ill, and Aunt Olivia took her away. When the same time of year comes round it all comes back to her. She came into my room the other night and told me about it. That is why she was sad. Anna thought she would like it if I just went in to see her and say goodnight.''

"You were on affectionate terms with her?''

Candida said,

"I was very fond of her.''

CHAPTER 26

Inspector Rock made his report to the Chief Constable. "On the face of it, sir, it doesn't look like an accident. To start with—the position of the body, which is shown very clearly in the photographs. She couldn't possibly have fallen in the position in which she was found, and the position in which she was found doesn't account for the fractured skull. We ought to know a bit more after the post-mortem, but I think it's clear enough that she didn't just fall down those stairs. Miss Olivia Benevent is very bitter against Miss Sayle. She accuses her of murdering Miss Cara in order to succeed to the property."

"Does she succeed?"

"Well, yes, she does. And it is obviously a very sore point. Mr. Derek Burdon informs me that the Miss Benevents' grandfather came in for a lot of money from his mother, and he settled it, like the rest of the property, first on his son and his male heirs after him, and failing these on daughters and their descendants. The son had only the three daughters, Cara, Candida, and Olivia. If Cara had had children, everything would have gone to them—to the sons first, and then to the daughters in the order of their age. If she didn't have children, everything went to the next sister, Candida. Miss Sayle is her grand-daughter and only surviving descendant, so she gets the lot."

"Miss Olivia Benevent doesn't get anything?"

"Some property in Retley and a life-rent of about five hundred a year."

The Chief Constable had known the Miss Benevents in a distant social way for upwards of twenty years. He had never felt any urge to improve the acquaintance, but it enabled him to form a fairly accurate picture of Miss Olivia's reactions to being cut out by a great-niece. He was a lively little man, efficient at his job, but with a taste for lighter relaxation than was afforded by the Miss Benevents' circle. He rode to hounds, competed at point-to-points, and was in demand as a partner at local dances. Since he was under fifty, he considered that he could defer marrying for at least another five years. He raised his eyebrows.

"A bit rough on Olivia. But *murder*! What's the girl like?"

"Two or three and twenty—nice-looking—quiet. Made a good clear statement, as you see. The maid, Anna, says Miss Cara was very fond of her—it's in her statement. She says she fetched her because Miss Cara was crying and she thought it would comfort her to see Miss Sayle. Miss Sayle herself says she was very fond of her aunt."

Major Warrender picked up the typed copy of Miss Olivia Benevent's statement and frowned at it.

"She says she spoke to Miss Sayle outside her sister's door—let me see, that was the night of the Deanery party, wasn't it?—something about not upsetting her and that the girl said, 'What does it matter when you are as old as that? She will die soon anyhow.'" He put the paper down again. "Doesn't seem an awfully likely thing for a girl to say, somehow."

"No, sir."

"And the maid shilly shallies—she doesn't say she said it, doesn't say she didn't say it. Says she can't say what was said. Looks to me as if she didn't like to contradict Miss Olivia. And the girl says she was worried about Miss Cara and told Miss Olivia that she thought she was ill. The only thing they are all agreed about is that Miss Olivia struck Miss Sayle. A fairly odd thing to do unless there was something to account for it."

"The maid says Miss Olivia couldn't bear to have anyone remark on Miss Cara not being well."

Warrender nodded.

"Eccentric old party," he said. "Autocrat. Bullied her sister by all accounts. Up against the niece because she couldn't bully her, I shouldn't wonder."

"She's up against her all right. But Miss Sayle isn't the only one she's up against. You haven't looked at the butler's statement yet—Joseph Rossi. He is married to the maid Anna, by the way. He came in on rather an odd kind of scene yesterday morning. There was some sort of a quarrel between Miss Olivia and the young fellow Derek Burdon whom they call their secretary. She had him into the study immediately after breakfast. Miss Cara was there too. Joseph says he had occasion to come in and see to the fire, but if you ask me, I should say he was eavesdropping. Anyhow he says he heard voices raised. He heard one of the ladies say, 'Is this your gratitude?' and just as he was wondering whether he should go away and come back later, Miss Olivia screamed and Miss Cara cried out, 'No—no!' He opened the door and saw Miss Cara lying on the floor with Derek Burdon standing over her, and Miss Olivia was saying, 'You've killed her—you've killed her—you've killed her!'"

"What had he done?"

"His account of it is that Miss Olivia wanted him and Miss Sayle to make a match of it, but they didn't see it that way. They are very good friends, but Miss Sayle is engaged to somebody else, and so is he. He told Miss Olivia he was engaged, and that he was planning to get married and go into a garage business. She lost her temper, Miss Cara fainted, and Joseph came in. All quite straightforward, and much more likely than that there was any violence on Burdon's part. It links up with Miss Olivia striking Miss Sayle, and with what Joseph says further on. Here—down at the bottom of the page."

"What—this bit?"

"Yes, sir. It's what happened this morning."

Warrender read aloud: "'I came into the hall, and saw Miss Cara lying at the foot of the stairs. Miss Sayle was down on her knees beside her and Mr. Derek was looking over her shoulder. My wife Anna was sitting on the bottom step. She was crying. Miss Olivia came down the stairs in her dressing-gown. When she got to the bottom she stood looking at Miss Cara, and she said, 'Which of you killed her?'"

He broke off and said,

"Rather given to jumping to conclusions, isn't she? And a bit free with the temper. I suppose she didn't push Miss Cara over herself?"

"Well, sir, she had every reason not to, the property all going past her to Miss Sayle."

Major Warrender nodded.

"I suppose so. All the same, dishing out accusations of other people always seems a bit fishy to me."

He went on reading Joseph's statement.

CHAPTER 27

Miss Silver was enjoying the peaceful hour which follows afternoon tea. Louisa had been recalling a number of those family events which never seem to lose their interest for elderly ladies. Together they had recalled how Fanny's wilfulness had precipitated her into that disastrous marriage, and moralised over the painful consequences of Roger's determination to go to China. Louisa had been able to supply some hitherto unknown details in the matter of Millicent's divorce, and to assure her cousin that there was no truth whatever in the scandalous rumour that poor Henry had committed suicide. Miss Silver knitted and listened. Everything that people did or said was of interest, and Louisa was able to throw quite a fresh light upon both Henry and Millicent. Miss Arnold had just observed that, "What the housemaid said was, of course, quite conclusive," when the telephone bell rang. Louisa, lifting the receiver, heard Stephen Eversley's voice.

"Oh, is that you? Could I speak to Miss Silver?"

"Of course, my dear boy. I hope there is nothing wrong?"

"I'm afraid there is. Look here, Cousin Louisa, she does take things on professionally, doesn't she?"

"Who—Maud? Oh, yes, she does—but I really don't know——"

Miss Silver put down her knitting and came across the room. As she approached the instrument she could distinguish the sound of a man's voice, and that he seemed to be in something of a hurry.

"Oh, no!" said Louisa Arnold in a shocked voice. "Oh, yes, of course—but I don't suppose ... Well, perhaps you had better speak to her yourself."

Rightly judging this to be her cue, Miss Silver took possession of the receiver. As she put it to her ear she heard Stephen Eversley say,

"I would like to come and see her at once if I can."

With a faint preliminary cough she said,

"Miss Silver speaking. Am I right in thinking that you wish to see me?"

"Yes—yes, please."

"Then, you had better come round here."

"Yes, I'll come at once."

She hung up. Louisa was agog.

"Maud—he says Cara Benevent is dead! Some sort of accident! Do you know, I thought he sounded quite upset! And if he is, that must mean that he is really interested in Candida Sayle!"

When Stephen arrived it was clear that no secret was to be made of this interest. He said they were engaged, and went on, still with that hurry in his voice,

"Miss Silver—"

Miss Arnold broke in on a twittering note.

"My dear boy—what has happened? Poor Cara!"

He would rather have spoken to Miss Silver alone, but this was plainly impossible. Cousin Louisa was overflowing with interest, commiseration, and kindness, and he must endure them with as good a grace as he could muster. He said,

"I've been out all day, going into those plans with Lord Retborough. When I got in, there was a message to ring up Underhill. Burdon answered the call. He

195

told me Miss Cara was dead—some sort of an accident. And he fetched Candida. She said"—he began to pick his words with care—"she said Miss Olivia was very much upset."

"Oh, she must be!" said Louisa Arnold. "Oh, poor Olivia! It must be dreadful for her! She did bully Cara, but of course she was devoted to her too! That was why she was in such a state when people were saying that Cara meant to marry Alan Thompson! Of course there couldn't have been any truth in it, but it would upset her dreadfully all the same!"

Stephen went on with what he had been going to say.

"Well, she is so much upset now that she says she can't stay in the house."

"My dear!"

"Not even for a single night."

"Oh, my dear Stephen!"

He nodded.

"Actually, she has gone already."

"Gone! Where?"

Miss Silver had not spoken. She stood there quietly and listened. Stephen threw up a hand.

"It seems that she owns a house in Retley. It's been let, but the tenants went out a week ago. She has taken Joseph and gone there. Anna is to follow later."

"My *dear Stephen!*"

He spoke directly to Miss Silver.

"You see how it leaves Candida. She can't stay there alone with Burdon. I have come to ask if you will go to her."

Miss Arnold was prompt in hospitality.

"But she must come here! The room has just been spring-cleaned, and Eliza shall put bottles in the bed."

He really did feel grateful, and preoccupied as he was, he managed to show it.

"How frightfully good of you! But she doesn't feel that she ought to come away. I did say that when you knew we were engaged—you've been so kind about everything—but she thinks she ought to be there. You see, she comes in for everything now, and she feels responsible—she says it would look like running away. But she ought to have someone with her—like Miss Silver. Anna may have to go tomorrow, and you know how people talk. If Miss Silver only would, nobody could say a word."

Miss Silver had picked up her knitting. She said,

"Certainly, Mr. Eversley. I will just go and pack my things."

While he was driving her out to Underhill Stephen was a good deal more explicit than he had thought it prudent to be in front of his Cousin Louisa. What she heard from other sources was beyond his control, but Miss Olivia's monstrous accusation would not reach her through him. With Miss Silver there could be no concealments.

"She has gone mad of course. I suppose it's the shock or something, but she actually accuses Candida of Miss Cara's death. You see, the police don't think it's an accident, and Miss Olivia is pretending to believe that Candida is in some way responsible. That is why she won't stay in the house. And honestly, I'm thankful to feel that she isn't there. If she is insane enough to think that Candida would harm Miss Cara, she is quite mad enough to be dangerous herself."

Miss Silver said in a very composed voice,

"Will you tell me just what happened, Mr. Eversley?"

197

"That's just it—I don't know—nobody seems to. The maid, Anna, found Miss Cara lying at the foot of the stairs at seven o'clock this morning. The back of her head was injured, and she had been dead for some time. But she was lying on her face. Her own doctor and the police surgeon both say that she couldn't have moved after an injury like that, and that it couldn't have been caused by the fall. Miss Olivia is saying that Candida pushed her over the stairs, but quite apart from its being an insanely wicked thing to say, it makes nonsense in the face of the medical evidence. That is really all I know. I gather there had been rows, one with Candida and one with Derek Burdon, but she didn't want to talk about it on the telephone."

Miss Silver inclined her head in approval.

"It is always better to say too little than too much."

CHAPTER 28

Miss Silver had seen Candida Sayle across the drawing-room at the Deanery, her eyes bright, her colour high and pure. She had met her when the Miss Benevents brought her up to be introduced to Louisa Arnold, and she had admired the tone of her voice and her warm response to what Louisa had to say about her grandmother, the earlier Candida after whom she had been named. She took an interest in girls, and she had thought Candida Sayle a very charming one. She saw her now in the black dress which she had worn for Barbara, the bright colour all gone, the eyes with a look of strain that was painful to see. But the breeding held. Her thanks to Miss Silver for coming, her welcome, were all that the most exacting standard could demand.

The comfortable bedroom that had been prepared was next to her own. The bed, Miss Silver was glad to observe, was quite modern, and it was being warmed by two hot water-bottles. A small electric fire had been lighted. Her experience of country houses had not encouraged any great hope of such attentions, and while perfectly ready to do without them in the cause of duty, it was pleasant to find that they had been provided.

The evening passed as such evenings do. There was a meal prepared by Anna. There was conversation, supplied mainly by Miss Silver herself, and by Derek Burdon. Stephen had returned to Retley, Miss Silver applauding the good taste which dictated this course of action. Underhill might now have passed to Candida Sayle, but it was not for him or for her to obtrude that fact. Since Stephen had not been received there as a visitor by the Miss Benevents, both tact and breeding suggested that he should not immediately avail himself of so tragic a change in their circumstances.

Later Miss Silver had an opportunity of talking to Anna Rossi and to Derek Burdon. Both appeared to be more than willing. To Anna, her face swollen and her eyes red with weeping, it was an obvious relief to pour out everything she knew. There was no Miss Olivia there to check her, no Joseph to fix her with the look she so much resented or to say as he so often did, "Anna, you talk too much." After all, one had been given a tongue to use, and when terrible things happened, what was there to do except to let the tears spill out of your eyes and the words out of your mouth? If you did not weep, if you did not speak, the very heart dried up in you and you might as well be dead. The tears gushed afresh as she imparted these views to the little visiting lady who was so sympathetic, and who had come to take care of Miss Candida.

Derek also obliged with every appearance of frankness. Talking had never presented any difficulties to him, and like so many other people he found Miss Maud Silver quite extraordinarily easy to talk to. She listened, she made sympathetic reply, she maintained an interested and encouraging manner.

The opportunity for a conversation with Candida Sayle came when they went upstairs together at the end of the evening. To Candida it seemed as if the hours of that day had become lengthened out like shadows seen at sunset, until the time before she knew that Miss Cara was dead appeared to be indefinitely removed from this moment when she went with Miss Silver into her room and hoped that she had everything she wanted. Any hostess to any guest— But Miss Silver's response was not quite that of any guest to any hostess. She laid a hand on Candida's arm and said in her kindest voice,

"Oh, yes, indeed. But I am just wondering whether you are too tired to give me the opportunity of talking to you for a little."

Colour came into Candida's face. She had a quick realisation that the pressure of her own thoughts was no longer to be endured. With Stephen gone, there was no one to whom she could unburden herself— unless it was to this stranger. She said,

"No, no, of course not. It was so very good of you

to come. I wouldn't have asked you, but Stephen just did it. He said I couldn't stay here alone—it would make talk. You see, none of us knew what Aunt Olivia was going to do until she had done it. At least Joseph and Anna must have known, but she kept Anna in her room packing up her things, and she took Joseph with her. It wasn't until after five o'clock that we knew she had gone. Joseph took the cases down. Then he brought the car round to the side door and picked her up. Anna had been forbidden to say anything until they had gone. I didn't know what I ought to do. If Aunt Olivia felt she couldn't stay on in the same house as me, then I was the one who ought to have gone. I tried to get on to Stephen, but he wasn't back. Derek said he wouldn't stay if I went. You see, Aunt Olivia was saying all sorts of things about both of us, and there are a lot of valuable things in the house. He said we ought to ring up the police and ask them what to do about it, so we did, and the Inspector said I ought to stay. And then I got on to Stephen, and he said he would ask you to come."

Miss Silver had seated herself. Candida took the chair on the other side of the fire and leaned forward.

"Stephen says you know a good deal already—about my aunts, and Alan Thompson, and everything. It all seems to go a long way back."

Miss Silver had taken up her knitting. A grey stocking depended from the needles. It was the last of the set, and it was nearly finished. She said,

"It is always difficult to know where things begin. There are causes which lie a very long way back. There are jealousies, resentments, hatreds, which have their roots in the remote past."

Something in Candida answered this. It was like the string of a musical instrument which trembles in response to a distant note. She said, "Yes," and found what so many had found, that it was easier to talk to Miss Silver than it was to hold things back. She told her about Barbara, about coming here to stay, about meeting Stephen again—"You know, he really did save my life once long ago." And so on, through the time of her visit down to the last few days.

Miss Silver sat there and knitted. Sometimes she asked a question, but for the most part she was silent. Inspector Frank Abbott of Scotland Yard, a devoted admirer, has said of her that "she knows people." He has also observed that as far as she is concerned the human race is glass-fronted—"She sees right through them." But then it is, of course, notorious that he sometimes indulges himself in an extravagant way of speaking. Certainly it was not only Candida's words which received attention, but every change in her expression, every inflection of her voice, every variation in the manner in which certain names were pronounced were subjected to the same clear scrutiny.

The scene outside Miss Cara's door after the return from the Deanery party was gone over with the closest interest. Candida spoke quite steadily.

"Anna says Aunt Olivia won't ever let anyone talk about Aunt Cara being ill, but I didn't know that. I really did think she was ill, and I was worried, and I said so. That was when she—struck me."

Miss Silver had not been unaware of the slight remaining traces of that blow. She said, "Dear me!"

Candida went on.

"She hates me, you know, but even so, I think she must be mad. She has told Inspector Rock that she struck me because I said Aunt Cara was old and would die soon anyhow. She must be mad to say a thing like that, even if she does hate me."

"Why should she hate you, my dear?"

"Because of Underhill and the money. Aunt Cara told me about a dreadful thing she said when her sister Candida died—she was my grandmother, and I was called after her. She died about the same time as their father, and when the lawyer told Aunt Olivia that my grandmother's children would have everything after Aunt Cara she said that Candida was dead and she hoped her children would die too, and then *she* would come into her own."

"That was a dreadful thing to say."

"Aunt Cara cried about it. You know, they looked so much alike, but they weren't really. Aunt Cara was just a frightened little thing—she had been bullied all her life. But she was kind, and deep down inside her she wanted someone to be fond of. She was dreadfully unhappy about Alan Thompson. You know about him, don't you?"

Miss Silver might have said a good deal upon this point, but she contented herself with a simple, "Yes."

Candida went on telling her things—Nellie waking up with a cold hand touching her face and something that went crying through the room.

"And she wouldn't stay after that. She went in with Anna for the night, and she was off in the morning. But it was only poor Aunt Cara walking in her sleep—I'm sure about that. I asked Anna, but she wouldn't really say. Sometimes she talks a lot—sometimes she won't talk at all. When she won't talk, it's because there is something she is afraid about. She really is afraid of Aunt Olivia, you know, even after being with her all these years. The last thing she wanted was for Nellie to go, but she was afraid of telling her that the crying thing was just Aunt Cara wandering about in an unhappy dream."

Miss Silver's needles moved rhythmically. She wore the dark blue crêpe-de-chine and her bog-oak brooch in the form of a rose with an Irish pearl at its heart. Her small, neat features expressed a high degree of interest. Candida no longer found it possible to think of her as a stranger. She imparted a sense of kindness, security and common sense not often to be found outside the family circle. The frankness of speech which is natural there seemed natural now. The strain which the day had brought was relaxed. It was quite easy to tell her things. She went on.

"You know, I think the reason Anna was afraid was that she knew Nellie had locked her door, so if Aunt Cara had come in, it must have been by some other way. The walls in the old part of the house are very thick. I think there may be passages, and that Aunt Olivia would be very angry if anyone got to know about them. I know there is one in my room."

If Miss Silver was startled she did not allow it to appear. She went on knitting as she enquired,

"And how do you know that?"

"Someone came through my room in the middle of the night. I saw a crack of light where the bookcase is. There's a door there, but I haven't been able to find out how to open it. When I saw the light I pretended to be asleep—it was rather startling, you know—and someone came through the room and out by the door."

"Was it Miss Cara?"

"I don't know. Sometimes I think it was, and sometimes I think it couldn't have been—because of my being so frightened. I was, you know."

Miss Silver coughed.

"It was quite a startling occurrence."

Candida flushed.

"It was horrid," she said. "But if it had been Aunt Cara, I don't think I should have minded like I did. And whoever it was wasn't sleep-walking. It had a torch."

Miss Silver looked a mild enquiry.

"You do not say she."

Candida's colour brightened.

"I thought about its being Joseph, and that made me so angry that I went after it. But I was too late—whoever it was had gone."

Miss Silver said in a thoughtful voice,

"Why should anyone who was not sleep-walking have taken the risk of passing through your room?"

"I wondered if they knew just where the passage would come out. I thought if it was someone who was exploring——"

Miss Silver inclined her head.

"Yes, it might have been that way."

There was a little pause before Candida spoke again.

"I can't help wondering about Aunt Cara—whether she was walking in her sleep when she fell. She might have been. You know, I don't believe she would have been wandering about in the dark by herself if she had known what she was doing. The storm was so loud, and I think she would have been frightened. I did think she might be frightened. That is why I went along to her room."

"When was that?"

"I didn't look at the time. The wind was coming in those great noisy gusts. I thought Aunt Cara would be frightened, and I went along to her room."

"Did you go in?"

"Not really. I didn't want to wake her. I just stood there and listened. Of course the wind was too loud for me to hear anything, but I had put on the light at the end of the passage, and I thought if she was awake she would see me standing there. When I was sure that she must be asleep I shut the door and came away."

Miss Silver said, "Sure?" on an enquiring note. Her eyes were on Candida's face. She saw a look of trouble cross it. It led her to amplify the question.

"You were sure then that Miss Cara was asleep. Are you so sure about it now? Can you even be sure that she was in her room when you stood there looking in?"

The hand that was lying in Candida's lap closed hard upon itself. She was back in the half-lit passage with the cold of the door-sill under her bare feet, and she was looking into a dark room with the drone of the wind in her ears. The room was perfectly dark, the curtains were closely drawn. She couldn't see the bed, or the big mahogany wardrobe, or the washstand with its marble top. She couldn't see anything at all. She said in a stumbling voice,

"No—I'm not—sure——"

There was a silence. In the end Candida went on.

"Miss Silver, the Inspector says she wasn't killed by falling down those stairs." A shudder went over her. "You see, she was lying on her face, but it was the back of her head——" She broke off, struggling for composure. "If she didn't fall on the stairs, where did she fall—and how? He says someone must have moved her." Her voice dropped to a whisper. "There was dust on her slippers, and a cobweb on the tassel of her dressing-gown—I saw Anna brushing it off."

Miss Silver spoke quickly.

"She ought not to have done that."

"I don't think she was thinking about what she did. She was crying. I think it was just that she wanted to do something for Aunt Cara. You know, when anything has happened like that, you *don't* think. I didn't myself—not till afterwards. Then, when the Inspector said she must have been moved, I remembered the cobweb and the dust—and I wondered—about the passages—whether she went into them and fell—and got hurt. You see, there are stories. Aunt Olivia told me about its being unlucky to touch the Benevent Treasure. There was James Benevent in the eighteenth century—he was going to sell some of it. They said he was thrown from his horse at his own front door. His head was dreadfully injured and he died. A long time afterwards his grandson, Guy Benevent, was going to take some of the treasure. He was found quite near the house with his head broken. They said it was footpads. I don't know why Aunt Olivia told me all this, but she did. And when Derek and I were going through some of the old papers—we were supposed to be doing a family history—there was a rhyme:

> "'Touch not nor try,
> Sell not nor buy,
> Give not nor take,
> For dear life's sake.'

207

"So when I saw Aunt Cara, and the dust and the cobweb, I wondered whether she had been looking—for the treasure."

Miss Silver looked very grave indeed. She even stopped knitting for a moment.

"Did you tell the Inspector?"

"No, I didn't. He didn't ask me anything like that."

CHAPTER 29

Miss Silver did not feel called upon to make any comment. At the moment her connection with the case might be described as tenuous. Her professional assistance had been solicited by Stephen Eversley, but more in the capacity of a chaperone for Candida Sayle than as a private enquiry agent. He was, however, understandably disturbed by Miss Olivia's unbalanced accusation and anxious to provide Candida with what protection he could. In the circumstances, he could not himself remain at Underhill. So she was there as it were on guard, her position delicate, the scope of her activities quite undefined. So much for Stephen Eversley and Candida Sayle. There was also the fact that Mr. Puncheon had enlisted her services in connection with the disappearance of his stepson Alan Thompson. The link between the two cases was the link between Miss Cara and a young man whom she had loaded with benefits and had even planned to marry. His disappearance had broken her heart. Was it for him that she sought when she walked in the old house by night? Did she walk waking, or sleeping—by known or by unknown ways? And where in this well-kept house had she picked up dust on her slippers and a cobweb on the tassel of her dressing-gown? Miss Silver had been shown over the house. She had traversed a bewildering maze of passages, had looked into rooms used and unused. Everywhere there was neatness and order—polished floors and shining furniture—a smell of beeswax and turpentine before which any spider would have retired—not a speck of dust. What Anna had brushed away could not have come from any of these ordered places.

This old house had its secrets—and kept them. What was it that Cara Benevent went looking for, and by what hidden ways? And what was it that she had found? Death certainly. But death by accident—or by some sudden blow in the dark? And whose hands had lifted and carried her to where she was found at the foot of the stairs?

Miss Silver knitted steadily. As she turned the heel of Johnny Burkett's stocking she went over the people who had been in the house that night.

Joseph Rossi and Anna, his wife. Old trusted servants—what motive could either of them have? A legacy? Perhaps—murder has been done for such a thing before now. Forty years service in the one case, nearly twenty in the other. Strange things move beneath the surface of the years—an old resentment, a grudge growing slowly out of sight—envy, malice and all uncharitableness? People do not always love one another because they have lived for a long time in the same house. Familiarity may breed hatred.

Derek Burdon. A pleasant, likeable young man—but pleasant, likeable young men have faced a capital charge before now. She recalled what she knew about him. He had succeeded Alan Thompson as the Miss Benevents' protegé—an easy life—almost nominal duties—money in his pocket. And then a sudden break. He had been quite frank about it himself. The Miss Benevents wanted him to marry Candida, and it didn't suit either of them. She was engaged to Stephen Eversley, and he was engaged to Jenny Rainsford. He had become quite eager about his plans—"The old chap she works for wants to retire. He has got a small garage business. It's been going downhill a bit, but it can be worked up again. I do know something about cars, and of course Jenny has the whole thing at her fingers' ends. There's a house too, and we were planning to take it over. Well, yesterday morning it all came out, and there was a most frightful row. Not Miss Cara—she just sat there and hated every minute of it. But Miss Olivia went right off the deep end. She does sometimes, you know, and all you can do is to get under cover and wait for her to come round again. Only this time Miss Cara fainted. Joseph came in the middle of Miss Olivia telling me I had killed her, and of course he had to go and tell the police what she'd said, so they've been asking me a whole lot of questions about whether they were kicking me out, how much I stood to lose if they were, and whether I was down for anything in Miss Cara's will."

Miss Silver had looked at him in a very direct manner. "And are you?" she said. Derek appeared shocked. "I haven't the slightest idea. I've never thought about it." That might have been true, or it might not. There were people who did not think about those things. On the other hand, there were people who thought about them a great deal, and a young man who was getting married and taking over a run-down business would certainly find a legacy very useful.

She went on to the next name on her list—Olivia Benevent. The sister who had dominated Miss Cara since they were children. Louisa Arnold had talked about her a good deal. What Louisa said about people was not as a rule unkind, but she had had very little that was kind to say about Miss Olivia. She emerged as a ruthless and vindictive woman imposing her will upon the delicate elder sister, upon her father when he fell into ill health—in fact upon anyone who would allow himself to be dominated. "You know," Louisa had said, "I think that was partly why Cara was so foolish about Alan Thompson. He was someone she could talk to, if you know what I mean. He couldn't take her part openly—he would have been afraid to do that— but from something she said to me once I think he used to back her up in private, and that it even got as far as her complaining to him about Olivia. It would be such a relief, you know. Why, sometimes she came very near doing it to me, so it shows she had got it on her mind."

Miss Silver went back to these words and thought about them gravely. Had there come a moment when the delicate down-trodden sister had revolted and provoked some frightful loss of control? There were some grounds for supposing that a scene of this nature might have taken place. Miss Cara's heart had been set upon Alan Thompson, and she had lost him. Just how he had been induced or forced to disappear was a mystery that had never been cleared up. That he should have risked a paltry

211

theft when a few more days would have put him in a position to control Miss Cara's entire fortune was difficult to believe. He might at the eleventh hour have recoiled from the prospect of an unnatural marriage. But had he? Whatever the facts, to Miss Cara his disappearance was sheer tragedy. Now, after three years, she was threatened with a second break in the family circle. If she did not love Derek Burdon as she had loved Alan Thompson he was still very dear to her, and Olivia was driving him out. She had been so disturbed as to fall into a swoon. The last account of her state of mind that evening came from Anna, who spoke of her as very sad and crying all the time. She came to fetch Candida Sayle because she thought she might comfort her poor Miss Cara, but when they reached her door it was opened by Olivia Benevent. Anna's description of the scene sprang vividly to Miss Silver's mind. Miss Olivia in her black wrap tapping the floor with her foot and whispering fiercely, "She is not to be disturbed! Go back to your room and stay there!" And then the door shut and locked in Candida's face.

What had happened after that? No one knew except the woman who had shut and locked that door. Alan Thompson gone, Derek Burdon going, and Candida Sayle locked out. Had there been a scene between the sisters? There might have been, and it might have ended suddenly, terribly, with some act of violence. It was true that Olivia Benevent had everything to lose by her sister's death, but the woman who had struck her young niece in the face, and had been so far carried beyond normal control as to accuse her of murder, might have been betrayed into some dreadful passionate act. The proverb

212

which declares anger to be a brief madness presented itself. There were still darker possibilities. She regarded them steadily.

The last name to be considered was that of Candida Sayle. She gave it the same scrupulously fair attention that she had given to the others.

CHAPTER 30

When she had said good-night to Candida, Miss Silver went on sitting by the fire for some time. As she passed in review all the circumstances of the case, one point continually presented itself. However often she attempted to relegate it to a position of very little importance, she found that it persistently forced itself upon her attention. She would be considering the question of who among the household at Underhill could have lifted and carried Miss Cara to the place where she was found, when, pushing in upon her thought, would come this apparently irrelevant point. It cost her quite an effort to dismiss it and continue her train of thought. Joseph or Anna could certainly have done the lifting. Anna was a big woman, and Joseph though not tall was wiry. Miss Cara would have been a light burden for either of them. Derek, of course, could have done it with ease. Candida could have done it. But what about Olivia Benevent? Could she, under whatever stress of fear, have dragged or carried her sister any distance? Miss Silver remembered shaking hands with her at the Deanery party. The feeling of the hand that had taken

213

hers came back clearly. There had been no particular pressure, just the touch of a small bony hand, hard and firm. There was the suggestion of a bird's claw, dry and cold to the touch. The two sisters looked so much alike, but the touch of Miss Cara's hand had been soft and slack, just meeting her own and falling away. It occurred to her that if Olivia Benevent chose to do a thing she would make it her business to see that it was done, whereas Miss Cara would accept the first discouragement.

She began to consider why Olivia should have left Underhill, and immediately the point which she had been at pains to dismiss again obtruded itself. It was not only the question of why she had left Underhill, but of why she had taken Joseph with her. She was going to a furnished house which was her own property. It had just been vacated, and was presumably in perfect order. What she would require was someone to cook for her, someone to wait upon her. Exactly how the service at Underhill had been divided she was not perfectly clear, but Anna, even in her present distracted state, was an extremely good cook. The meal of which they had that evening partaken was sufficient proof of this, and in the matter of personal attendance it would have seemed more likely, and certainly more suitable, that she should be preferred to Joseph. Yet it was Joseph who had been taken, and Anna who had been left.

It was some time before she rose and began her preparations for bed. They culminated, as always, in the substitution of the strong net which it was her practice to wear at night for the almost invisible one which controlled the neatly curled fringe by day. This accomplished, the blue dressing-gown trimmed with hand-made crochet was hung over the back of

214

a convenient chair, the black felt slippers with their blue tufts placed side-by-side below, the bedside lamp switched on, the overhead light extinguished. It was her habit to read a passage of Scripture before she slept. She did so now. In the psalm of her selection there occurred a verse which she could not help considering extremely apposite—chiming in with her thoughts and indicating the firmness of her trust in what she called Providence. It ran:

"When the wicked, even my enemies and my foes, came upon me to eat up my flesh, they stumbled and fell."

She read on, she closed the book, and laid it down. She switched off the bedside light and passed into the calm and healthful slumber to which she was accustomed.

In three other rooms the occupants slept or waked. Derek Burdon was one of those who slept. There was a weight upon his heart, upon his spirits. He had found himself unable to throw it off. The long, accustomed ease of his life at Underhill had been shattered. It had just gone on from one day to another without thought and without care. There was no need to exert himself, to plan, to struggle, to wonder what was going to happen next. Instead, there was money in his pocket and the ground agreeably firm beneath his feet. To retain all this he had only to be himself—to smile and make himself agreeable, to play the piano, to drive the car, to be the adopted nephew of two kind old dears. And now catastrophe—the sudden slash of violence cutting across the picture—Miss Cara horribly dead, Miss Olivia horribly changed. He had not seen that side of her before, and it shook him. Old ladies might be crotchety and particular—it was part of the game to soothe·

them down and keep them happy. But the naked fury with which Olivia Benevent had turned upon him was something quite beyond him to understand. It was as if she had stripped herself to the very bones. It was a thing quite out of nature. In its way it shocked him even more than the fact that Miss Cara was dead. There was a weight upon him, and it went down into his sleep and stayed there.

Anna had knelt and prayed. The tears ran down—words broke from her. Sometimes she leaned her forehead on the hands which clasped one another, straining. Sometimes she got up from her knees and paced the room, her lips moving, her breast heaving with sobs. She wore a very full cotton nightgown made from an ancestral pattern. There must have been seven or eight yards of stuff in it. It fell about her in classic folds, darkening the olive tint of her skin, whilst over all there floated the nimbus of her wild white hair. There came a time when she went to her bed and fell upon it, weeping into the pillow.

In the end she slept, and stood at the edge of a dream looking in upon it. Waking or sleeping, what she saw was the thing which she most feared to see. If she had been awake she could have shut her eyes and turned her head. She could have bidden her feet to carry her away from it. Her very terror would have speeded them. She would have run as you run when death is at your heels. But she was asleep. Her feet would not run, and her eyes would not close. And no good if they did, because the picture was there in her mind. You cannot close your eyes to your own thoughts, nor, however swiftly you run, can you out-distance them. She stood and looked upon her dream with open eyes and with a shrinking heart.

Candida had laid down her burden. The interminable hours of the day were done. Nobody and nothing could make her live them over again. They were gone, and they would not come back. She had talked the weight of them from her heart. It was just as if she had been straining every nerve to climb a hill and now she had come to the place where the path led down again. All she had to do was to set her feet upon it and let it take her where it would. She was almost too tired to think.

She must undress. Why? There was a glass of hot milk by the bedside. Anna—how kind—— She had hardly eaten anything all day. She took the glass of milk in her hand and sat down by the fire. Drinking it was the last thing she was to remember.

CHAPTER 31

The morning came, and with it Anna in a flowered wrapper, her lids still swollen from yesterday's weeping. She had slept uneasily and waked to a new and burdened day. She moved with weighted limbs, the tray she carried was heavy in her hand. She set it down, answered gravely when Miss Silver spoke to her, and went on her way. It took her to the room next door, where Candida should be sleeping, but when she knocked there was no answer. She had in one hand the cup of tea which she had taken from Miss Silver's tray. With the other she knocked again, after which she turned the handle and went in.

With her first step across the threshold the cup tilted and fell. She stood there, holding the saucer in a rigid grip and staring, not at the broken cup and the pool of tea which spread from it, but at the empty ordered room. The bed was made, and it had not been slept in. As it was now, so it had been when her shaking hands had left it at some time during the dreadful hours of yesterday morning. She remembered that the counterpane had fallen a little crooked at the head, and that she had looked back at it from the doorway and thought, "What does it matter? Miss Cara is dead." She looked at it now, and saw it was as it had been then. Her eyes moved slowly from the bed to the window, to the bookcase, the hearth, the dressing-table. There was something there—a piece of paper with a line of writing on it. She crossed the room swiftly and set the saucer down. The hand that had held it lifted the paper. The writing was smudged and blotted—a mere scrawl. It ran:

"Good-bye. I can't go on."

Anna continued to look at it until the words began to run into one another. Then she went back by the way that she had come.

This time she did not knock at Miss Silver's door. She wrenched at the handle and pushed it like a blind woman feeling her way. Miss Silver saw her come. She set down her cup upon the tray and took the paper which was thrust at her.

Anna had begun to shake and to weep again.

"She is gone! First the one, and then the other! Miss Cara first, and then Miss Candida! But why— oh, *Dio mio*, why!"

Miss Silver looked gravely at the paper with its shaky scrawl.

"Is this Miss Sayle's writing?"

Anna threw up her hands.

"How do I know?"

"But you must have seen it. Pray sit down and compose yourself. You must have seen Miss Sayle's writing."

"How should I?" sobbed Anna. "Miss Olivia writes to her—she writes back—it is one letter among all the letters that come! I do not look at them, I do not notice them, I do not know which is from Miss Candida! I only know that she was here, and that she is gone, and that God knows what has become of her, or what is to become of us all!"

Miss Silver was getting out of bed, reaching for the blue dressing-gown, putting on the black felt slippers. She came into Candida's room with Anna following her, sobbing and talking all the time.

"The bed! You see no one has slept there! It is the way I leave it! Last night Miss Candida says to me she will turn down your bed and hers and she will put in the hot water-bottles. 'You have enough to do without that,' she says. And it is true what she says—there is enough for the one pair of hands! She is so good, Miss Candida—so kind! And Mr. Derek too! He comes out last night, and he says, 'Let me help you with the washing-up.' I say, 'No, no—Miss Olivia would not like it,' and he says, 'Darling, she won't know.' It is the way they have, these young people, to call everyone darling. It means nothing, but he says it as if he means it, and he stays until everything is finished. He and Miss Candida, they are kind. Why should these things happen?"

Miss Silver let the words go by her.

She went to the bed and turned back the eiderdown. There had been a hot water-bottle in her own bed last night. There was one in this bed now. Does a girl who is going to run away put a hot water-bottle in her bed? She went to and fro in the room. In the end she opened the wardrobe door and spoke.

"Anna, come here. That is the dress she wore last night, is it not?"

The black dress trailed from its hanger, one shoulder slipping so that it hung askew. Anna caught her breath.

"Yes—yes—that is what she wore—my poor Miss Candida!"

"Then what is missing?"

"The grey coat and skirt—the grey coat—that is what she would wear if she went out. And the little grey hat—it would be in the drawer . . . No, she has taken it! And the handbag—she has taken that too! And the outdoor shoes—see, here are the ones she wore last night—she would not go out in these! *Dio mio!* Where has she gone, and why?"

Miss Silver said,

"If she has gone, then one of the doors would be unlocked, or a window. Wake Mr. Derek and get him to come down with you and try them all whilst I dress."

But when Anna was gone Miss Silver did not proceed to her own room immediately. She closed the door and then went over to the bookcase and examined it. Strictly speaking, it was not a bookcase at all but a set of shelves fitted into the recess between the fireplace and the wall which took the windows. The shelves ran from the floor to within a couple of feet of the ceiling. A strip of carved wood framed them on either side, and a simulated cornice decorated the top.

Miss Silver stood looking at the shelves. Taking out some of the books, she discovered that there was a wooden backing. Candida Sayle had spoken of waking in the night and seeing first a streak of light, and then the opening of a door in this recess. Shelves with a wooden backing could be contrived to mask a door. Candida might have dreamed of that opening door. She took these two possibilities with her to her own room.

Anna's return with Derek Burdon found her fully dressed, her hair in neatly plaited coils behind and netted fringe in front. She wore the olive-green cashmere now relegated to morning use, and the warm fluffy scarf, so comfortable, so cosy, which had been her niece Ethel's present to her at Christmas. Shading as it did from lilac to purple, she considered it not only very pleasing in itself but a delicate tribute to the fact that she was now in a house of mourning.

At the sound of approaching footsteps she made haste to open the door. Derek Burdon was in his dressing-gown, an ornate affair which emphasised his pallor. It appeared that the side door by which Miss Olivia had left was not only unlocked but was actually standing ajar. A handkerchief picked up in the courtyard just outside was soaked by the rain which had fallen during the night. Anna identified it as one of a set embroidered by Barbara Sayle during her long illness. It bore in one corner a finely worked capital "C."

Invited to examine the note which had been found in Candida's room, Derek stared at the uneven writing and said that, so far as he could tell, it would be hers.

Miss Silver looked at him with grave enquiry.

"You were working with her upon the family papers. You must have seen her writing."

"Well, yes, I have—yes, of course—but not so very much of it. We were mostly sorting—we hadn't

221

really got to the writing stage. There never seemed to be a lot of time. I say, Miss Silver—you don't really think—she has—gone away?"

She said, "It is too soon to make up our minds about that. What I must do at once is to ring up Mr. Eversley."

Stephen picked up the receiver and heard her voice. He said, "Miss Silver——" And then she was saying,

"Mr. Eversley, can you come out here at once?"

He said quickly, "Is anything wrong?"

"There has been a development. I would like to see you."

"Is there anything wrong? Not Candida—"

The primness of her tone was accentuated.

"I would rather not say any more over the telephone. I would be glad to see you as soon as possible."

She rang off. He was left in a state of mounting apprehension.

Miss Silver was half way to the door, when the bell rang again. About to lift the receiver, she changed her mind. She had spoken to Stephen from the study. It occurred to her that this second call might more suitably be answered by Anna. Proceeding to the door, she opened it, and at a glance there Anna was, at no distance at all, her hands clasped at her breast, her whole attitude that of one who strains to listen. With her usual calm, Miss Silver said,

"Will you see who it is?" and as Anna came forward, she turned and followed her into the room. Standing beside the instrument she could not only hear Anna's shaky, "Who is there?" but what was unmistakably Olivia Benevent's voice in reply. It was quite clear and sharp, and it said,

"Is that you, Anna?"

"Yes—yes—"

"Why do you speak like that? Is anything the matter? You should really pull yourself together! I am ringing up to say that I find I have left a great many things behind me. Joseph will drive me over during the morning, and you had better be ready to come back with us. Have your own things packed by the time I come, and then you can see about mine. I do not wish to see either Mr. Derek or Miss Sayle—you will tell them so! They must respect my wish to be alone whilst I am preparing to leave Underhill. It has been my home during the whole of my life, and—" The hard voice checked for a moment and then went on again. "I do not suppose that I shall ever see it again. You will make them understand that I am not to be intruded upon!"

The voice ceased. The audience was over. A little click upon the line announced that the connection had been broken. Anna's hands were shaking so much that the receiver slipped from them and fell.

CHAPTER 32

In real life there is no ringing down the curtain between the acts. There are moments when such an interval would be more than welcome, but there is, there can be, no such relief. Beds must be made, meals must be prepared, and however reluctantly, some effort must be made to partake of them. Miss

Silver's invariable common sense imposed this point of view. Rooms were aired and tidied, coffee was made and a meal produced. By the time that Stephen Eversley arrived everyone was steadier.

It was Miss Silver who told him what had happened. She showed him Candida's note and asked him if he could identify the writing, only to hear that he had never seen it.

"We met practically every day." He spoke with stiff lips, his face grey and rigid as he remembered those meetings. "We never wrote—we never had to. What does Derek say?"

"He says it might be hers. He has only seen an occasional note, made when they were working on the family papers, and mostly in pencil."

"Miss Silver, you saw her, you talked to her. She didn't say anything to make you think she meant to go away?"

She let her thoughts go back to that conversation by the fire. Could she truthfully say that there had been nothing to justify the supposition that Candida might have been overcome by a sudden impulse to leave Underhill? She had received a severe shock, a monstrous accusation had been brought against her. Was it probable or even possible that her common sense and self-control had given way and left her at the mercy of a blind instinct for flight? Most unwise, most ill-judged, was Miss Silver's mental comment. But when did panic regard either judgment or wisdom?

Stephen controlled himself. He could see that she was thinking. He must give her time. When at last she spoke, it was with gravity and kindness.

"We sat by my bedroom fire and she talked to me for quite a long time. She told me that the Miss Bene-

vents had been very kind until the night of the
Deanery party when Miss Olivia struck her. It was
while she was talking about this incident that she
said, 'I didn't see how I could stay. I meant to leave
in the morning as soon as I was dressed, but Anna
persuaded me not to. She said it was just Aunt Olivia
losing her temper—she was like that, and I wouldn't
hear any more about it. She said Aunt Cara would
miss me.' And then she caught her breath and said,
'Oh, why did I listen to her—why didn't I go?' "

"She said that?"

Miss Silver inclined her head.

"I have given you her exact words."

"Was there anything else?"

"I do not think so, except that she spoke of Underhill with distaste. She said it was an old house,
and she supposed there must have been happy
people in it from time to time, but that Miss Olivia
only seemed to remember the ones who had come
to a violent end."

"What did she mean by that?"

"You have heard of the Benevent Treasure?" Then,
as he nodded, "There seems to have been some belief
that it was unlucky to handle it. The two last Benevents to do so did die suddenly and violently."

"How?"

"One was thrown from his horse at his own front
door. He received a bad head injury and never recovered consciousness. The other, his grandson, was
supposed to have been set upon by footpads. He
also received an injury to his head."

Stephen's eyes met hers with a look of horror.

"What do you mean?"

"I am repeating what was said to me. I asked no

questions, because I did not think the moment a suitable one. Nor do I think that this is a moment to explore its possibilities. What we must do, and that without delay, is to effect an entrance into the passages which Candida believed to exist between the walls in the old part of the house."

"Passages!"

"She believed that one of them opened into her room. She told me she had waked in the night to see a streak of light in the recess between the fireplace and the window. There are shelves there, and from her description they may conceal a door. She spoke of someone coming through the room from that direction with a torch held low. It may have been a dream, but it may not. If this door exists, we must locate it without delay. Miss Olivia has just rung up to say that she will be coming over to fetch the rest of her things. If she arrives and Candida is still absent, neither you nor I will be in a position to conduct a search. I think we should lose no time."

But time was not to be permitted them. They had hardly reached Candida's room, and Stephen had done no more than take a look at the book-lined recess, when Derek Burdon came knocking at the door.

"Look here," he said, "Miss Olivia has just arrived. I was at my window and I saw Joseph drive up. Did you know she was coming over?"

Miss Silver said, "Dear me!" It was the strongest expression she permitted herself. It appeared to be surprised from her, for she made haste to tone it down by saying, "Yes, she rang up just now. She must have come straight from the telephone. She spoke to Anna and told her that she would be fetching the rest of her things and taking her back."

Derek looked relieved.

"Then we just keep out of the way, don't you think? By the by, Mrs. Bell hasn't turned up—the daily, you know. Anna says she wasn't too keen about stopping yesterday. She was going on about getting mixed up with the police and not liking it. So if Anna is going too, it puts us in a bit of a spot, doesn't it?"

Miss Silver had opened her lips to speak, when a sound reached them from the passage. Derek had left the door open, and what they all heard was the sound of footsteps. A moment later Olivia Benevent stood upon the threshold looking in. She was in black from head to foot. A deep mourning veil was thrown back. It framed the sallow face and fell in folds about her shoulders. Her black eyes looked from one to the other in a scornful question. The brows above them were arched as if in surprise. She took her time before she spoke.

"Derek—you are still here? I imagined that you were leaving us. . . . Miss Silver, is it not? Louisa Arnold introduced you, I believe. I hardly expected to meet you here. . . . And Mr. Eversley—I hoped we had made it quite clear that we did not propose to employ you further."

It was Miss Silver who answered her. She said with quiet composure,

"I came last night, Miss Benevent, on Miss Sayle's invitation. It did not seem right to her friends that she should be here without an older woman to countenance her."

Her calm look met Miss Olivia's insolent one without giving way to it.

Miss Benevent came a step into the room.

"In view of what Anna has just told me my plans

227

are altered. Since Candida has seen fit to leave Underhill, there is no occasion for me to do so. I have sent Joseph to fetch what I took away with me. As he and Anna will be here and Mrs. Bell will doubtless return, I shall be well provided with household help and need make no demands upon Miss Silver. As for you, Mr. Eversley, I hope I have made myself clear. Your services are not required."

Thoughts presented themselves to Miss Silver's mind. The legal position was known to Miss Benevent. She had left Underhill in that knowledge. The house and its contents had passed to Candida Sayle. If she now returned, what gave her the assurance that the situation had changed? What supported her in the assumption that the field was clear before her, and that Candida would not return? Only such an assumption would warrant the tone she was now adopting. She said with something more than her usual dignity,

"In all the circumstances, I think you must agree the police should be informed that Miss Sayle has disappeared."

Stephen said, "Miss Silver—"

Olivia Benevent gave a short laugh.

"And do you suppose she will thank you for that? It is obvious that Mr. Eversley does not think so. Ring them up by all means if you think it wise. I imagine they will arrive at the same conclusion that I do myself. I have made no secret of the fact that I believe the girl to be responsible for my sister's death. Anna tells me that she left a note which practically amounts to a confession—'I can't go on. Good-bye' or some such matter. I am afraid I shall be obliged to think very poorly of your intelligence if you do not conclude, as I do, that she has felt unable to brazen it out any longer. The police had been put on their guard, I myself had accused her, and she has, quite simply, run away. If you wish to use the telephone you can do so, but after that I must ask you to leave the house."

"Miss Benevent——"

Stephen had got no further than that, when Miss Silver's hand was laid upon his arm. It was to him that she spoke.

"I do not believe that any useful purpose will be served by continuing this conversation." She addressed herself again to Miss Olivia. "I think the police will wish to see those of us who spent the night here. Neither I nor Mr. Eversley accept what you suggest with regard to Miss Sayle."

Derek Burdon had effaced himself. With Miss Olivia's advance into the room, he had edged his way towards the door. When Miss Silver and Stephen emerged he was waiting for them.

Three miles away in Retley Inspector Rock was called to the telephone.

CHAPTER 33

Candida opened her eyes upon an even darkness. A momentary consciousness of this darkness just touched her and was gone again. But next time it came it reached the point at which it became thought.

Darkness——

Then, after an undefined interval, the thought again, and with it a question.

It was quite, quite dark—why?

Time passed before she got any further than that. Gradually the question began to impress itself, to demand an answer. There wasn't any light at all—the darkness was absolute. Even in the deepest middle of the night there is some shading, some thinning of the blackness, where a window cuts the wall. Unless there are thick curtains tightly drawn. But she never drew her curtains or shut the windows at night. She should have been able to see two narrow oblongs hanging like pictures on the wall to her left.

She became aware that she was lying on her back. If she wanted to see the windows she must turn on to her left side. It wasn't easy. Her body didn't feel as if it belonged to her. She made it obey, but looking as far to the left as she could, there was still no break in the darkness, no window in that impenetrable wall. The question in her mind had become insistent. Feeling, sensation, consciousness flowed back, evenly now and without those dizzy intervals when they had seemed to ebb.

The bed was very hard. She had lost her pillow. She put out her hand and groped. It touched a cold, unyielding substance that was certainly not a bed. It was cold—it was hard—it was damp.

It was stone.

She tried to sit up, but her head swam. At the third attempt she was on her hands and knees. Her head ached, but it was steadier. Her hands pressed down upon a stone floor. She pushed herself into a half-sitting position, one hand still on the stone.

There had been a moment of awful fear, just there on the edge of thought. Now it was gone. There was space over her. She was not closed in. She wasn't—*buried*. When she stretched her arm above her head there was nothing there. Only darkness, only air. Nothing to prevent her from getting to her feet.

She wasn't quite ready for that. She stayed leaning on her hand. Presently she sat right up and tried to think. The last thing she remembered was drinking the glass of milk which Anna had put beside her bed. After that nothing—just nothing at all. She put up a hand to her throat and let it slide down again, touching, feeling. She had been wearing her black dress, but she wasn't wearing it now. But she hadn't undressed. What she was touching wasn't a night-gown. There was a silk shirt, and the lapel of a coat. Someone had taken off her dress and put her into these clothes—her grey coat and skirt and the outdoor coat that went with them. She was even wearing her little grey felt hat.

She sat and thought about this. She was in her outdoor things, but she wasn't out of doors. Why? It didn't seem to make sense. She had on her outdoor shoes. Why had she put them on? The answer came with astonishing certainty, "I didn't." Then, after a long strange pause, "Someone did."

There really was no getting away from it. Someone had drugged the milk, and changed her clothes, and brought her here. But why? The answer forced its way—"To get rid of me."

She put her head in her hands and tried to think. To have sight and to have no use for it—to batter against this wall of darkness and to feel it just flow back again like air, like water, like fear itself! She pressed her hands down close upon her eyelids and held them there. If you did that, even in a lighted room you would not expect to see.

She got herself steady again and began gradually and methodically to feel about her. She might be in a cellar, or in one of the passages. The air was heavy and the floor damp. She had got to find out where she was, and she had got to be careful. There might be some hole or some pit into which she could fall, as poor Aunt Cara had done. Quick and clear there came up the picture of Anna brushing away the dust from Miss Cara's slippers, the cobweb from the tassel of her dressing-gown. If it was in such a place as this that she had come by the cobweb and the dust, then it was in such a place as this that she had come by her death. But how had she come to such a place at all? Of her own free will, or drugged as Candida had been drugged?

She began to move cautiously on her hands and knees, feeling before her. Almost at once she touched something smooth—first leather, and then a metal clasp. Her handbag—her own handbag.

Of course if she was to disappear, her handbag must go with her. She couldn't be supposed to have run away in a thin black dress and indoor shoes. She must be dressed for a journey, and she must wear a hat and have a handbag with her. Was it poor sobbing Anna who had thought of all these things? She couldn't believe it. Yet Anna had acted a part before now. She might have been pushed, threatened . . . She had no need to think who might have threatened her. A voice in her own mind said quick and clear, "She would never have hurt Aunt Cara." And like an echo another answered it, "How do you know what anyone will do?"

People have just so much resistance and no more. Not everyone can endure to the end. Anna had been conditioned by forty years of service—forty years of bondage during which she had been driven by another will than her own, a very hard and ruthless will.

These things did not come to Candida as logical, consecutive thoughts. They were there, as the pictures are there on the walls of a room into which you have strayed. You did not bring them into the room, but they are there, and if you look that way they are most plainly to be seen. The one she could see most plainly of all was the dark picture of Olivia Benevent's hatred.

She had stopped moving, her hand on the bag. Now she sat back and opened it. The first things that she felt were a purse, a handkerchief. Her hand went beyond them. It touched something cold. There, at the bottom of the bag, fallen down by its own weight, was an electric torch.

CHAPTER 34

Inspector Rock sat looking at Miss Silver. As he was to remark to the Chief Constable later, everything did seem to be piling up. The post-mortem had proved that the injury which had caused Miss Cara Benevent's death was the result of a blow from a piece of rusty iron. The rust had scaled off and there were unmistakable traces of it in the wound. There could be no question at all but that it was murder. A couple of men were going through the house room by room in search of anything which could have been used as the weapon. The Superintendent would have been here if he had not gone down with a sudden attack of influenza. He himself was to report direct to the Chief Constable, and meanwhile he was to exercise all possible vigilance, resource, and tact. A short interview with Miss Olivia Benevent had left him with no illusions as to the difficulty of combining these qualities. Old ladies were tricky at the best of times, and single old ladies who hadn't had anyone to cross them for donkey's years were of the trickiest of the lot. In his own family there had been a cousin of his mother's, old Miss Emily Wick, who was a caution. Said to have money in the bank, and a proper Hitler in petticoats with all the relations saying, "Yes, Cousin Emily" when she said yes, and "No, Cousin Emily" when she said no. A trial, that's what she was, and a bee in her bonnet about the woman who looked after her wanting to poison her for her money—"But she won't get a penny." And as it turned out, nobody did, because she was living on an annuity and there wasn't even enough of it left to bury her. When Miss Olivia Benevent sat there and went on about her niece having murdered Miss Cara she put him strongly in mind of old Cousin Emily Wick. And now here was Miss Candida Sayle gone off into the blue, and everyone saying they hadn't a notion how, or why, or where. All except Miss Olivia, who stood there as if she had swallowed the poker and stuck to it that the girl had run away because her conscience wouldn't let her stay.

He sat and looked at Miss Silver, who up to now had been just an elderly lady in the background. He gathered that she was a relative of Miss Arnold's, and that she had come over on the previous evening to keep Candida Sayle company at Mr. Stephen Eversley's request. Miss Arnold was the daughter of old Canon Arnold, and as such beyond social criticism. In fact the whole set-up was not only respectable but in the highest degree select. His experienced glance found in Miss Silver a type with which life in a cathedral town had made him familiar—elderly ladies who sat on committees, took stalls in church bazaars, and engaged in a hundred and one ecclesiastical activities. She was, it is true, of a slightly earlier pattern, her manner more formal and her dress more out of date.

Their interview, however, had not proceeded very far before he became aware of a welcome difference. Where most of these ladies were apt to be diffuse and flustered in making anything that resembled a statement, Miss Maud Silver was both cool and succinct. She presented him with the clearest possible picture of the previous evening and what had passed between herself and Miss Sayle. He had left her to the last, and what she said tallied perfectly with the statements made by Derek Burdon, Stephen Eversley, and the maid Anna. When she had finished speaking he regarded her with respect. She had stuck to the point, she had avoided personal comment, and she had given him a strong impression of verbal and factual accuracy. He found himself asking for what had been withheld.

"You came into the house last night without knowing any of these people?"

She sat there very composedly in her olive-green cashmere and the shaded woollen wrap, her hands folded in her lap, her feet placed neatly side-by-side upon the study carpet. In the interests of accuracy she made a slight correction.

"I have some acquaintance with Mr. Eversley. Mr. Burdon and Miss Sayle were introduced to me during a musical evening at the Deanery. I had no more than a few formal words with either of them."

"And the Miss Benevents?"

"I met them on the same occasion. My cousin Miss Arnold has known them all her life."

"Was Miss Olivia Benevent here when you arrived last night?"

"No. She had already left when Mr. Eversley rang me up."

"You knew that he and Miss Sayle were engaged?"

She gave a small discreet cough.

"He came round to see myself and Miss Arnold, and I think I may say that it was understood. Miss Arnold at once offered the hospitality of her house."

"It was refused?"

"In the absence of Miss Olivia Benevent Miss Sayle considered herself responsible for the household at Underhill."

"And you came out here at once?"

"As soon as I had packed a suit-case."

"Miss Silver, I am going to ask you what impression the household made upon you. None of these people were really known to you—I should like to hear how they struck you."

As she returned his rather direct look he became aware that he really did want to know what she thought about Candida Sayle, about Derek Burdon, about Stephen Eversley, about Anna Rossi. He wondered whether she was going to tell him. And then she was doing so.

"I found Miss Sayle very frank and simple. Miss Cara's death had obviously been a great shock, and so had Miss Olivia's accusation."

"Enough of a shock to frighten her into running away?"

"I should not have said so. The first impact of the shock was wearing off. She spoke naturally and simply of Miss Cara, who she said had been very kind to her, and for whom she had, I thought, a good deal of affection."

He said, "That sort of thing can be put on, you know."

She coughed again, this time on a note of reproof.

"I was for some years engaged in the scholastic profession. I am accustomed to young people. If one has experience, insincerity is not difficult to detect."

He found himself with a surprised conviction that it would be extremely difficult to tell her a lie, and that if you did so it would be immediately stripped to its bare bones. Others had, of course, had this feeling before him, but he was not to know about that. He said,

"And you found Miss Sayle sincere?"

"That was the impression she made upon me."

"No evidence of a guilty conscience."

"No, Inspector."

He was more impressed than he would have been by protestations. He continued,

"How did Mr. Burdon strike you?"

"He has a great deal of charm, and he has been accustomed to rely upon it. The Miss Benevents have been very indulgent, and I believe he did what he could to repay their kindness. He spoke of Miss Cara with affection, and of Miss Olivia with surprise and regret at her present attitude. He gives me the impression that he has an easy-going nature, a kind heart, and an indolent disposition."

Since this agreed not only with what was said in the town but with his own judgment, Rock accepted it without comment.

"And Mr. Eversley?" he said.

Miss Silver said in her temperate way,

"You are probably aware that he is related to my

cousin, Miss Arnold. I suppose he may be considered a distant connection of my own. His uncle's firm enjoys a high reputation, and I believe he does it no discredit. There is no reason to suppose him to be anything but a clever, intelligent young man with a good character and good prospects who is honestly and sincerely in love with Miss Sayle. You may be aware that some part at least of Miss Olivia Benevent's anger proceeds from the fact that she hoped to make a match between her and Derek Burdon."

The Inspector said, "Yes——" in rather an absentminded tone. He was thinking that Miss Silver appeared to be very well informed. He went on,

"And Anna Rossi—what do you think of her?"

Miss Silver smiled.

"She is, of course, Italian by birth. I understand that she came to this country at an early age, and there is very little foreign accent. The foreign temperament is, however, present to a marked degree. She is excitable and emotional, and makes no attempt to restrain the expression of her feelings. I believe her attachment to Miss Cara Benevent to have been genuine, and I think she has become fond of Miss Sayle. She stands a good deal in awe of Miss Olivia and is very much afraid of provoking her anger."

Rock found himself impressed not only by what she said, but by the manner in which she said it. Ladies, and especially elderly ladies, were often quick to observe, but he had found in the main that their judgment was apt to be swayed by personal feeling. In any case, they usually had too much to say about it. In Miss Silver he found a moderation, a restraint, and an economy of words quite outside his experience. Also, and above all, he was aware of an intelligence which stimulated his own. Miss Silver's marked success in the schoolroom had been largely due to the fact that, whilst making knowledge seem desirable, she was able to awake in her pupils the consciousness of their ability to attain it. The timid found themselves becoming confident, the intelligent stimulated. All had found themselves capable of more than they supposed. As Frank Abbott once remarked, "She strikes sparks out of you." Inspector Rock was aware of this, though he could not, perhaps, have put it into words. What he did was to lean forward and say,

"Miss Silver—what has happened to Miss Sayle?"

Her reply was grave.

"I do not believe that she has run away."

"Then where is she?"

"I believe her to be somewhere in this house."

"What do you mean?"

She told him what Candida had told her. Anna's niece Nellie waking behind a locked door to hear something that went to and fro in the room and wept, taking refuge for a night with Anna, and going away next day. Candida Sayle waking to see light coming through a crack where bookshelves masked what seemed to be a solid wall and being aware of someone passing through her room with a torch held low. Anna brushing dust from Miss Cara's slippers and a cobweb from the tassel of her dressing-gown.

"I think you must see, Inspector, that these things point to the fact that there are concealed passages in this old house. There is a family story about a hidden treasure. It has not been considered lucky for anyone to interfere with it. Miss Sayle repeated a curious old rhyme which she and Derek Burdon had come across while going through some family papers:

> "'Touch not nor try,
> Sell not nor buy,
> Give not nor take,
> For dear life's sake.'

"They considered that it referred to the treasure, and she told me of two instances which appear to bear this out. Both occurred in the eighteenth century. In the first, a Benevent was found at his own front door. He had a severe head injury, and it was said that he had fallen or been thrown from his horse. In the second, his grandson was found dead or dying, also quite near to the house. He too had a head injury, and was said to have been set upon by footpads."

Rock said, "What have you got in your mind?"

She continued as if he had not spoken.

"Both these men were believed to have interfered with the Benevent Treasure. Both were found quite near the house with fatal injuries to the head."

Rock repeated his question,

"What have you got in your mind?"

She replied with a question of her own.

"What have you got in yours, Inspector?" Then, after a pause during which he remained silent, she continued.

"There is said to be a hidden treasure. There is some evidence that there are hidden passages. My cousin Miss Arnold informs me that this house was an old one when the founder of the Benevent family bought it and added on to it in the seventeenth century. He was said to have brought the treasure with him from Italy. So old a house might very well have afforded him a secret hiding-place. It is not unknown, especially in Italy, for such hiding-places to be contrived so as to be difficult or even dangerous of approach. Does it not strike you as a strange coincidence that these eighteenth-century Benevents, associated with an attempt to withdraw the treasure, should both have received head injuries from which they died, and that Miss Cara should now have met with a similar accident? In your own opinion that was not due to a fall at the place where she was found. Miss Sayle should have informed you that there was dust upon Miss Cara's felt slippers and a cobweb on the tassel of her dressing-gown. She saw Anna brush them away. I may say that this was under the first shock of finding her mistress dead. She thought Anna acted instinctively, and it was only much later that she began to think what these traces might imply. Underhill is a very well kept house. I have been into every room, and there is no place where dust or a cobweb could have been picked up. But they are what one might expect in a secret passage. If Miss Cara came by her injury in such a place, the same thing may have happened to James Benevent and his grandson in the eighteenth century. If the secret of the house was to be preserved, the bodies must be moved and some story produced that would explain the injuries. There seems to be no doubt that Miss Cara's body was moved. The eighteenth-century cases may have suggested this course of action."

He was more impressed than he cared to admit. The particles of rust found in the wound came to his mind. Rust—dust—and a cobweb. None of these three things were to be found in a well kept house. He had been over every part of it himself, and they had no place there. He said abruptly,

"If these passages exist, what should take Miss

241

Cara into them, and in the middle of the night?"

He got a sober look, a sober response.

"She was a most unhappy woman. I think she could not rest. May I ask whether you are aware of the circumstances surrounding the disappearance of Mr. Alan Thompson about three years ago?"

If he was startled he did not allow himself to show it.

"I heard the talk that was going round. The matter was never brought to the police officially."

"I believe not. It was put about, was it not, that he had taken money and a diamond brooch belonging to Miss Cara?"

"That was the talk."

"Should you have thought that a likely story if you had known that Miss Cara was within a few days of marrying him, and that had she done so she could have left him a life-interest in the whole of her property?"

He was surprised into a sudden movement.

"Who told you that?"

The sage-green dress had a pocket. She produced a card and proffered it. He read in neat inconspicuous type,

Miss Maud Silver
15 Montague Mansions
Leaham Street

There was a telephone number, and in the bottom left-hand corner the words, "Private Enquiries." He was less surprised than he would have been half an hour ago.

She said sedately,

"The young man's step-father commissioned me

to make some enquiries. In the course of them the daily help who was working here at the time of Mr. Thompson's disappearance told me that Miss Cara had given him a coin which she believed to be a lucky charm. She said he wore it always about his neck on a chain. At some time subsequent to his disappearance she was doing Miss Olivia's room, when she noticed Miss Olivia's bunch of keys depending from the keyhole of a drawer which had always been kept locked. She said that the drawer was open, but I do not credit this. I think the key was in the lock, and that she could not resist gratifying her curiosity. Be that as it may, she was very much startled to find that the drawer contained not only the coin which Mr. Thompson had so constantly worn, but also the missing diamond brooch. I may say that I went to see her because I was told she had declared that Alan Thompson had never left Underhill. I got no more out of her than I have told you. She was, in fact, very reluctant to speak of the matter at all. As far as she did speak, I believe her to have been telling the truth. If Alan Thompson did not take the brooch which he was accused of taking, he may not have taken the money either. He really had very little reason to do so. Miss Cara was on the eve of marrying him——"

He interrupted her sharply.

"How do you know that?"

"Colonel Gatling of Hilton St. John spoke of it to Stephen Eversley. His brother, the Reverend Cyril Gatling, had agreed to marry them. He was a good deal exercised about the matter, and wrote down his misgivings in a diary which came into Colonel Gatling's possession after his death. He had, of course, no right to repeat what he had learned from so private a source."

Rock said, "If she was going to marry him—" He left it at that.

"Precisely. He had no inducement to disappear."

"He may have felt he couldn't face the marriage."

Miss Silver gave a slight disapproving cough.

"From what my enquiries have brought to light, I do not fancy that he would have scrupled at what was so evidently to his advantage. By all accounts Miss Cara would have given him anything he wanted. I cannot believe that he would have turned his back upon such a favourable prospect. Even if the story stood alone, I should find it difficult to believe. Taken in conjunction with the two eighteenth-century cases and with recent events, it appears to me to tax credulity too far."

"You suggest——"

She said gravely,

"Mr. Thompson disappeared. Miss Sayle has disappeared. In both these cases there was a threat to Miss Olivia Benevent. If her sister married, she lost everything except a very moderate life-interest. When her sister died she was in a similar position. She reacted by accusing Miss Sayle of being responsible for the death. She has forbidden Mr. Eversley the house, and she is dismissing Mr. Burdon and myself. I am quite unable to believe that Miss Sayle has disappeared voluntarily. I am afraid that she may have been tricked or enticed into the passages, or even taken there by force. That they are dangerous is certain. I feel that a search-warrant should be procured without delay, and that there should be a thorough investigation. Mr. Eversley, as an architect, would be in a position to give the most valuable assistance. Miss Benevent is in a hurry to get rid of him. As you can see, the matter is extremely urgent. We do not know what has happened already, but I am sure there is no time to be lost."

CHAPTER 35

After a short but decisive encounter with Miss Olivia Benevent Inspector Rock retired upon his Chief Constable. It was all very well to be told to use tact and to handle her with kid gloves. You couldn't use tact with a tank, or handle an atomic bomb with kid gloves. He would not have dreamed of allowing these or similar exaggerated expressions to escape into speech, but they thronged his mind and set up quite a disturbance there.

Major Warrender heard him with sympathy.

"Formidable person," he said. "But look here—this search-warrant—what's your own idea about it? It's an awkward position to my way of thinking. She has made no objection to your searching the house?"

"No, sir."

"To be sure, it wasn't for her to say one way or another, except as a matter of courtesy—not with Miss Sayle there."

"That's just it, sir, Miss Sayle isn't there now, and Miss Olivia has got the bit between her teeth. When I asked her about hidden passages she just said there weren't any. When I told her that her sister's body had certainly been moved, and that Anna Rossi had

245

been seen to brush dust from her slippers and re-move a cobweb from the tassel of her dressing-gown, she sent for Anna and put it to her that she hadn't done any such thing."

"Oh, come, Rock, you shouldn't have let her do that!"

"How was I going to stop her, sir? She just said, 'You had better ask Anna about that,' and she rang the bell. And then before the woman was well inside the door she was putting it to her—'The Inspector says you brushed some dust from Miss Cara's slip-pers and a cobweb from her dressing-gown. I have assured him it's all nonsense, but you had better tell him so yourself.'"

"And what did Anna say?"

"Stood and looked at her like a dog that thinks it's going to be beaten. And when I put it to her the way it ought to have been put, she flared up and said how could there be any dust or cobwebs the way the house was kept? And I said, 'I'm not talking about the parts of the house I've seen, but you've got some secret passages here, haven't you?' And all she could do was to stare at me and say she had never heard of any such thing. And then she began to cry and go on about her poor Miss Cara."

"You ought to have seen her alone," said Major Warrender.

Inspector Rock considered that the Chief Constable was being wise after the event.

The question of a search-warrant hung uneasily between them. Just what Major Warrender would have done if he had been left to himself, it is difficult to say. As it turned out, he was not to be left to himself. The arrival of Stephen Eversley and Miss Maud Silver precipitated a decision. Stephen was grey and grim, Miss Silver decorously determined. Both were insistent that Candida Sayle could have no possible reason to run away, and that in fact she had not done so.

Major Warrender tapped on his writing-table.

"And you suggest——"

"That she has not left Underhill," said Stephen Eversley. Miss Silver took up the tale.

"Miss Sayle informed me of her belief that the house contained a secret passage or passages. Someone had come through her room in the night." She described Candida's experience and went on to repeat her description of having seen dust and a cobweb on Miss Cara, and Anna brushing them away. Her manner was calm and persuasive. She concluded, "If such passages exist, as indeed they do in so many old houses, what we fear is that Miss Sayle found the entrance to one of them, probably the one which opened on her own room, and that she may have been induced to explore it. We fear that she may have met with an accident."

Major Warrender tapped again.

"Is there any evidence as to the existence of these passages?"

She had only got as far as "Miss Sayle——" when he interrupted her.

"Well, you see, that's just it, it's all Miss Sayle. There's no evidence except hers, and quite frankly, what does it amount to? She could quite easily have been dreaming. Miss Benevent denies that any such passages exist."

Stephen said,

"And isn't that what she would do if they were a family secret? Look here, sir, if those passages don't exist, why won't she let me satisfy myself that they' don't? She had me there because she had got fussed about cracks in the oldest part of the house, but she wouldn't let me make a proper examination, and when I said I must have more light in the cellars and wanted to bring in a powerful electric lamp, she wouldn't hear of it—put me off and wrote to say they wouldn't require my services. Even from what I was allowed to see I can tell you there's plenty of room where those passages could run. It's the front of the house that's been built on to. The older part was old in the sixteenth century, and the walls there are thick enough for anything."

"And that's true, sir," said Inspector Rock.

Miss Silver coughed in the manner in which she had been accustomed to call a class to attention. Her eyes rested upon Major Warrender with an expression of mild authority.

"There really appears to be no reason why Miss Benevent should adopt an obstructive attitude. May I point out that she has no right either to give or to withhold permission for a thorough search of the house? Underhill was the property of Miss Cara Benevent, and she is dead. It has now passed to Miss Candida Sayle. You may confirm this by ringing up Mr. Tampling, who is the family solicitor. He is also my cousin Miss Arnold's legal adviser, and the reason for my presence in Retley being to help her in a matter of family business, I have some slight acquaintance with him myself. He should, I think, be told that Miss Sayle has disappeared. As her representative, his presence would seem to be highly desirable if a search is to be made."

Major Warrender experienced some relief. He would not, it appeared, be obliged to face Miss Olivia Benevent without support, if indeed he had to face her at all. He looked at Miss Silver with gratitude, for of course what she said was perfectly true. Olivia Benevent had really no legal status. It was not she but Candida Sayle who was Cara Benevent's heir. He reached for the telephone and rang up Mr. Tampling.

CHAPTER 36

In the darkness Candida remained motionless, her hand on the torch. Brushing past handkerchief and purse, it had closed on the smooth, cold metal and become frozen there. For the moment thought was frozen too. Then gradually it came to life again, questioning, clamouring for an answer. How had the torch got into her bag?

It wasn't hers. She had brought no such thing to Underhill. There was a torch of Barbara's packed up in one of the boxes she had left in store, an old battered thing which had gone through the war in the days when Barbara Sayle was a warden and had come out of it with a veteran's scars. There was a dent on the rim which held the glass . . . . Her fingers moved on the thing she held—unclipped glass and a smooth metal ring. This couldn't be Barbara's torch. It lay there under her hand new and undented, and whoever it belonged to, it was not she who had put it into her bag. Then who? There was an answer to that—the same person or the same people who had dressed her in her outdoor clothes and brought her here.

But why? As to the clothes, the answer was not far to seek. It was meant to look as if she had run away. She had been accused, and she had run away. The picture was clear enough. But the torch—that didn't account for the torch. She had been put into this dark place and left there to its terrors. Then why the mercy of the torch? She thought it would have taken more than one person to carry her. Perhaps it had come to one of them how dreadful it might be to die in the dark. Perhaps—her thought broke off.

Since she had the torch, it was all that mattered. Then why did she delay to use it? In the depths of her mind she knew the answer. It was because it gave her a little hope which she was loth to lose. She could stay there with the torch under her hand and feel that she could break the darkness. She had only to move her finger on the switch and there would be light. But was there any chance that the torch would have been put in her bag if it was going to help her? She could not think.... Suppose she pressed on the switch and no light came—could anyone be cruel enough to make such a mock of hope? She didn't know. She had stumbled into a nightmare where anything might happen.

Suppose the light came on and showed her something more dreadful than the dark—some trap, some pit, or just the blank unbroken walls of a tomb. Perhaps the torch was there to show her how little hope there was.

All this time she had been dulled by the drug, but the effect was waning. Quick and suddenly her courage rose. If you don't do everything you can, you will always be beaten and you will deserve it. If you don't fight on even after it doesn't seem to be any good, you are not worth saving. She lifted the torch out of the bag and pressed the switch.

The beam was bright and strong. It cut the darkness and came to rest no more than a yard away, splashing its light against the dull surface of a wall. She turned it this way and that. There was a wall on either side of her and a roof above. She thought the roof would be six foot over her head as she sat, perhaps more, perhaps less. She was sitting back upon her heels with the bag in her lap. The passage ran away in front of her.

Her feet and ankles were cramped. She got up on to her feet and stood waiting for the blood to come back into them. She was dizzy enough for her first step to take her to the wall with a hand stretched out and groping for it. The air was heavy. Turning the torch the other way, she could see that the passage went away to the right. She didn't know whether to go on or to go back. As her head cleared she became aware that the wall against which she was leaning was made of brick. With nothing to sway her choice, she went step by step in the direction towards which she had been facing when the light came on. Ten paces brought her to a turn. The passage narrowed and the roof was nearer. She came to a flight of steps, very narrow, very steep, and climbed them. Ten steps going up, and at the head of them a small square platform and a door. She went down on her knees and set the torch beside her, propping it with her bag.

The door was about two and a half foot high by two foot wide. It was made of old weathered oak. The light showed up the grain and the dry grey surface of the wood. It was all dry here—dry and dusty. Not damp like the passage below. She put out her hand to the oak and pushed against it. It was as solid as the floor upon which she was kneeling. There was no handle to the door.

CHAPTER 37

Mr. Tampling was a little grey man. He had a bright enquiring eye and a tendency to romance which he made it his business to hold in check. He considered that it should be kept in its place, where it afforded him a good deal of secret pleasure. He was now in his early sixties, and he had known Miss Olivia Benevent ever since he could remember. His father, his grandfather, and his great-grandfather had handled the Benevents' affairs. When he had first come into the firm as a very young man Miss Olivia had patronised him. She was a few years the elder, and she had not only behaved as if those few years were a good many more, but she had very obviously regarded him from the other side of a social rubicon which could never be crossed. He made up his mind about her then, and had never seen any occasion to alter it. He was sorry for Miss Cara, who was obviously quite incapable of standing up for herself, and he had done his best to protect her interests. He was now quite prepared to do his best for Candida Sayle, and since he was an executor of the will under which she inherited, he was in a position to do so. He expressed himself as shocked at her disappearance and concerned for her safety.

As he waited for the Chief Constable to pick him up, this concern increased. He was remembering a conversation with Miss Olivia Benevent after her father's death. It had been necessary for him to remind her that it was not she but Miss Cara who inherited the estate, and that, apart from Miss Cara's right to assign a life-rent of the property to her husband in the event of her marriage, it would pass at her death to her sister Candida Sayle.

She had stared back at him with cold anger.

"My sister Candida is dead."

"I believe she had children."

"A son and a daughter. What has that to do with it?"

"The son would inherit. Failing him or his children, the daughter would do so."

He had never been able to forget her look, her words. She had not raised her voice. She had said that she hoped no child of Candida Sayle's would survive, and she had said it as if she were cursing them. He had been most profoundly shocked, and he had not forgotten. He remembered that Miss Cara had cried out, and that Olivia had quelled her with a look. He could see poor Cara now with the tears running down her face, catching her breath and murmuring, "Oh, no—no—that is a dreadful thing to say!"

Miss Olivia was in the drawing-room when Joseph informed her of Mr. Tampling's arrival.

"There is another gentleman with him—Major Warrender—and the Police Inspector."

She sat very upright, her plain dead black relieved against the white brocaded chair. She had her embroidery-frame upon her lap, and a needle

253

threaded with scarlet silk in her hand. There were three handsome rings on the third finger. They crowded one another, but the diamonds flashed bravely. She said in a measured voice,

"Major Warrender is the Chief Constable. I have not sent for him, or for Mr. Tampling, but I will see them."

She looked very small and black as they came round the lacquer screen into the big white room. She was setting a stitch in her embroidery, and she did not look up until they were half way across the floor. She did not rise to meet them. There was a cold stare from the shallow black eyes, a rising of the narrow arched brows, and a slight, a very slight inclination of the head. After which she addressed herself to Major Warrender.

"May I ask the reason for this visit? My sister is very recently dead. Is there to be no consideration for my grief?" The tone was even harsher than the words. She turned to Mr. Tampling. "I do not quite know why you are here, but since you are, you can perhaps tell me whether I am obliged to put up with these intrusions."

He took the word from Major Warrender, who was only too glad to let him have it.

"Miss Benevent, I must advise you that it would be very unwise for you to refuse to co-operate with the police. The Chief Constable informs me that Miss Cara's death cannot be attributed to an accident. I was her legal adviser, and I am an executor under your grandfather's will. The estate has devolved upon Miss Candida Sayle. I am informed that she has disappeared. In the circumstances, I feel sure you must see that every possible assistance should be given to the police. There is no desire to intrude upon your privacy, but you are not in a position to withhold all possible facilities for a very complete search of the house."

She appeared to stiffen. He guessed at the forced control of a formidable temper. When she spoke, it was without any expression at all.

"The house has already been searched."

He had not met Candida Sayle, but he knew now that he had seen her. On a day a week ago in Stephen Eversley's car. They were talking together and laughing, and he had thought to himself that young Eversley was a lucky man. The picture came back to him now—a young man quite obviously in love and a girl with bright hair and sparkling eyes, the air of youth and happiness which surrounded them. He turned from it to the dead weight of Miss Olivia's resistance.

"There have been developments since the search was conducted. Major Warrender will tell you that he is not satisfied." He turned to the Chief Constable. Miss Olivia also turned to fix him with that cold resentful stare. He said,

"Miss Benevent, Miss Sayle has disappeared. There is a suggestion that she may have strayed into some passage in the older part of the house and have found herself unable to get out. If you know of any such place——"

"I do not. Miss Sayle is not here."

"Then where is she?"

She lifted a hand and let it fall again. It held the needle with the scarlet thread.

"How should I know? I believe her to be responsible for my sister's death. When she found that the police would not accept it as an accident she became frightened and she has run away. You would be better employed in trying to trace her. You are wasting your time here."

With the last word, her attention appeared to be withdrawn. She lifted the embroidery-frame and took a fine, smooth stitch. Mr. Tampling came up to her and spoke in a low voice. She might not have heard him. He said,

"This is very unwise. I have to tell you that there is a search-warrant. Major Warrender does not wish to use it. As Miss Sayle's nearest relative you must be deeply interested in her being found. I would urge you in the strongest terms——"

She looked up then, scanned him briefly, and said,

"I do not know what more you want. I have told you my opinion. Major Warrender will do as he pleases. Miss Sayle's whereabouts do not interest me." She went back to her embroidery again.

Joseph was waiting in the hall, the quiet decorous manservant, resentful of an affront to the house he served, but concealing it deftly. To have the police back again when it was to be hoped they had seen the last of them, and with the police Mr. Eversley who had been forbidden the house, and that Miss Silver who had come as it were out of nowhere! He had expressed himself with a good deal of freedom on the subject of Miss Maud Silver. One had only to see her for five minutes to tell what sort she was. He had a good deal to say about it to his wife Anna.

"If there is one grain of dust in a room, she will see it! If anyone whispers a word in the middle of the night, she will hear it! I had only to set my eyes on her and I knew!"

He was asked to produce his wife, and did so. She had been crying again. Upstairs in the room that had been Candida Sayle's she was questioned, and went on crying. She didn't know about a passage that opened here. She didn't know about any passage at all. If there were such a thing, it would be secret. She would not know about it—she would not want to know. Such places were horrible—they had been made for some bad purpose. Nothing would make her enter one. In a place like that, who could know what there might be? Mice, or even rats! Or some pit into which you might fall and never be heard of again! She called God to witness that nothing would make her set foot in such a place.

Rock said, "She knows something." To which Miss Silver replied,

"I do not think she knows, but I think she is afraid."

"What is she afraid of?"

She said gravely,

"Of Miss Olivia—of what has happened to Miss Cara—of what may be happening to Miss Sayle."

"You don't think——"

She dropped her voice to its lowest tone.

"Inspector, I too am very much afraid."

Stephen Eversley had not spoken at all. He went straight from the door to the recess between the chimney-breast and the side wall of the house. Shelves filled with books from the floor almost to the ceiling, a carved border to simulate a bookcase. He began to take the books out of the shelves. Presently the other two men joined him.

It is astonishing how much room books can take up. Even the smallest bookcase when emptied appears to have given up double the number of books which it could have been supposed to contain. The piles upon the floor grew high. Sometimes they overbalanced and fell. The books had to be carried farther back into the room. There was no dust. The empty shelves were clean. The first thing Stephen discovered was that they were not fastened to the wall. There were wooden side-pieces and a wooden back. There was, in fact, what amounted to the shell of a bookcase fastened into the recess, but by what means it did not appear.

There could be a door here, and if there was, there must be some means of opening it. He did not believe that Candida had been dreaming when she saw someone come from the recess and pass through the room with a torch held low. His mind became concentrated on the task of finding the opening.

The other two men stood back and watched him. He had the skill and the incentive which were beyond anything they could supply. Anna's breath still came unevenly, but she no longer sobbed aloud, and her tears had ceased to flow. When Miss Silver touched her on the arm she rose and followed her to the room next door. Bidden to sit down, she said in a distressed voice,

"Miss Olivia will not like it. I must go back to her."

She was overborne by a manner of calm authority.

"Not just yet, Anna. I want to talk to you—about Miss Candida. You have served the Benevents for a long time, have you not?"

"For forty years." There was pride in her tone.

"And you loved Miss Cara?"

"God knows I loved her!"

"Miss Candida is also of the family, and I think Miss Cara loved her."

"Yes, yes, she loved her—my poor Miss Cara!"

"Then will you think what she would have wished you to do? You do not believe that Miss Candida has run away, do you? You do not believe that she had anything to do with Miss Cara's death. You know very well that she had not anything to do with Miss Cara's death. You know very well that she had no reason to run away. If there is anything else that you know, you must tell it before it is too late. Do you want for all the rest of your life to have to think, 'I could have saved her, but I would not speak'?"

Anna's hands twisted in her lap. She said in a tone of agony,

"What can I do?"

"You can tell me what you know."

"*Dio mio*, there is nothing—they would kill me!"

"You will be protected. Where did Miss Cara get the blow that killed her?"

The twisting hands came up in a gesture of despair.

"How do I know? I will tell you, and you shall judge. There are secret places—that is all I know. It is not my business—I do not look, I do not speak. I have seen dust on my poor Miss Cara's slippers. I think sometimes that she walks in her sleep, but I do not ask. There is a night I miss her from her room and I come looking for her. I think perhaps she has gone to Mr. Alan's room to grieve for him. So I come this way, and she comes out of his room, walking in her dream. She comes by me and she is talking to herself. 'I can't find him,' she says, 'I can't find him!' And, 'They have taken him away!' She goes back to her room, and she is crying all the way. I help her out of her dressing-gown, and there is dust on it and cobweb, so I think she has been in the secret places and I am very much afraid."

"Why were you afraid?"

Anna drew in her breath sharply.

"Because of what old Mr. Benevent told me."

"What did he tell you?"

Anna's voice dropped to what could only just be heard.

"He was very old," she said. "He would talk to himself, and he would talk to me. He tells me about the Treasure—how it is quite safe in a secret place. 'Quite safe,' he says, and laughs to himself. 'A man may walk over it and not know it is there. He may go up, and he may go down, and he will not know. And if he knew, and if he went, it would never do him any good.' And then he would take hold of me by my hand hard—*hard*, and he would say, 'Yes, it is safe—quite safe.' But not to go near it, never to go near it—not for anything in the world. Not to give and not to take—there was something about that in a rhyme."

Miss Silver quoted it gravely:

> "'Touch not nor try,
> Sell not nor buy,
> Give not nor take,
> For dear life's sake.'"

Anna stared from her reddened eyes.

"Who told you that?"

Her look was held.

"It was Miss Candida. Anna—where is Miss Candida?"

Anna put her hands up and covered her face.

"O *Dio mio*—I think she is dead!"

CHAPTER 38

Candida did not know how much time had gone by. Perhaps the effect of the drug had not quite worn off, perhaps the heavy air of this small confined space had dulled her senses, but after she had come upon the door which had no handle everything seemed to stand still. She couldn't move the door, she couldn't go on, and there was no strength in her to go back. She wasn't afraid any longer—everything was too hazy for that. But she remembered that she must save the battery of the torch, and she switched it off. She didn't remember anything after that for quite a long time.

She woke to a cramped position and stiff limbs, and for a moment she did not know where she was. With returning memory, she put on the torch again. There was no sense in staying here. The door wouldn't move, and the air was fresher below. She went down the steps and back along the way that she had come. There must be other ways out of these passages. There was the one behind the bookcase in her room, and certainly one in the room which Nellie had had, or how could Miss Cara have come into it walking in her sleep? There might be a dozen ways in, a dozen ways out. Any one of them would serve her turn, but she must find it before the light began to fail.

She came back to the place from which she had started. At least she thought it was that place, because looking back, she had seen, or thought she had seen, that the passage ran away to the right. She went on and found that the right-hand bend had become a turn. There was something that lay across the path. The light fell on it. It was an iron bar coated with rust. She stepped across it without thinking what it might be.

The passage ran on a few feet and ended in a kind of hollow cave or niche. The niche was narrower than the passage, and it was raised above it. The beam of the torch played over it and showed an iron-bound box or chest with the lid thrown back. It filled the niche and it disclosed, piled up within, the treasure which Ugo di Benevento had stolen three hundred years ago.

At the first glance she had held the torch too high, but even then she had no doubt as to what she had stumbled upon. There was a dish or platter standing on its edge and leaning against one of the hinges. There was a pair of candlesticks fallen in a St. Andrew's cross. There were other things. She remembered that there had been a golden dish—no, 'sundry golden plates and dishes'—in the list which she and Derek had read, sitting safely in the daylight with the table between them. They had looked across the three-hundred-year gap, and Derek had warned her to have nothing to do with the Treasure. She could remember that he had said to let it alone. And then he had spoken about Alan Thompson—just his name and, "I've got a feeling he *didn't* leave it alone."

It was something like that—in her mind, but vaguely, with memory playing on it as the beam of the torch played on the hidden things in the niche.

The beam was still too high. The hand that held the torch was rigid, reluctant to bring it down. She did not direct it consciously, but it began to move as if she could no longer hold it up. The shimmering light slid over the stones of a necklace. They were great red stones, and they were linked with diamonds. It slid lower. Now what it touched was not stone, but bone. Fleshless bones of a skeleton hand which clutched the edge of the chest.

Lower, down the shape of an arm, to a heap of huddled clothes pressed close against the niche. Someone had knelt there to clutch at the Treasure—had knelt—and clutched—and died. Even to Candida's failing senses there could be no doubt as to who that someone had been. She had no doubt at all that it was Alan Thompson who had laid hands on the Benevento Treasure and died for it. She took a wavering step backwards and went down.

CHAPTER 39

The back of the bookcase swung in. Stephen stepped back with the chisel in his hand and said,

"There!"

Major Warrender said, "Well, I don't know, I'm sure," his tone a doubting one, because it had been necessary to force an opening and he couldn't help seeing that some damage had been done. Of course it would have been a good deal worse if the damage had been done and no opening found. He turned for reassurance to Mr. Tampling and surprised an unexpected gleam in his eye. For the moment the streak of romance had got the upper hand of him. Candida

Sayle had said that there was a secret passage, and there was one. The wooden back of the recess was a door, and it stood open.

Miss Silver had returned to the room. She looked gravely at the dark entry which the open door disclosed. She looked at Stephen Eversley's face. He took the powerful electric lamp with which he had provided himself and passed into the gap. There was a small platform and steps that led from it. He went down, the light withdrawing as he did so and leaving only a reflected glow. When he got to the bottom he called back.

"There are ten steps. Someone ought to stay behind to see we don't get shut in."

There was a delay whilst Rock went to fetch the constable who had been told to wait in the car. On his return they climbed down after Stephen. There was an old worn handrail stapled to the wall, and they were glad of it. The steps were high and irregular.

When they had come to the bottom there was a short length of passage. It was dark, and narrow, and dusty. Miss Silver reflected upon the probable presence of spiders. If Miss Cara had wandered here, there might very easily have been dust upon her slippers and a cobweb on the tassel of her gown. But she wondered, very deeply she wondered, whether she could have come this way or climbed that steep, irregular stair in a dream. There might, of course, be other and easier ways into the passages.

There were certainly other ways. They came to a place where this one divided. There were steps that went up and steps that went down. Stephen left them standing in the dark and climbed, taking the light with him. It dwindled and was gone. They stood close together, feeling the heaviness of the air and the weight of the dark. Only to Mr. Tampling was the experience other than an anxious and sinister one. Not all his concern for Candida—and he was truly concerned for her—could deny him the thrill of adventure. Buried memories of stories in the *Boy's Own Paper* read surreptitiously by candlelight when he ought to have been enjoying his lawful slumbers woke up and magicked him. The passage under the castle moat—secret ways that led to the smuggler's cave—the skeleton . . . Well, thank goodness there could be no skeleton here. They stood together, touching one another, and did not move. After a long time, the light glimmered and returned. Stephen came back. He said briefly,

"There is a way out into several of the rooms. All quite easy to open from this side. We are at ground-floor level here. Those other steps will take us to the cellar level. I've always thought that if there was a hiding-place, there would be an entrance to it from those cellars. Miss Olivia wouldn't let me examine them, you know."

He went on before them with the light. The steps were easier here. They led by way of a short passage into a small brick-lined chamber. But this did not lead to anywhere at all. It was empty. The air was heavy. The beam of the torch travelled over all the walls in turn. They showed an unbroken surface.

Miss Silver gave her slight hortatory cough.

"I think," she said, "that a review of some of the facts would be beneficial. This is an old house. It was old when Ugo di Benevento bought it and built on to it. I think we may assume that these passages were part of the original building. But would he have considered them a sufficiently safe hiding-place for the

Benevento Treasure? I believe not. He could have no certainty that their existence was not known. I believe that he would have constructed a hiding-place which was known only to himself."

Major Warrender said,

"To make sure of that he would have had to do all the work himself."

"He may have done so, or he may have taken means to ensure that whoever did the work would never speak of it."

With a thrill that was only partly horror Mr. Tampling recalled that dead men tell no tales.

Miss Silver continued.

"We have not found any place where Miss Cara could have met with a fatal accident. It seems likely that she had been in these passages, but I think we must conclude that she died, or was murdered, elsewhere. I do not think it possible that her body could have been taken to where it was found by way of the steep steps and narrow passages which we have traversed. There would have been a great deal more than a little dust upon her clothing if that had been the case. She may have walked through one of the passages, but I think her body must have been brought back by some easier way."

Thoughts which Stephen had been holding by main force thrust past his desperate guard. By what way had Candida gone—by what way had she been taken? And if they found her, what was it they would find—herself, or only the body she had worn? He had no answer to these things. He said harshly,

"Miss Silver is right. If there was such a thing as the Benevento Treasure, it wouldn't have been hidden where anyone who knew the house might stumble on it. And if Miss Cara came by her death whilst she was looking for it, she must certainly have been taken back into the house by some easier way than the one by which we have come. Only as to where she was murdered—if she really *was* murdered—there simply isn't any evidence. And what does it matter? What we have to do is to find this other hiding-place—if it exists."

He had started out to say, "What we have to do is to find Candida," but he couldn't say it. He turned abruptly and went back along the passage leading to the steps. There was something—passed over at the time but coming back as one of those impressions which come, and go, and come again. It was something to do with the passage. The light had been focussed ahead of him as they came through it, the cellar door had been in view. Now it was the passage itself which had his whole attention—rough brick walls, propped by wooden posts and crossed between every two posts by a wooden lateral. Old cottages had half-timbering like that, but what was it doing in an underground passage?

The answer came with the question. One of these squares could be a door.

The light ran up and down, and there was the latch, fitted smoothly against one of the wooden uprights. A turn of the hand and the door swung outwards. He stooped, and came up again. The lifted lamp showed him where he was—in the main cellar of Underhill.

CHAPTER 40

It was all to do again. And there was no clue. As the others came through the gap and joined him, Stephen was looking about him with something very like despair in his heart. This was the main cellar of the house, with an easy flight of steps going up to a passage behind the kitchen, and a second flight which led to the courtyard at the side of the house. Along the far wall there was a row of doors. When Miss Olivia had brought him down here she had dismissed them briefly.

"The wine-cellar. Coals. Wood. The others are empty."

He had not been permitted to examine any of them. When he had said bluntly that he could not make a satisfactory report without a much more detailed examination he had been put in what Miss Olivia considered to be his place. Any of the cellars might conceal an opening, and "The wine-cellar is locked." He found he was saying these words aloud.

It was Miss Silver who answered him.

"Is it your opinion that the entrance to this hiding-place would be in a locked cellar? It is not mine."

"Why?"

She said in her usual composed manner.

"It would attract too much attention. The locked room would be the very first to be investigated. The aim would rather be to put the Treasure in a place which would attract no attention at all."

Stephen said bitterly. "This place is about thirty by twenty—there is plenty of choice."

She came nearer to him and put a hand on his arm.

"Have you thought about the steps—the ones coming down from the house? Or the others?"

He stared at her.

"What do you mean?"

"I talked to Anna. She is in great distress about Candida. She had grown fond of her. I asked her whether she could bear to think for the rest of her life that she might have saved her and had refrained. She cried bitterly, and said what could she do? She was very much afraid. She said, 'They would kill me!' I told her that she would be protected, and that she must tell what she knew. She declared with vehemence that she knew nothing—only that there were secret places, and that she had seen the dust on Miss Cara's shoes, and that she was very much afraid. When I pressed her she said it was because of what old Mr. Benevent had told her."

They were all listening, but as far as she and Stephen Eversley were concerned they might have been alone. He reached out and took her by the arm.

"What did he tell her?"

Miss Silver repeated what Anna had said.

"He was very old, and he used to talk about the Treasure. He said it was quite safe in a secret place— 'A man may walk over it and not know it is there. He may go up, and he may go down, and he will not know. And if he knew, and if he went, it would never do him any good.' There is a rhyme about it, you know, among the family papers:

"'Touch not nor try,
Sell not nor buy,
Give not nor take,
For dear life's sake.'"

His hand closed on her. He said in a hard voice,
"An old man in his dotage babbling. What a clue!"

"Old men remember the past."

"Say it again."

She repeated the words.

"'A man may walk over it and he will not know.
He may go up and he may go down, and he will not
know.'"

He let go of her abruptly and went over to the
steps which led to the house, but before reaching
them he swerved and crossed diagonally to the flight
which gave upon the courtyard. It was set in a corner,
but a little away from the wall. There was a space
there wide enough for a man to enter. A little straw
lay about, as if carelessly dropped. It was old trodden
straw. He came into the narrow place with the electric
lamp in his hand. *He may go up, and he may go down,
and he will not know.* This unregarded corner might
be passed a thousand times. The steps were of
stone—old steps, hollowed by the passing of many
feet. The wall on the other side was also of stone—
big square blocks of it, quarried from the hill beyond
and set in place three hundred, four hundred years
ago. If there were a secret entrance to Ugo di Benevento's hiding-place it might very well be here. A
tunnel dug from this point would pass under the
courtyard. There might be such a tunnel. The steps
would screen it. His mind was quite clear, quite logical. A hundred men might search for a hundred days
and never find the entrance. The light passed back-

wards and forwards, up and down. It showed stone and straw, and a little round black thing that lay at his foot. He stooped and picked it up, and it was a shoe-button.

Just an ordinary black shoe-button.

He held it in the palm of his hand and the light fell on it. Miss Silver's voice seemed to come from a long way off.

"What is it?"

He turned so that she could see the button on his palm.

"Candida has shoes with a strap and a button like this."

The words horrified him. If Candida had come this way, how had she come? And why had the button come off her shoe? Frightful images rose before his thought. If she had been dragged along this rough floor, the button might have caught and been wrenched— —

Miss Silver said quickly and insistently,

"It means that this is the place. It means that we are on the right track."

Mr. Trampling was at some disadvantage. Both the Chief Constable and Inspector Rock were taller than he was, especially the Inspector. He really could not see what was happening. It occurred to him that if he went a little way up the steps he would be able to see very well. He saw Miss Silver step aside, and he saw the Inspector take the lamp whilst Stephen Eversley examined the wall. There was no hand-rail to the steps, so to be sure of keeping his balance Mr. Trampling kneeled down upon the fifth step, which gave him a very good view. He heard the Chief Constable say, "Well, it all looks as solid as the Cathedral to me."

271

And then the thing happened. Rock made a step forward and slipped on the mouldy straw. He had the lamp in his right hand, and with his left he thrust out against the wall to recover his balance. The slip landed him in a heavy plunging step with all his weight behind it. He came down sprawling, because the wall against which he thrust had given way.

Stephen snatched the lamp and held it up. Rock got to his knees and stared at the slanting hole in the wall, which had been a solid block of stone. Stephen leaned across him and pushed it. It swung in like a door. The chance of a heavy man coming down with all his weight upon a stone slab in the floor while he pitched against just the right block in the wall had released the mechanism which controlled the entrance to Ugo di Benevento's hiding-place. Mr. Tampling from his vantage point could see the open doorway, narrow and low, and beyond it a platform of bricks, and steps that went down into the dark.

There was another of those delays whilst Rock went for the constable who had been left on guard in Candida's room. The entrance there was no longer of any importance. It was this one which must be guarded now. The longest minutes of Stephen's life dragged by. By the clock there were no more than four of them—in terms of heart-wrung suspense they seemed to have no end and no beginning. If there had been a second lamp, he could have gone on, but there was no second lamp.

The footsteps of the two men returning broke in upon the strain. The Chief Constable looked at the hole in the wall and decided to take no chances. He had no fancy for being trapped underground, and he told Rock to stay with the constable.

Stephen went in, and the light went with him

down the steps. On the inner side the stone was faced with wood. Against this door Candida had beat in vain—on this small brick platform she had sunk down in despair. There was nothing to tell them these things.

They followed Stephen to the foot of the steps and along the passage which ran under the courtyard and tunnelled into the hill. The lamp which he held picked up an iron bar flung down across the path. He checked momentarily. The light fell on it. It showed a coating of rust—and something else— shreds of hair that had been soaked in blood. They all stood looking at it.

For a moment there was just one picture in every mind—Miss Cara dead at the foot of the stairs in her own house. But not killed by any fall from those stairs—struck down here by this rusty bar in this strange place. Stephen stepped over the bar and threw the light ahead.

Mr. Tampling's excitement had reached a dizzying height. He now saw what Candida had seen, but far more brightly illumined—the cave or niche which had closed the passage, the iron-bound box that filled it, the raised lid and the Treasure within. The light dazzled on the golden dish, the candle-sticks, the stones of a fabulous necklace. It struck fire from the stones—blood-red fire. And then——

He saw the skeleton hand that had clutched at the Treasure and fallen upon death—the bones and the rags which were all that were left of Alan Thompson. And nearer, right across their path, Candida Sayle, her face hidden against the arm thrown out to save herself as she fell.

The lamp was thrust on Major Warrender, and Stephen was on his knees, saying her name.

"Candida—Candida—Candida!"

She came back to the sound of his voice, and she was never to forget it. After the darkness that had been like death, after the burial of hope and life itself, to wake with his arms about her and his voice calling her name——

She opened her eyes, and the place was light. Stephen was holding her as if he would never let her go. She said, "I found the treasure—don't touch it—it killed poor Alan——"

CHAPTER 41

Joseph came into the drawing-room, his dark skin yellow and damp with sweat. Miss Olivia was working at her embroidery. She looked up and said sharply,

"What is the matter?"

"They are down in the cellar—they have found the opening!"

"Impossible!"

His voice grated.

"I tell you they have found it! The Inspector came up—he went to the bedroom and fetched the constable. I followed them to the top of the cellar stairs. From there I can see that the secret door is open and that they are all there. The Inspector and the young man stay, and the others go down into the passage. You know what they will find. What do we do—what do we say?"

She looked at him very directly.

"Do? Say? We have only to be perfectly clear and firm, and to be very much surprised. There are some passages in the house which have always been a family secret, but we do not know of any others—if there is one in the cellar, we know nothing about it. There have been stories about a treasure, but I have never believed them. If there was anyone so foolish as to go looking for it, he did so at his own risk. If he met with a fatal accident, it was without any knowledge or responsibility of mine. And if Miss Sayle was foolish enough to follow his example, I cannot hold myself responsible for that."

"She will say——"

"She can say anything she likes, and she can prove nothing at all. She will say she drank a glass of milk and after that she remembers nothing. And the answer is that she was walking in her sleep. It is either that, or she has made up the whole story. She has found out something about the passages—she has been working on the family papers, and she takes it into her head to explore at night when everybody is asleep. A much more likely story than that she was drugged and shut up there in the dark to die."

He said in an approving voice,

"It is a good story—if they will believe it." Then, after a pause, "Anna is the one I am afraid of."

"She is a fool—and she knows nothing."

He said in what was almost a pettish voice,

"She looks at me as if—as if——"

"As if what?"

"As if she found me—horrible!"

Her glance just touched him scornfully.

"Perhaps she does—perhaps——" She spoke suddenly and vehemently. "How did my sister die?"

He stood his ground.

"I have told you. She walked in her sleep. I followed her in case she should come to harm. She was wringing her hands and saying, 'I can't find him— I can't find him!' She went down into the cellar and opened the secret door. I could not let her go into such a place alone—I went after her. When she came to where the Treasure is she saw Mr. Alan lying there, and she cried out. His hand was on the necklace, and she went to take hold of it. The lid of the chest came down and struck her, and she died. I pushed it up, and I pulled her away, but she was dead. I came and told you, and we carried her to where she was found. You know all this."

There was a sense of unbearable strain. They were too much intent upon one another to have been aware that the door behind the tall black lacquer screen had opened. There was no design in that soft opening. It was not Miss Silver's wont to enter or leave a room with any jarring sound, but when she heard Miss Olivia say, "How did my sister die?" she came no more than one step inside the door and put up a hand to check the advance of Mr. Tampling, who was immediately behind her. They stood there upon the threshhold, listening, and heard Joseph tell his tale, and when he had said, "You know all this," they heard Miss Olivia answer him. The words came tense with feeling.

"I know what you have told me."

Joseph said, "I have told you the truth."

Within the room, and beyond their sight, Miss Olivia let the embroidery-frame drop upon her knee. The hand which held the needle came down too, the thread of scarlet silk trailing. She said,

"You are lying."

"*Madam!*"

Her eyes were on him, sombre and intent.

"You are lying. You say she was walking in her sleep. I have seen her walk like that, and so have you. Are you going to tell me that she took a torch in her hand to light her through a dream? But you say you *saw* her go down into the cellar and open the secret door. There are lights in the house, but what light is there in that dark place?"

He said on a stubborn note,

"I had a torch."

"I tell you, you had not! You would not have dared to follow her with a torch in your hand—you would not have dared!"

"Do you think I followed her in the dark?"

"I do not! It was she who had the torch. And she was not walking in her sleep, she was awake, because it had come to her that Mr. Alan must be there. I did not think that she would ever dare to go into that place alone. She had gone once with me, and she came near to fainting with fright. I did not think she would ever go alone."

He said with impatience,

"What does it matter who had the torch? The rest is as I said."

"No."

The word was like a blow and he exclaimed against it.

"Is this a time to question and to quarrel? We have to know what we are to do, what we are to say."

"I must have the truth from you. My sister did not die as you have said. There was no hand there for her to touch—there were only bones. Do you ask me to believe that she would have touched dead bones? I tell you she would have fainted, or she would have screamed and run away. And she would have done

277

nothing to set off the spring and let down the lid of the chest upon her head. I think she cried out and turned to run away. I think you tried to stop her, perhaps to reason with her, and she would not listen. I think you had to stop her because you could not stop her mouth. I think she died because you knew what she might tell."

He cried out.

"I never laid a hand on Mr. Alan!"

"There was no need to lay a hand upon him. He snatched at the Treasure and it killed him, as it has killed before, and may again."

His voice rose.

"And who showed him the way to the Treasure? It was not Miss Cara! And who else knew the secret? Only you, madam—only you! You showed him how to open the door, and if the Treasure had not killed him he would have died down there as Miss Sayle was meant to die! No food, no water, and no way out—it would not have taken long!"

There was a silence. Miss Olivia broke it.

"If you had not followed me that night you would have known nothing, and you could have done nothing. You have been a long time in my service. Not as long as Anna, but long enough. I think you killed my sister. How do you expect me to reward you for that?"

He stood staring at her. She went on in the same toneless voice.

"If my plan had succeeded, I would have rewarded you and sent you away, but now—if Candida lives, there is nothing for either of us. She will have Underhill, and she will marry and have children to come after her. She should have been dead, but I think she is alive, and there is nothing more that I can do. So you shall have your reward for killing my sister."

It was when Joseph cried out that he had never laid a hand on Alan Thompson that Inspector Rock came up quietly behind Miss Silver and Mr. Tampling. At Miss Olivia's words he pushed past the end of the screen and strode into the room.

CHAPTER 42

Candida lay on her bed and Stephen knelt beside her. Her hand clung to his. If she shut her eyes she might slip back into the dream again. He said, "I won't let you," and she held his hand.

Anna came in with a tray, and she drank the most delicious draught she had ever tasted—hot milky tea to assuage her thirst and comfort her parched throat. Anna was crying. She tried not to, but the tears ran down. She took up one of Candida's hands and kissed it, and went away back to the kitchen to boil an egg and make toast. When she was gone, Candida caught at Stephen's arm.

"Will you take me away from here? I can't stay in this house. I don't want to see it again—*ever!*"

He said,

"You shan't—I'll see to that. Louisa Arnold will take you in. I'll drive you out there as soon as you've had something to eat."

She was sitting up now with his arm round her.

"I'm all right—I'm quite strong—I only want to get away."

She pressed against him and dropped her voice.

"It was Alan Thompson—there in the passage—wasn't it?"

He nodded.

"I expect so. There's a spring that brings the lid of the chest down if anyone touches the Treasure. He grabbed at it, and it killed him."

"How—horrible! But it wasn't—murder—"

He said slowly and doubtfully, "I—don't—know—"

"What do you mean?"

"I don't think anyone laid hands on him. But do you think Miss Olivia meant to let him live and marry her sister? How do you suppose he knew how to open that hidden door? We only found it by a lucky chance, and that's not the sort of thing you would expect to happen twice."

"Aunt Cara might have shown him the way."

"If she had she would have warned him not to touch the treasure. There's a rhyme about it, isn't there—

"'Touch not nor take,
For dear life's sake'?"

"Yes—yes, there is."

He said grimly,

"I think Miss Olivia showed him the secret door, and I think she meant him to touch—and take what was coming to him."

A shudder ran over her.

"Let's get away, Stephen—quickly, quickly!"

Louisa Arnold was most agreeably thrilled. Apart from the fact that she had an extremely kind heart, her house was to be enlivened by a love affair, the solution of a three-years-old mystery, and by a really

280

shocking scandal. The love affair showed every sign of leading up to an early wedding, and since Stephen was certainly a cousin, and Candida an orphan, from what house could they more suitably be married? She had her mother's wedding-veil laid away in lavender—and there could never have been a happier marriage than hers to dear Papa. As to the solution of the mystery, there seemed to be no doubt that the skeleton found in Underhill was that of poor Alan Thompson, and in regard to the scandal, there really never had been one of so resounding a nature. Was it possible that Miss Olivia Benevent was actually suspected of having murdered her sister?

There was a school of thought which answered this question in the affirmative but softened the conclusion by declaring Miss Olivia to be out of her mind. By others the part of first murderer was assigned to Joseph, and a good many people discovered that they had always thought there was something sinister about him. It having become known that Miss Silver had accompanied the police during their search of Underhill, Louisa Arnold found herself in the enviable position of being considered a positive Fount of Information. It was gratifying in the extreme, but she did feel that dear Maud might have given her a little more to come and go upon. Discretion was all very well, but who more reliable than one's own cousin? And to sum it all up, "Dear Papa always told me everything."

At the news that the inquest had been adjourned, Miss Louisa restrained herself no longer.

"Do you mean to tell me that nobody has been arrested?"

Miss Silver had embarked upon a jumper in a particularly pleasing shade of blue for her niece Ethel

Burkett. About an inch of it stuck out from the needles like a frill. The wool was exceptionally soft, and she was trying a new pattern. She looked mildly at Louisa and said,

"Joseph Rossi has been detained."

"Detained! And what's the good of that, I should like to know! Do you mean to tell me that he didn't murder poor Cara and then pretend she had been killed by falling down the stairs?"

"The police will have to decide whether there is a case that they can take into court."

Miss Louisa tossed her head.

"He probably killed poor Alan Thompson too!"

"I do not think so."

Louisa Arnold leaned forward.

"Do you know, I saw one of those chests in a museum. I am so vexed that I can't remember where it was, but it was during that trip that Papa and I took the year after Mamma died. We only had a fortnight, and we saw so many places that they all ran together in my head and I can't remember where I saw that chest, but it was just like what everyone is saying about the one at Underhill. There was a spring in the lid, and if you touched anything in the chest there was a horrible sort of hasp that came down and hit you. And they say that this is what Alan Thompson must have done. Unless you really do think Joseph killed him."

Miss Silver made no reply, and after a moment Louisa continued her speculations.

"Do you know, the thing I find hardest to understand is the part about poor Cara. I just can't believe she went down into a dark cellar in the middle of the night—unless she was walking in her sleep. Do you think she was?"

"I think she was looking for Alan Thompson, but whether she was awake or asleep, I cannot say. She may have been suspecting his death for a long time. She may have been very much afraid, and she may suddenly have felt that she could not bear the suspense any longer."

There was a pause. Louisa's voice went down into a whisper. She said,

"Do you think—Olivia killed her?"

"Oh, no. There was no reason for her to do so. Miss Cara's death was the greatest misfortune that could have happened to her."

"Well, it wasn't the chest. Cara wouldn't have touched it with poor Alan lying there dead."

"No."

The whisper became insistent.

"Then it was Joseph."

Miss Silver said, "That is not for us to say."

Miss Arnold flushed. The effect, with her white hair and blue eyes, was becoming, but it conveyed the fact that her patience was now exhausted.

"And I suppose you will not talk about Olivia either?"

"I believe it would be better if we did not discuss her at the moment, Louisa."

Louisa Arnold really was obliged to leave the room.

Others were, unfortunately, compelled to discuss Miss Olivia Benevent. When all was said and done, there was only the slightest evidence on which to build a case against her. Miss Silver and Mr. Tampling had stood behind a screen and heard Joseph and Miss Olivia accuse one another. What they said could be true, or it could be false, for each denied what the other had said. When, just at the end, Miss

283

Olivia said, "If Candida lives, there will be nothing for either of us. She will have Underhill, and she will marry and have children to come after her. She should have been dead, but I think she is alive, and there is nothing more that I can do." When she said that, there was an admission which could perhaps have been used. But it rested upon Miss Silver's evidence alone, since Mr. Tampling, appealed to for confirmation, declared himself unable to supply it. They were at some distance from the speakers, and he felt himself quite unable to swear to anything that had been said. Not that he wished to cast any doubt upon Miss Silver's recollection. She appeared to be a most accurate and observant person, but he must really not be asked to swear to anything himself.

And then, whilst all this was going on, Olivia Benevent died. There was no blurring of her senses. She had set aside a legacy for Joseph, a legacy for Anna, and she asked to see Candida Sayle. But Candida was out, and when she came she came too late. They did not tell her of Miss Olivia's last words. She sat propped up against half a dozen pillows, and when she knew that Candida would be too late she used her hard-won breath to say,

"I wanted to curse her. She would have remembered that."

CHAPTER 43

Miss Silver had rather a touching interview with Mr. Puncheon. She was hardly prepared for the warmth of his gratitude or the generous size of the fee which he pressed upon her acceptance.

"It will be very good of you if you will take it," he said. "My sister is comfortably provided for, and I have no other kith or kin. If poor Alan had been different and had lived, I should have left him what I have, so it is only right that you should accept a proper reward for clearing his name. The false accusation against him killed my wife. It not only did that, but——" He hesitated, took off his glasses, and looked at her with moistened eyes. "I wonder if you will understand me when I say that it seemed to come between us. I could take no comfort in recollecting the happy times we had had together—the trouble about Alan seemed to cloud it all. But now that he is cleared, I have that comfort again. I think I told you that I was very fond of my wife. Perhaps you can understand how I feel."

Miss Silver understood very well. She said so with great kindness.

The case of Joseph Rossi was a considerable headache for the police. Though it was extremely probable that he had murdered Miss Cara to prevent her giving the alarm and bringing Alan Thompson's death and the whereabouts of the Treasure to light, there really was a conspicuous lack of any evidence likely to secure a verdict of guilty if he were brought before a jury. Miss Silver had heard Miss Olivia accuse him, but he had denied the accusation, and being dead she could not be called upon to substantiate it. It was remembered that she had brought a similar and quite unfounded accusation against her niece Miss Candida Sayle. The papers went to the Public Prosecutor, and they probably gave him a headache too. The whole thing smelled to heaven, but where was the evidence? Miss Cara Benevent had been found dead with her skull smashed in, and the body had certainly been moved. There was the evidence of one witness to a conversation between Miss Olivia Benevent and Joseph Rossi, according to which the moving of the body was admitted between them, but the defence would of course represent this action in quite another light than that of guilt. Confronted by a terrible emergency, an old lady and her devoted servant had taken what steps they might to preserve a long treasured family secret. It had probably never occurred to them that they were doing anything illegal. All very easy and plausible.

The iron bar, which might have supplied some evidence, was, to put it baldly, a washout. It bore traces of having been used to cause the fatal injury, but it was too deeply rusted to carry any man's fingerprints. How it came to the place where it was found, there was nothing to show. It could have been snatched up by Joseph Rossi and used to silence a frightened woman, or it could have been in some way part of the trap which guarded the Benevento Treasure. Word went back to the county police that there were not sufficient grounds for a prosecution, and Joseph Rossi was discharged.

He walked in upon his wife Anna, who was still

at the house in Retley where Miss Olivia had died. There was some good furniture there, and Mr. Tampling was paying her a wage as caretaker. She had opened the door, and he was in the hall almost before she realised that it was he.

"You don't seem very pleased to see me," he said.

She had turned very pale. She went back a step.

"It is just—that I am—surprised."

He went through into the kitchen and sat down.

"Well, cook me a meal—and it had better be a good one! How much money have you got in the house?"

She stood on the other side of the table and stared at him.

"I don't know."

The words were slow and reluctant. His came back quick and cold.

"Then find out! I'm not staying here to be pointed at! I'll take what you've got and be off! You can send me more later! Did Miss Olivia leave you anything?"

She would have liked to lie, but she was too much afraid. Her eyes widened in her dark, anxious face.

"I—she——"

"She did! How much?"

"It was just—some money—in a parcel——"

"I said, 'How much?'"

She moistened her lips with her tongue.

"It was—a hundred pounds—in notes."

He reached across the table and caught her by the wrist.

"You are lying! Even she wouldn't do that —after forty years!"

She tried to step back, but he held her.

"There is money to come when the lawyer has settled everything. An annuity—for me."

"How much?"

"I do not know. They say I will be taken care of. There is something for you too—a parcel with money in it. There was one for you and one for me. She gave them to me when she was dying."

He let go of her wrist.

"Get them!"

She went without a word, her mind in a confusion of fear. She had always been afraid of Joseph—always. But at Underhill there had been Miss Olivia over them both, and even Joseph had been afraid of Miss Olivia. Now there was no one but him and her, and the money between them. He would take the money, hers as well as his, and she would be left. That was better than if he made her go with him— much, much better. There was a trembling in her limbs when she thought that he might make her go with him.

She was talking to herself as she went up the stairs.

"No, Anna, no, he does not want you—he has never wanted you. And you need not go. You can say that you must stay here and get the money that is to come from the lawyer. Yes, you can say that. But he will not want you to come."

The money was in the room that she was using, put away under the mattress of the bed. She got it out now. There were two parcels, done up with paper and string and written on in Miss Olivia's hand, "Anna" on the one, and "Joseph" on the other. The packet marked "Anna" was much thinner and flatter than the other. She had opened it and done it up again, so that she knew exactly what was in it— twenty five-pound notes doubled in half and laid in a little cardboard box. She had seen the box in Miss Olivia's hand a week before she died.

The other parcel was much bulkier. It too had been

prepared beforehand, only the name had been put on it after Miss Olivia had been taken ill. Anna's legacy was already addressed, but it was a dying hand that had written Joseph's name.

He looked up as she came back into the kitchen with the packages in either hand. He had lighted a cigarette, and the smoke and the acrid smell of it hung upon the air. He rolled his own cigarettes and he liked them strong. He looked at her package first.

"You have opened it?"

"Yes."

"You said there was a hundred pounds."

"Yes."

He took his own and tore the paper off. A bundle of dirty one-pound notes came into view and he stared at them. They might have come from some low gambling dive. They reeked of tobacco. It was difficult to believe that Miss Olivia could have brought herself to handle them. There was no message, no enclosure of any kind, only his name on the outside wrapping. He laid down his cigarette on the table and began to count them. The notes must have got damp, for they stuck to one another. He licked his forefinger to separate them. He had a trick of it when he counted money, or even when he turned the pages of a book. That the notes were rank did not disturb him unduly. The finger went to his mouth again and again.

"Thirty—thirty-one—thirty-two——"

He thought there would be a hundred. With Anna's hundred, not too bad, and there was the annuity to come.

He went on with his counting.

"Forty—forty-one—forty-two——"

The cigarette smoke came up in his throat and nose. He waved it away.

"Fifty—fifty-one—fifty-two——"

He began to lose count.

"Sixty-five—sixty-seven—sixty-nine——"

Anna stood on the other side of the table and watched his finger rise and fall. She saw the sweat come on his brow. His voice wandered, and the notes fell from his hand. He said, "I'm ill." And then, on a gasping breath, "I'm—poisoned——" His eyes accused her. His voice would have accused Olivia Benevent, but it choked in his throat.

He was dead before the doctor came.

CHAPTER 44

Retley buzzed. There was another inquest, and another funeral at which there would no doubt have been the usual gathering together of the morbid-minded if it had not taken place at eight o'clock in the morning and the secret very well kept. As it was, a mere handful of people drifted in to watch Anna in a long black veil stand with bowed head above Joseph Rossi's grave. Miss Silver stood beside her, extending the kindly support she was so well fitted to give. She had removed the bunch of flowers from her second-best hat, which like all her other hats was plain in shape and black in colour, and had further satisfied her sense of decorum by the substitution of a plain black woollen scarf for the yellowish fur tippet which usually completed her winter coat. She would not let Anna go through such an ordeal alone, and nothing could have been kinder than voice and manner as, the ceremony completed, she led her back to where her niece Nellie awaited them with breakfast laid out on the table and a good strong brew of tea. Nellie had been perfectly willing to come down, and she would take Anna back with her, but go to Joseph Rossi's funeral she would not.

"And I'm sure it's ever so good of you to do it, Miss Silver, but I couldn't, not for anything in the world. If ever anyone was well rid of a murdering good-for-nothing, it's poor Auntie, and the less said about it the better."

Candida saw them before they left Retley. Anna was to have a pension, but to her tearful protestations that all she wanted was to come back and serve her dear Miss Candida there was no response.

Candida Sayle had very little response for anyone during this time. She went to Derek Burdon's wedding, which was also at eight in the morning, and she kissed him and Jenny and wished them well, but her lips were cold and her eyes looked far away. She sat in Mr. Tampling's office and discussed the necessary business in what was almost a mechanical manner. Since she would never live at Underhill, would he please suggest what could be done with the place. He looked at her with concern. She was not wearing black, but in her plain grey coat and skirt she had the air of a mourning ghost. The bright colour which he remembered with admiration was all gone. There were violet shadows under the eyes which seemed to look past him.

"The house has been in the family for a very long time."

291

She said, "Too long——" And then, "I don't want to have anything to do with it—ever. Or with the things that were found there—that horrible Treasure."

"It is extremely valuable, Miss Sayle."

"Yes. It has cost people's lives—I don't want to have anything to do with it. I thought perhaps the Retley museum——"

He felt a secret excitement and satisfaction, but he constrained himself to say soberly,

"It might be considered. But you should not do anything in a hurry. In any case, probate must be obtained before you can make any disposal. Since the things may be considered to be in the nature of heirlooms, it may not be in your power to make an outright gift, but the museum would doubtless be very glad to have them on loan, and meanwhile they are perfectly safe in the County Bank."

It was after this interview that Stephen found it increasingly difficult to see her. With arrears of work to be overtaken, his time was not his own, and when he did arrive at Miss Arnold's house in the evening it would be to find that Candida had gone to bed early, or that she sat through the meal eating practically nothing, only to slip away as soon as it was over.

"I'm sorry, but I don't feel like talking." Or, "It's no good—I'm really too tired."

As the door closed behind her, Miss Louisa was voluble in explanation.

"Well, you see, my dear boy, she has had a shock, and you must give her time to get over it. I recollect a cousin of ours who was just the same after her engagement was broken off. You will remember her, Maud—Lily Mottram—really a very sweet creature, but a little inclined to be melancholy. Well, as I said, after her engagement was broken off they really thought she was going into a decline. He had a good deal of money and a nice place in Derbyshire—or was it Dorset—but I'm afraid *not* very steady, so perhaps it was all for the best. But she didn't sleep and she didn't eat, and they really didn't know what to do with her, only fortunately she met a very nice steady young man who was a partner in a shipping firm, so it all turned out very well in the end, and I think they had six children. At least I know there were five, because when the fifth one arrived she wanted to call him Quintus, but her husband didn't like the idea at all. I believe they had quite a tiff about it."

Just how this rather tactless anecdote could be said to apply to himself and Candida, Stephen could not determine. A little later, Miss Arnold having left the room, he addressed himself to Miss Silver.

"Look here, we can't go on like this. I've got to see her. She goes and sees Tampling—she sees other people. It's only when I come along that she's too tired to sit up any longer and has to go to bed."

Miss Silver looked at him kindly across Ethel Burkett's blue jumper.

"She has had a shock."

"Of course she's had a shock. We've all had shocks, but we don't go on having them. She ought to want to see me, and she doesn't. There's something on her mind, and I want to know what it is. If I could see her—really see her——"

"Yes, I think it would be advisable." She devoted a moment to consideration, and then continued. "I think it possible that Louisa and I may be out at tea-time tomorrow. There is an expedition we have

293

talked of making—a visit to the daughter of an old family friend at Laleham. We thought of hiring a car. It is practically settled, and the final details can be arranged on the telephone. Could you be free at tea-time?"

"Yes. I've got to see her."

She said very composedly,

"Then it will be best if you just walk in. I will see that the door is left unlocked."

He came into his cousin's drawing-room next day to find Candida behind the tea-table. At the moment of his entry Eliza Peck was setting down a Victorian teapot and hot water-jug.

"Just happened to see him, and the kettle on the boil, so I made the tea and stepped along, for I said to myself, 'Well, the door's not locked, and if he doesn't know how to let himself in by now he never will do, and that's that.'"

Candida sat pale and silent until the door was shut and they were alone. Then she said,

"How did she know you were here?"

Stephen laughed.

"Saw me out of the window, I should think. Now, darling, what is all this?"

"I told you not to come."

"And Miss Silver told me she and Cousin Louisa would be out to tea."

"She hadn't any business to."

Stephen insinuated himself on the tea sofa beside her.

"Darling, if Miss Silver always confined herself to minding her own business, I've got an idea that quite a lot of people would be sorry, ourselves included."

Candida edged away from him. When she had got

as far as she could she turned to face him, her hands clasped tightly in her lap.

"I didn't want to see you, because I wanted to think."

"And have you thought?"

She had perhaps expected a protest. What she got was a look of grave attention. Perhaps this was going to be easier than she had expected. It was strange that this should make her feel as if nothing mattered any more. She said in a low shaken voice,

"Yes, I've thought."

"Well?"

"I'm going away."

"Where are you going to?"

She took as deep a breath as she could.

"There's someone who used to work for Aunt Barbara—she has a room that she lets. I thought I'd go there."

"It doesn't sound like a good place to be married from."

She looked at him in a lost kind of way.

"Stephen, I don't think I can marry you."

"Is that what you were thinking about?"

"Yes."

"What a waste of time. I don't love you any more—or you don't love me any more? Which is it?"

She shook her head.

"No—it's not that. It—it's all the things that have been happening. They are Benevent things—they haven't got anything to do with you. I don't think you ought to be dragged into them. I don't think there ought to be any more Benevents."

He nodded.

"A plague-sticken lot. And you propose to go

295

into quarantine the rest of your life—is that it?"

"Something like that."

"Then it's about the most morbid thing I ever heard in my life! Do you suppose there is a family on this earth who couldn't rake up a bad hat or two if they really went to work? Look here, darling, I take it you've heard Cousin Louisa talk about the Benevent sisters. Your grandmother broke away, and she was all right. Cara was in Olivia's pocket. She would always have been in somebody's pocket—it was just too bad that it happened to be Olivia's. And look at Olivia herself. All that force and determination and will, and no outlet except to boss Miss Cara! Their father paid their bills, but he never gave them a penny to spend for themselves. Louisa says they had to go to him for money to put in the plate at church. That kind of tyranny does things to people—they either break away, or it breaks them. Or they turn into tyrants themselves as soon as they get a chance, and that's what happened to Olivia. Our children are not going to be like that, if that is what you were thinking about."

She said, "No——" on a long shaken breath. And then, "No—they won't—will they?"

He took her hands, and felt how cold they were.

"Darling, do come off it! It's such a waste of time! You've had a shock, and we've all been through hell, but it's over. What do you suppose I felt like when I knew you were somewhere under that damned hill and I didn't know whether you were dead or alive? Do you suppose there is any need for you to rub it in? But it's over, finished, done with, unless we keep digging it up and making ourselves go through it again. We've got our lives before us, and we are going to make a good job of them—together. We're going to be happy."

The resistance had gone out of her. She let him put his arms round her and felt the past slip by them and away.